"I said not to split the group," Cat said.

"So what?" Davyn demanded . . . "You don't get to decide how I feel, Cat."

"Well then who does?" asked Cat. "Because you do not seem to be capable of making reliable decisions on your own."

"What does *that* mean?"

"It means that we cannot trust you," Cat said. "We have never been able to trust you. You knew the truth about Maddoc and what he was doing to Nearra from the very beginning. You are a liar, Davyn."

"Yes," Davyn said. "I'm a liar. I'm a manipulator. I'm rotten to the core. But at least I know who and what I am. You're a failure, Cat. And what's more, you're a coward . . . Why don't you just quit before someone else dies?"

## THE NEW ADVENTURES

# THE NEW ADVENTURES
## VOLUME
## 6

# DRAGON DAY

## STAN BROWN

### COVER & INTERIOR ART
**Vinod Rams**

MIRROR
STONE

# DRAGON DAY

©2005 Wizards of the Coast, Inc.

Art by Vinod Rams
Cartography by Dennis Kauth
First Printing: March 2005
Library of Congress Catalog Card Number: 2004114592

9 8 7 6 5 4 3 2

US ISBN: 0-7869-3622-3
ISBN13: 978-0-7869-3622-9
620-17720-001-EN

U.S., CANADA,
ASIA, PACIFIC, & LATIN AMERICA
Wizards of the Coast, Inc.
P.O. Box 707
Renton, WA 98057-0707
+1-800-324-6496

EUROPEAN HEADQUARTERS
Wizards of the Coast, Belgium
T Hofveld 6d
1702 Groot-Bijgaarden
Belgium
+322 457 3350

Visit our web site at **www.mirrorstonebooks.com**

FOR SARAH, BENJAMIN, SEAN, GARRETT, AND
GB3—THE NEXT GENERATION

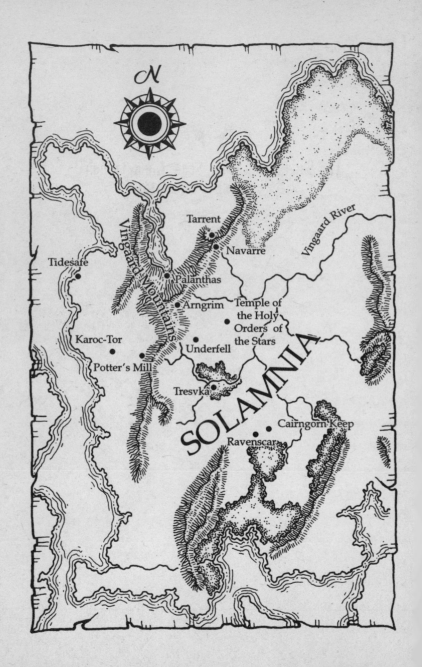

# Contents

The Laughing Mermaid's door burst from its hinges. Seconds later a burly silhouette belonging to one of the Bursur brothers, filled the open doorway. Under his arm he carried what one might have thought was a large sack of potatoes until, of course, one noticed that the shape was squirming to get free.

"You don't look as tough as a platinum dragon," Galdon Bursur said as he started to rock his captive forward and back with long arcs of his powerful arms. "Maybe you can fly like the kingfisher."

With a powerful thrust Galdon threw the smaller man high into the air. So high, in fact, that the massive blacksmith was able to take three long strides onto the square while his victim shrieked and pin wheeled through the air. Immediately the doorway was filled with two nearly identical silhouettes—the other Bursur brothers, Hannod and Jandor, who giggled brainlessly at their elder brother's antics. They followed Galdon into the night and the doorway filled with a half-dozen other, less burly shapes.

Adyn Thinreed landed like the sack of potatoes he'd recently resembled, his breath escaped in a loud, pained grunt. He wore the robes of a student cleric and acolyte from a temple dedicated to the gods of old, but they were so big on him that he was unable to do anything useful with his hands unless the sleeves were rolled up and cinched at the elbow. Adyn was thin and not especially tall, he had a mass of curly, dirty blonde hair on his head, and his smile (along with the sparkle in his eye) was usually enough to get him out of most difficult situations.

Unfortunately for him, tonight in the tiny, cliff-side fishing village of Tidesafe, his grin had not been quite charming enough.

Disoriented, Adyn lay very still. Loose dirt and small rocks pressed against his right cheek, so he decided that the stars he saw out of his barely open left eye were real and not the result of having landed too hard on his head.

"Nope," Galdon Bursur said. "You don't fly well either."

Derisive laughter came from all around. Apparently most of the inn's patrons had followed them onto the square. The crowd formed a loose ring around Galdon and Adyn, close enough so they could see what would happen next, but far enough back that they were not likely to get accidentally pulled into the confrontation. But before the beating could continue, a small man pushed his way through the crowd and walked directly to where Adyn lay.

"Seems to me that your faith in Paladine is a little misplaced," said Fostben Bursur, father of the brothers who were giving Adyn so much trouble. "Wouldn't you agree?"

Adyn tried to sit up, but his head was still spinning. Although he did manage to get himself righted to the point that he had both knees on the ground again, he only managed this feat by pressing his face into the dirt.

"P-Paladine is king," he said in a wavering voice. "He is first among the gods."

A murmur rose. Some in the crowd snickered. Others spat on

the ground. But no one showed even the slightest sign of agreeing with Adyn's words.

The old man knelt until he could look Adyn in the eye. A strand of long white hair fell across the man's leathery, wrinkled face. It hung in the air between the two, arcing back and forth like the pendulum of a gnomish device.

"Paladine is a feckless thug," he said.

The crowd grunted its approval.

"Tha's right, Pa," called Jandor Bursur, the youngest of the brothers, though it seemed he didn't actually understand the words his father had used. Hannod, the middle child, simply giggled maniacally—the only sound Adyn had heard him make.

"Paladine punished a world full of innocent souls," Fostben continued. "He punished them—punished us—for twelve generations because one man displeased him. Paladine, who had been the protector, the loving father for all of Krynn, withheld from us his blessing because of something we did not do. And worse, he turned his back on us completely. Because the King-priest of Istar failed in his duties, Paladine the mighty, Paladine the righteous, Paladine the spiteful turned his back on all his children for more than three hundred years."

Again the crowd voiced its approval. But this time the people of Tidesafe stepped closer, tightening the circle and giving Adyn the feeling of being locked in a very small room.

Summoning all his will, Adyn forced his head to stop spinning, rose to his knees, and looked the old man in the eye.

"The world had become a wicked place," he said with a strong, clear voice. "The Kingpriest may have been the most guilty, but man, elf, and dwarf alike had wandered from the righteous path. We needed to be taught the error of our ways. We needed to be shown that every deed has a consequence. We needed—"

"We needed guidance!" shouted Fostben. "We needed Paladine

to hand down measured justice, and to see that the righteous prospered while the wicked failed. We needed the 'king of the gods' to lead his flock. Instead, what did we get? We got neglected. We were left in the dark to fend for ourselves—no guidance, no support, and no blessings. And Paladine wasn't the only one. Oh no, all the gods turned their backs on the world, on the people who had offered them nothing but devotion and prayers. They turned their backs on us all."

"But not the moons," called someone from the crowd.

The rest of the crowd answered with one voice, "The moons."

"No, not the moons," Fostben said, picking up the cadence, making it feel like a sacred chant. "The faithful moons. The predictable moons. When all the other gods abandoned us, only the moons remained. Only the moons shed their light into the dark void left by Paladine and his ilk."

The old man's eyes were wild, filled with the kind of euphoric glee that Adyn had seen from time to time in the gazes of street preachers, warriors on their way to battle, and those wracked by fever dreams. The young priest looked away to see how the crowd was reacting. He immediately regretted it. All around him the crowd inched closer and closer, chanting, "The moons . . . the moons . . . the moons!"

"I do not dispute the power of the moons," Adyn said. "Solinari, Lunitari, and Nuitari have always been important figures in the court of Paladine. They control the tides and bring magic to the world. Who could doubt their power? That you found happiness in their service, even through the long, dark Age of Despair does nothing but fill my heart with joy."

The old man threw his head back and cackled mirthlessly.

"You are so like your god," he finally said. "Filled to the brim with arrogance. Our devotion to the moons is just a quaint aberration to you. Now that Paladine has deigned to return his gaze to the world you expect us to fall back into line, to accept the old order with Paladine as lord above all. Well, we won't have it. We won't acknowledge Paladine."

"Can't we each worship in our own ways?" said Adyn. "And consider ourselves brethren in the sight of the gods?" He held out his arms with his hands open, as if to welcome a long lost friend with a warm embrace.

"Certainly," Fostben said. But Adyn thought his tone was much less than agreeable.

"I can ask nothing more," said Adyn and moved to go back inside the Laughing Mermaid planning to head straight up to his room. He was only passing through Tidesafe on his way to Palanthas, and after a few hours of sleep he could get up with the sunrise and go on his way, before the Bursur family had slept off all they ale they'd been drinking he hoped. He took about a half-dozen steps though, and found his way blocked by the hulking body of Galdon Bursur. The giant of a man had purposely stood in the acolyte's way, but now looked away so that Adyn could not make eye contact.

Obviously Galdon wanted to pick a fight, but Adyn would not allow himself to be goaded.

"Pardon me for being so clumsy," he said bowing slightly and took a step backward to go around Galdon. That's when he bumped into Hannod Bursur, who had silently stepped right behind Adyn.

"I wasn't watching where I was going," said Adyn, although annoyance at these petty tricks was clear in his voice. "Please forgive me."

He turned to his left and found that Jandor Bursur had stepped into the space there. With only one way left to go, Adyn turned to his right and found himself nose-to-nose with Fostben.

"There's no place in this town for those who worship false gods," the elder Bursur said.

"Wh-what?" stammered Adyn. "What do you mean 'false gods'? I thought we just agreed—"

"Aye," Fostben said. "We agreed that we would each worship in our own ways. I and everyone else in Tidesafe give our devotions to the moons—the constant moons."

The crowd replied, "The moons!"

"You, on the other hand," the old man continued, "give your allegiance to a sham. You pray to a god who is not there, who performs no miracles and never makes himself known. If that is not worshipping a false god, I don't know what is."

"How can you say that?" Adyn pleaded. "Didn't Paladine just help the armies of good defeat the Dragonarmies? Didn't Mishikal bring her first priestess back from the grave to carry word of the gods' return to the world? Haven't the ancient constellations returned to the sky, showing us that the gods of old once again look down on all we do?"

"Legends and lies!" the old man shouted. "I cannot put any faith into stories sung by wandering minstrels when I have seen the power of the moons with my own eyes."

"Then you have no faith," said Adyn.

It was Fostben's turn to be shocked into momentary silence.

"You know that the three moons exist," Adyn continued, "and you know that they grant you spellcasting power. There is no manner of faith in putting your belief behind something you know is real. Faith requires that you believe in something because you feel it to be true—feel it in your heart and your soul despite the lack of proof."

Fostben remained tongue-tied.

"I've always believed in the powers of the moons," Adyn continued. "I had faith in their power just as I did in Paladine's and all the gods'. I did not require proof because I knew it in my heart to be true."

Adyn looked at the crowd, which no longer seemed nearly as threatening. Clearly they were considering his words. He flashed them his most dazzling smile and hoped for the best.

"All of the gods have power beyond mortal understanding," he said. " Yet they still need one another. They know that in spite of their differences, they are stronger together than apart. They know that infighting weakens them all. The same is true for people. We need one another. No matter our differences, if we set them aside and work together we are stronger than we could ever be as individuals."

The crowd was so quiet that Adyn could hear the sound of the surf crashing against the rocks at the base of the cliff.

"That is what my faith in Paladine gives me," he said.

Fostben's head hung against his chest and his arms lay still at his side. His mouth was moving and his shoulders shook slightly. Adyn wondered if he was crying. Perhaps the acolyte had been too harsh in his rebuke. While he had hoped to secure his own safety, he never intended to crush the old man's faith.

These thoughts fled when Fostben raised his chin. His ancient eyes crackled with arcane energy and his lips mouthed unpronounceable rhymes. He pointed a gnarled finger at Adyn, accusing him.

"This is what my gods have given me," Fostben said, his voice echoing like thunder from an ocean storm that has not yet made landfall.

A tiny ball of fire shot from the old man's fingertip and flew toward Adyn. When it reached the acolyte it exploded into a gigantic flower of flame.

Adyn once again found himself flying through the air, tumbling head over heals. But this time instead of landing on the packed dirt of the town square, he hit something that felt more like a rock, then hit it again, and again. Only after the fifth hit did he realize that he was not hitting the same rock over and over—he was tumbling down the cliff and striking a different rock each time. After two more bounces his journey ended with him lying face-up on a stony beach. Adyn could hear waves crashing and feel the foamy water roll just under his head before it pulled back to the sea.

Although he was bruised and sore, Adyn didn't think he had any truly serious injuries. A few minor healing spells would make him right as rain.

"Paladine be praised," he said quietly as he sat up.

Some might curse their god for putting them through such a painful ordeal, but Adyn preferred to think that Paladine pulled him from a dragon's mouth just before the jaws snapped shut. He knew, as always, that he could count on Paladine to preserve him when all hope seemed to be gone.

"Look," cried a voice from the top of the cliff. "He's still alive!"

"Well, get some torches and go after him!" This second voice belonged to Fostben Bursur. "We can't have him crawling off to Palanthas and spreading lies about us."

Adyn could hear the sound of scuffling on the clifftop above. They would not be long delayed.

"Paladine helps those who help themselves," he said as he gingerly got to his feet and limped down the beach away from the not so quiet little town of Tidesafe.

# 1 Assessing the Damage

Catriona stared into the campfire. She was weary to the bone, tired enough to sleep for a day or more, but she was afraid to close her eyes—afraid because of all the things that had happened, all the changes she had witnessed and been party to. Catriona was afraid that if she went to sleep she would forget something, something important.

She was afraid she might forget Nearra, as innocent a soul as she'd ever met in her travels, and the reason she'd joined this unlikely band of adventurers. Poor Nearra. Her body and mind had been taken over by the spirit of an ancient sorceress named Asvoria. Catriona had tried to save her friend, to purge Asvoria's spirit and allow her friend to live a normal life again. She would have given her life to restore Nearra.

But it wasn't Catriona who gave up her life—it was Elidor. The elf may have been a little too willing to bend rules (and even laws), but he was a good person and a stalwart companion. He deserved better than to die at the hands of Asvoria's shapeshifter, Ophion. And he certainly deserved better than for Catriona to allow his killer to escape. She should have laid down her life before allowing Elidor's noble sacrifice to be squandered. Catriona was afraid she would never be able to make up for this dereliction of duty.

Even if the group was able to track down Asvoria and Ophion, get to them before Nearra's possession became permanent, and exact rightful vengeance for Elidor's death, Catriona was afraid of how many more people—how many more of her friends— would die in the process.

Most of all, though, Catriona was afraid that if she went to sleep she might forget the horrible events of a week ago. She was afraid that when she woke up in the morning she would think this was all just a nightmare. Then, as reality set in, she would have to relive the same gasping, hollow disbelief that she experienced when she watched Elidor's body fall. She would have to feel the same icy emptiness that filled her as she watched Asvoria escape. She would have to live with the numbing sense of despair that replaced the pain and filled her now. And nothing frightened Catriona more than that.

Brushing her red mop of hair out of her eyes, Catriona poked the fire with the elm switch on which she'd cooked her evening's meal. The flames leaped and danced as she jostled the logs. Each crackle sounded like the footfall of an approaching enemy, each pop like a fireball spell cast at her feet. Still she continued to poke. Any noise was better than the silence.

"Will you stop that?" called out Davyn as he wrapped fresh bandages around his chest. Although Davyn sat with his back to the fire, Catriona could see the stab wounds and magical burns that the young man suffered in their recent battle. They were healing nicely, but the great number of them weakened Davyn and he had to make frequent rest stops as the group returned from Navarre. "For once can't we just have some peace and quiet? You're worse than Sindri."

"Hey!" Sindri cried. "I've been good, haven't I?"

"That's what I was saying," Davyn replied. "We finally get you to sit still and be quiet, and suddenly Cat can't stop fidgeting."

Tonight, as Catriona poked the fire and tried to forget the death and suffering she'd witnessed, tonight she would try to hide from her dismay at having once again failed to live up to the standards she'd set for herself.

"Did you hear a word I said?" Davyn asked.

She hadn't. But she felt no need to say so.

"Do you think it's important that we talk?" asked Sindri. "I mean, a lot happened recently—a lot of things I've never seen before, and a lot of things I never wanted to see, but important things. I mean, nothing's ever going to be the same again. Nothing. So maybe it's important that we talk about it. Maybe just a little?"

Poor Sindri. As hard as this was on Cat, she was certain that it was worse for the kender. He was so innocent, so full of life. It was said that a kender never felt fear, but looking at Sindri Cat knew for certain that he felt pain and sorrow.

Sindri Suncatcher claimed to be a wizard—the greatest kender wizard ever—despite the fact that everyone knew that kender could not cast spells. Nearra was just about the only person to humor Sindri in his delusion. Cat knew that Sindri was distraught when Asvoria took control of Nearra's body, but she also knew he believed that he would find a way to use magic to save his friend. Now, with Elidor's death and Asvoria's escape, even he seemed ready to accept that this goal might be beyond his power.

"I don't want to talk about anything," Cat said. Her voice echoed in the night as dry and cracked as the sound of the campfire, and she realized she hadn't said more than a handful of words all day.

"It's not like there's anything to talk about," Davyn added. "Elidor's dead and Nearra might as well be. We broke Asvoria's sword and left Maddoc in a haunted tomb. The end. We're done."

"Oh no," Sindri said. "There's still a lot to do. We've got to figure out where Asvoria went. It's not too late to save Nearra—I know it's not. We destroyed the Aegis, so she's still not unbeatable. All we have to do is find her lair and—"

"No," Catriona said. "What we have to do is return Elidor's effects to his family."

They all looked at the tightly wrapped woolen bundle sitting next to their gear.

Elidor died in Navarre. Rather than drag his remains through the forest for days, only to have to figure out how to get his body back home, they had gathered his effects—his throwing knives, lock picks, and other personal items—and wrapped them in his cloak. Then they had left their friend in the place where he had given his life. The bundle was all that remained of their friend.

"Sure," Davyn said. "We can take Elidor's belongings back to his family. Maybe we'll even tell them where to find him— maybe *they* can go and give him a proper funeral."

"There wasn't time," mumbled Cat. It pained her to think about how they weren't even able to lay Elidor to rest with the honor and ceremony he deserved.

"Right. Whatever," Davyn said. "But we had time to go through his gear."

Cat flinched at these words. Sorting through Elidor's belongings was one of the most difficult things she'd ever done. The whole time she felt like she was invading his privacy, betraying his trust and friendship. But it allowed them to determine where to find his family. The decorative etchings on his daggers marked them as family heirlooms made by a Kagonesti weaponsmith who lived on the island of Southern Ergoth.

"Our first order of business is tending to our honored dead," said Cat.

"Then what?" asked Davyn. "Go after Asvoria so that we can join Elidor as spirits in the Gray? Forget it. We lost. It's over."

"Is that what you're afraid of? Death?" Catriona replied. "There are worse fates than death, Davyn. Just ask Nearra. Technically she is still alive. Indeed, she is more powerful than she could have ever imagined. With Asvoria in control, Nearra's body will likely never be in physical peril again. It is just too bad that her mind has to be completely imprisoned to gain that security. But then it wouldn't bother you very much, since you helped make her that way."

"I didn't know I was doing that," Davyn said, his voice low and throaty. "Maddoc tricked me just as much as he did Nearra." There was no longer any love left between Davyn and Maddoc, the man he had called "Father" since the day his real parents were taken from him. The old man had built the entire relationship with his adopted son on lies and manipulations, including how he was using Nearra.

Once their greatest enemy, Maddoc had joined Davyn and his friends on their most recent quest to save Nearra telling them that his plans had backfired. Asvoria had used her ancient powers to strip Maddoc of his ability to use magic and left him helpless. Whereas once he wanted to be her ally, now Maddoc claimed he wanted to defeat her. When the old man was injured during the battle in Navarre, he told the companions to leave him there, saying that when he rested for a while he would make his way back to civilization—it was more important to him that they carry on the fight.

"You know it's true," Davyn said. "I've worked as hard as

anyone to rid Nearra of that ancient witch's spirit. I've given my blood and sweat to the cause. I . . . I care deeply about Nearra—more deeply than I think she ever knew."

"And yet," said Cat, "you are willing to abandon her to this horrible fate."

"There's nothing we can do!" Davyn shouted. "We tried. We did our best and we barely escaped with our lives. And Elidor lost his. What makes you think the next time would be any different? What makes you think that next time it won't be you that Asvoria kills?"

"There are more important things than simply living," said Catriona. "Honor, courage, and commitment to my friends—all of these I am willing to fight for, I am willing to die for."

"Well maybe I'm not," he said.

Davyn's sandy brown hair fell across his eyes. He finished wrapping his wounds and put on his tunic. It seemed to Cat he was purposely making it difficult to look him in the eyes, as though he was trying not to be seen—or to see reality around him.

In her heart Cat didn't blame him, in fact—she was ashamed to admit—she actually shared that feeling. The group had faced many dangers in the time they had been together. Some they'd defeated, others they'd avoided, and still others they'd tricked their way around, but they'd always come out the other side whole. With Elidor's death, nothing would ever be the same again.

"I've always wondered what the Gray was like," Sindri said breaking the uncomfortable silence. "I'd like to visit there some day."

Both Davyn and Catriona switched their glares from each other onto the kender.

"If she has her way," Davyn said, "we'll all get to visit sooner than we'd like."

"And if you listen to Davyn," Cat replied, "You may put it off for many years, but you will always live in the shadow of your own fear."

"I meant using magic," said Sindri. "I know I'll go there when I die, but I'd like to use my spells to travel there while I'm still alive. You know, so I can enjoy it."

Cat's and Davyn's eyes went wide, and they burst into laughter. Whether the kender had intended it or not, he'd managed to break the mood. He joined in the laughter as well.

Soon enough, though, the laughter fell away, leaving the three young friends looking awkwardly at one another.

"We'd better get some sleep," Davyn said. "We're almost to the coast, but who knows how long it will take us to reach a town."

"Yes," agreed Catriona. "If luck is with us, though, it will have a port where we can book passage to Southern Ergoth to carry the sad news back to Elidor's family. From there we can—"

"Let's take it one day at a time, okay, Cat?" Davyn said, his voice heavy with sadness and sleep.

"You know," Sindri said, "Maddoc showed me a lot of neat spells. I could probably teleport us to a town, or maybe even to Southern Ergoth. I've never been there, but—"

"No!" Cat and Davyn said as one.

Sindri scrunched up his face and groaned.

"I only wanted to help," he said.

"It will be a great help if you'd stop talking about magic," Davyn said as he unfurled his bedroll.

"Yes, my friends" said Cat. "The last thing we need is to bring more magical misfortune down on our heads."

Although her tone was kinder than Davyn's, the words didn't seem to make Sindri feel any better.

"Okay," the kender finally said. "Let's just get some rest. We can talk about it again in the morning."

The only response that came was noncommittal grunts from the blanket-draped lumps that lay on either side of him. Catriona and Davyn lay facing away from one another, leaving Sindri alone in the middle. He sighed and stretched out to stare up at the stars.

Before long, all three were snoring lightly.

# 2

## A FORK IN THE ROAD

The skies were overcast when the group woke the following morning. An undulating ceiling of gray seemed to cover the entire world, and the friends' moods were not much brighter. Davyn immediately gathered up the group's water skins and took them to a nearby stream so they would have fresh water for their journey. Catriona struck camp and arranged her and Sindri's packs. It was Sindri's turn to prepare breakfast, so he boiled a pot of rice, throwing in the remainder of the previous night's rabbit along with a few wild vegetables that he scrounged from the woods nearby. Rather than babble on about whatever topic crossed his mind, he quietly fiddled with what he claimed was a wand that he had somehow summoned in his sleep. And even though they thought it looked more like a twig the kender had rolled on during the night, no one said any such thing.

All of them went about their business silently. If one needed something from another, they exchanged only the minimum number of words required to get their thoughts across. Polite phrases such as "please" and "thank you" were omitted by mutual consent. This sped up the morning ritual considerably. There were 17 no discussions about what lay ahead, what course the group would take after they reached civilization, or (most importantly) what had transpired the night before. Even Sindri, who usually wouldn't stay quiet long enough to get a mouthful of food down, ate in silence. He fiddled with his twig, but he did so without saying a word.

When breakfast was done and the gear stowed, the group set off carrying their silence with them. Like the morning meal, the trip seemed to go more quickly than anticipated.

As they stepped out of the forest, they had to cover their eyes to adjust to the brightness. A strong southerly wind had broken up the even gray ceiling letting blue skies and bright shafts of sunlight peek through. The remaining clouds were whipped into large, dark puffy shapes that floated ominously from the horizon toward the shore.

Luck remained on their side. A town came into view just as swollen droplets of rain began to splatter on the beach, rocks, and the group itself. They broke into a run and managed to get under the eave of a bakery before they were soaked completely.

A wooden table and benches were set up under the awning, obviously in hopes that customers would sit and eat their bread or cakes, encouraging them to buy more after they finished their first round. While the others took places around the table, Cat went into the shop. She returned bearing a small loaf of bread for each of them. Before digging in, the friends pulled dry shirts from their packs and lay particularly soaked items out on the table so that they might be only unpleasantly damp by the time they were repacked.

The baker himself followed close behind Cat. He was a tall man who sported a mustache so thick that it was a wonder he could get any food into his mouth at all, let alone enough to sustain his round belly. He carried a large pot of tea in one hand and three clay mugs in the other.

Soon the companions were drinking tea and eating bread so fresh that a plume of steam escaped when they first broke the crust. Despite the coziness of the situation, Cat and Davyn remained stony faced and taciturn.

"That certainly chases the chill away," Sindri said finally. His cheeks were puffed with bread, and he held onto his mug with both hands. It wasn't much of a conversation starter, but it was a good try for the kender.

"Don't worry," the baker said. "The rain'll stop before too long. This time of year it falls off and on like this all day. It's the storms at night that you need to watch out for."

As if to prove him right, the rain began to ease. Instead of a driving downpour it was now nothing more than a gentle sprinkle.

"Are you planning to stay in town?" the baker asked. "Lila and Old Rag at the inn will be glad for a guest or two. I can see that they give you their best rooms."

The group exchanged glances.

"We are not sure how long we'll be staying in town, good sir," said Catriona. "It depends on how long it takes us to book passage on a ship heading west."

Masts could be seen over the roofs of the town, indicating that the pier was big enough to handle relatively large vessels. Given their position on the coast, that also meant this town was likely to be a popular port of call for ships sailing to or from the islands of the Sirrion Sea.

"Well, there's a ship called *Miller's Dream* that was supposed to weigh anchor this morning," the baker said. "But with the weather and all, I don't think she's actually been able to leave yet."

Cat glanced over the rooftops.

"There's her mast there," the baker said and pointed. "The one flying the Ergothian flag."

The group burst into whirlwind of activity, shaking out their drying clothes and stuffing everything back into their packs as quickly as they could. Sindri had to stand on the bench to reach all the various items he'd emptied from his pack. Where he'd gotten such things as a brooch with the cameo of a young noblewoman, a pressed flower folded in expensive parchment, and a steel piece that was bent in half—let alone why he carried them wherever he went—remained a mystery. Sindri was, after all, a kender, and it was not wise for members of other races to try to make logical sense out of the items in his collection.

As Sindri reached for his set of eight pieces of mismatched silverware, the bench slid out from beneath his feet. The kender tumbled head over heels across the table, knocking over Catriona and spilling the contents of both their packs.

"Sindri!" Cat yelled.

"I'm sorry," said the kender, his voice muffled by the tunic covering his face.

"For once," Cat said, "just once can you concentrate on what you are doing? Can you just stay focused long enough to get one thing done without destroying something along the way?"

She began grabbing items from the ground and carelessly stuffing them back into her pack. All the while she continued to mutter, putting particular emphasis on certain unintelligible words.

"Calm down," said Davyn, who had already secured his few items. "I'll run over and talk to the captain. If they're still looking for passengers they'll certainly be willing to wait an extra ten minutes."

"No!" Cat said, the force of her reply stopping Davyn in his tracks. "Do not separate the party—it makes us too vulnerable."

"Vulnerable to what?" asked Davyn. "We're in a fishing village, Cat."

Catriona continued to fill her pack as quickly as she could. All the while her eyes darted back and forth, scanning the rooftops and nearby buildings for unseen dangers.

"We've been attacked in more peaceful settings than this," she said. "Letting your guard down only invites disaster."

Davyn put his hands on his hips and glared at her.

"You can't go through life expecting enemies to be lurking around every corner," he said.

"I don't," Catriona said. "Just around the corners we fail to secure. How can I protect you—"

"You don't have to protect me." Davyn's voice had dropped to a near whisper, but still managed to convey a deep, abiding anger at the suggestion.

Catriona stopped with her hand still stuffed deep in her pack.

"That's what friends do," she said firmly. "They look out for one another. They stand by one another when the going gets rough. They protect one another when danger lurks."

"But danger isn't lurking everywhere, Cat," said Sindri as he stuffed his bag full of every item within reach, including one of Catriona's tunics, an empty mug that belonged to the baker, and Davyn's half-eaten bread. "You never really know where it is until it finds you."

"Exactly, my point," Catriona said. "We have to be constantly on guard. That's the only way to protect ourselves."

"No one can be on guard all the time," said Davyn. "Even you need to rest, Cat."

"Which is why we need to protect each other," she said as she stuffed the last of her belongings into her pack. "If we do not, then there is no hope for any of us. If we falter for even an instant, one of us may fall."

"Like Nearra," Sindri said sadly. "Or Elidor."

"That was not my fault!" Davyn shouted. He pivoted on his heel and marched toward the port.

"Fault?" said Sindri, but there was no one left to answer him. Cat had already started running after Davyn.

When she got close enough, Cat grabbed Davyn by the shoulder and spun him around. "I said not to split the group," she said.

"So what?" Davyn demanded. "Who made you the leader? Why do you even think that we'd want you as leader?"

"That is not what this is about—" said Cat.

"No," he said. "You may not want it to be about this, but you don't get to decide how I feel, Cat. In fact, you don't get to decide anything about me."

"Well then who does?" asked Cat. "Because you do not seem to be capable of making reliable decisions on your own."

"What does *that* mean?"

"It means that we cannot trust you," Cat said. "We have never been able to trust you, it just took us a while to figure it out. You knew the truth about Maddoc and what he was doing to Nearra from the very beginning, and yet you brought us into your group."

"If you'll remember," he growled back, "I didn't want you or Sindri to join us in the first place. And *you* were the one who invited Elidor into the group."

"Yes," she answered. "And who among that group, including yourself, would not be better off today if you had only been truthful with us? Would Nearra be a prisoner in her own body? Would we be stuck in the middle of nowhere? Would Elidor be dead?"

All the blood drained from Davyn's face, and for a moment Cat thought he might be about to pass out. Still, she couldn't stop. Now that she had begun letting out all the anger and sorrow she'd kept pent up in her heart, she just couldn't stop.

"All of this is your fault," she said. "You are a liar, Davyn, and you'll never be anything more than a liar."

"Yes," Davyn said. The color returned to his cheeks, but it didn't stop until his face was beet red. "I'm a liar. I'm a manipulator. I'm rotten to the core. But at least I know who and what I am. You strut around ordering everyone around like you're some Solamnic Knight in her castle."

"I am not a knight," said Cat.

"No, you're not," he continued. "And you never will be. You're a failure, Cat. And what's more, you're a coward."

"C-coward?" she stammered.

"You think we can't see how scared you are every time you go into battle?" Davyn said. "You took an oath to protect Nearra and you've failed in every way possible. And still you keep acting all righteous, talking about honor and telling us all what we 'must do' and how we must do it. You talk about duty, but it's all a sham. You have no duties and you certainly have no honor. All you have is the strange ability to get innocent people killed."

Now it was Cat who was stunned into momentary silence.

"Why don't you just give up, Cat?" Davyn said in a dark, hurtful whisper. "Why don't you just quit before someone else dies?"

Just then Sindri came running around the corner, having finally stuffed all his belongings into his pack. "What are you waiting for slow pokes?" he said, a mischievous grin on his face as he raced past them toward the docks. "We're going on a boat. This is going to be fun!"

# CHAPTER 3

## OUT WITH THE TIDE

There were three merchant vessels at anchor, but the largest and most impressive one was *Miller's Dream*. Catriona didn't know much about ships, but this one looked especially strong and sturdy. It had three masts, raised decks to the fore and aft, and a hatch large enough to allow a griffin to fly into the cargo hold below which, she guessed, was large enough to comfortably house a dozen or more of the beasts.

The ship teemed with activity. Sailors crawled along the masts poking, prodding, and some even sewing the sails. Others bustled about the deck polishing the ship's brass fittings, mopping the deck, and carrying barrels and crates into the hold. A few pairs of sailors sat on scaffolds suspended from the deck by rope, each pair performing a different task—applying tar to weather worn planks of wood, scraping barnacles from the hull, and applying a fresh coat of paint to the ship's name along the prow.

It was clear that *Miller's Dream* was not going to sail in the next few minutes.

Although Sindri had run on, Catriona was ready to finish her argument with Davyn. In her head she prepared a dozen devastating replies—retorts so deadly accurate and personally stinging that they would leave Davyn completely speechless.

But rather than point out more of her failings, Davyn jogged onto the pier after Sindri. When he reached *Miller's Dream* he cupped his hands around his mouth and shouted, "May I please speak to the captain?"

So, he was just going to pretend that they hadn't argued. He was going to continue on with their business. He was going to wait and restart the conversation at another time when she didn't have the perfect replies ready. Well, she could play that game, too. She would wait—she would bide her time until he decided he was good and ready to continue the argument. And all the while she would keep her answers as well honed and ready as she kept her sword.

But one tiny worry nagged at the back of Cat's mind and, try as she might, she could not dismiss it. What if Davyn was right? That one thought kept her from pressing the matter, from running up to Davyn and telling him just how wrong he was. In fact, the doubt quickly became so heavy that it kept Cat from running at all. She walked slowly down the pier until she came to where her friends waited.

"This is Captain Shirrah," Davyn said. "He says there is still a single cabin available for the journey."

"For a price," said Shirrah. He was a tall man with a hard-looking jaw and flat nose. His dark mahogany skin spoke of his Ergothian heritage, and the keen glint in his eyes revealed his experience. This was a man who looked like he had sailed from one end of Ansalon to the other, who had seen things that would cause even a seasoned warrior's knees to knock, and had come out the other end of the voyage stronger for it. Captain Shirrah was a leader, not just by rank, but by earning the respect of all those who served with him. Catriona could see it in his bearing and hear it in his voice.

"A price we have nearly finished negotiating," Davyn said.

"True enough," said the captain. With a broad sweep of his hand he invited the group to cross the gangplank. "Welcome aboard the *Miller's Dream*. Mr. Therogart, the second mate, will show you to your cabin. Once we are under way, I will be happy to show you around the ship."

"Aye-aye, Captain." Like most dwarves, Mr. Therogart stood about four feet tall and was nearly that broad across the shoulders. The top of his head was covered by a bright blue bandanna, but there was no doubt about the color of his hair. Therogart's chin, neck, and upper chest were completely obscured by as thick and black a beard as Cat had ever seen. As he stood at the top of the gangplank, hands on hips, he seemed pleasant enough. In fact, Cat thought the dwarf was even smiling down at them—either that or his moustache had a natural upward curl.

"Go ahead," Davyn said to Cat, his voice lower than usual. "Make sure Sindri actually makes it to the cabin. You can trust me enough to book our passage, can't you?"

Cat nodded, but did not smile.

Sindri began to sprint across the wooden plank that connected the pier to the ship. It rocked and bobbed with each step, sending Sindri springing higher and higher into the air.

"I wish all roads were like this," he said, bouncing again. "It's almost like flying. That's a pretty difficult spell, though, and I won't be able to cast it for a while. It'd be nice to be able to do this more in the meanwhile so I can get used to the feeling."

As he reached the top of the gangplank, Sindri bent his knees to take a final tremendous leap. He didn't get more than a few inches into the air because a pair of thick, calloused dwarf hands clasped him around the midsection.

"No leaping onboard," Second Mate Therogart said in a flat, gravelly voice. "That's rule twelve."

Sindri's whole body sagged in the dwarf's grasp.

"That's not fun," he said. "Hey! How many rules are there on this ship?"

"Oh, a great many," grumbled Therogart. "Don't worry, I'll make sure you learn them—every last one."

The dwarf put Sindri's feet on the deck, but kept one hand firmly placed on the kender's head.

"Follow me," he said and led the way toward the rear of the ship, guiding Sindri from the top of the kender's bushy head. "Where's your topknot lad?"

"I don't wear one," said Sindri, but his voice seemed far away and preoccupied.

"I wouldn't have to squeeze your skull quite so hard if you had a handle for me to hold onto," Therogart said.

"Oh, I don't mind," said the kender, who by this time was completely absorbed by all the activity around him.

"He thinks this looks more wizardly," Cat said indicating Sindri's hair, which was parted in the middle and hanging straight down past his shoulders.

"Aye, that it does," the second mate said with a chuckle. "A kender wizard. What will they think of next?"

Therogart brought Cat and Sindri to the rear of the ship and in through a door that led underneath the raised aft deck. Inside was a dark, cramped hallway and stairs going down into the bowels of *Miller's Dream.* He explained that the stairs went down to the crew's quarters, the galley, and the holds.

"You're free to wander down there if you like," he said. "But I don't advise it. The crew gets bored when we're too long at sea and they could decide to have a bit of sport with you. Nothing life-threatening, mind you, but they might help themselves to anything of value you are carrying."

"They could try," said Catriona. "Still, your point is taken. We will consider the lower decks off limits. Particularly you, Sindri."

The kender sighed, but didn't say anything. Clearly he got the message.

"That there is the captain's quarters," Therogart continued. "That's off-limits to everyone unless you have a specific invitation from the captain." With a flick of his wrist he turned Sindri's eyes to meet his. "Do I make myself clear?"

Again, the kender sighed.

"Aye-aye," said Sindri. Then he perked up so completely that he seemed to grow six inches taller. "Hey, I sure sounded like a sailor for a minute there."

Therogart turned the kender's eyes forward again as Sindri started rattling off every nautical term he could think of.

"This is your cabin," the second mate said as they reached a door at the end of the hall. He opened it and revealed the room beyond. It was large enough to hold a two-person bunk, two hammocks, and a wooden chair, but not much more. There were no windows or portholes, but a lantern was secured to the far wall and another hung suspended from the ceiling.

"Thank you," Catriona said to Therogart as he shut the door. "This will do perfectly."

"Oh! A hammock!" cried Sindri. "I'm sleeping in one of the hammocks!"

Catriona rolled her eyes.

"That is all we need," she said. "You will be bouncing and spinning all night and none of us will get any sleep."

"Not all night," Sindri said.

"I think it would best for everyone if you took the bunk," Cat said.

"All right," the kender said, doing nothing to mask his disappointment. But he perked up when he started to climb into the bed. "Hey! There's a latch on the bunk."

Without a moment's hesitation, Sindri unhooked the latch and the bed pivoted on a hidden hinge until the mattress was flush against the cabin wall and the whole structure had transformed into a writing desk.

"Wow!" cried Sindri. Then he clapped his hands joyously. "Now I have somewhere to study! Maddoc taught me a lot on the way to Navarre and I wrote it all down, but he said the only way to improve is to practice."

"I was wondering how this trip could become more unpleasant," Cat said. Truthfully, she'd only meant to think the words but out they tumbled from her lips.

Sindri looked at her with a wounded expression.

"What do you mean?" he asked.

"Nothing," said Cat. "It is just, how do you know those spells won't blow a hole in the side of the ship?"

"You don't have any faith in me do you, Cat?" Sindri said. Then after a little thought, he added, "You don't trust me at all."

"That is not true," Catriona said. "I do trust you, Sindri. I just don't trust that magic Maddoc was teaching you. It is foul magic—evil magic."

"There's no such thing," the kender said. "Magic is magic. It's not good or evil. It all depends on the caster."

"It depends on the color of their robes, Sindri," said Cat. "The Black Robes are power hungry manipulators, and Maddoc's robes were as black as they come."

"Well I'm not a Black Robe and you still don't trust me," the kender said, putting his hands on his hips and looking defiantly at his friend. "You don't trust any of us, Cat. You made it clear this morning that you didn't trust Davyn to go off on his own, even after he's turned his back on Maddoc. That's why you're always so nervous and over-protective, isn't it—because you really don't trust any of us?"

Catriona shook her head. "No," she said. "It's just that there are so many powerful forces aligned against us, and we never seem to do the smart thing—"

"So we're stupid, is that it?" Sindri asked pointedly.

"That's not what I meant at all," said Catriona.

"But that's what you think," Sindri continued. "You think we're all stupid because we don't listen to you. And you think if we would, then everything would be better."

Something inside Catriona snapped and her patience evaporated.

"Well, I fail to see how it could be much worse," she said bitterly. "Elidor is dead. Nearra is as good as dead."

"And how would you have made things better?" asked Sindri.

"In the first place," Catriona answered, "I would have kept us all together and focused on a plan of action. Between your wandering and Davyn's bungled manipulation we wasted weeks that could have been used to—"

Catriona heard a low creaking sound carry through the walls. For the first time, she noticed that the ship was rocking gently from side to side.

"We're under way," she said.

"We are?" said Sindri. "I wanted to see them weigh the anchor."

"That's just a phrase," Cat said. "They don't actually weigh the anchor."

"Either way," said Sindri, "I wanted to be on deck when we set sail. I wanted to watch the land get smaller and smaller until it wasn't there at all. Maybe there's still time to see that. Let's head up to the deck and—"

Catriona stepped in front of the door.

"Where is Davyn?" she asked.

"I don't know," said Sindri as he tried to squeeze through Cat's legs to get to the door.

"If we are this far underway," Catriona said, "then why hasn't Davyn joined us? Where is he?"

Sindri stopped squirming for a moment and thought.

"He's probably on deck watching the shore like I want to be," he said. "Let's go find him."

Catriona nodded. Just as she was turning to open the door, someone knocked. She pulled the door open, prepared to chastise Davyn for not rejoining them immediately.

"This is for you," Captain Shirrah said and handed her a piece of paper that had been folded in half. "It's from your friend."

# CHAPTER

# 4    STORMY SEAS

"What does it say? What does it say?"

Sindri danced under, between, and around Catriona's legs as she unfolded the paper. He tried to find a spot from which he could read the note, but when it became clear that no such position existed and that Cat had no intention of holding the page at a more accommodating angle, the kender leaped up and tried to snatch the page from his friend's hand.

Catriona had spent enough time around Sindri to anticipate this behavior and nimbly pulled the note out of reach. She stood there with one hand raised above her head and looked balefully at Sindri.

"How can I possibly know the answer to that question when you will not be still long enough for me to read it?"

The kender stopped in mid hop, balanced on one leg with his arms wildly akimbo.

"We look to be sailing into a bit of rough weather," Captain Shirrah interjected. "I suggest you stay in your cabin until it's passed. Judging by the look on that young man's face as he went ashore, the note will give you plenty to talk about in the meanwhile." He spun on his heel and strode down the corridor, closing the door behind him.

"What's it say?" Sindri asked. His voice was calm and relaxed, as though he was sitting on a comfortable cushion instead of standing in an acrobatic pose.

"I will read it aloud," said Cat.

Sindri sank to the floor, sat cross-legged at Catriona's feet, and adopted a sulky pose—elbows resting on knees, balled fists supporting his sagging chin. Cat did her best to ignore him.

Holding the paper at arm's length, grasping it with both hands like a town crier reading an official proclamation, Cat read the note.

"Goodbye."

"That's all he wrote?" Sindri whined, but a glare from Cat silenced him. She continued to read.

> Goodbye, my friends. We've traveled a long way together and covered ground we never expected to see. From the start we've had our differences. Yet we were always able to get past them because of our common goal: to save Nearra. We may have quibbled from time to time about how best to accomplish this, but we pulled together because that was the only way to get the job done.
>
> We were fighting a losing battle. We all knew it. We were racing against an hourglass whose sands we could not see. It's time to recognize that the hourglass has been drained. We've run out of time, and all the good intentions under the moons cannot change the fact that we failed in our mission. Perhaps you are too stubborn to admit it, but the battle has been lost. To continue fighting is pointless. The only thing to be gained is a meaningless death for a cause that no longer exists.

I've misled you all from the moment we met. I've told so many different lies that I can't tell the truth from the stories I want to believe. I honestly can't think how much blame I actually deserve for what's happened to Nearra, but the truth is that I am at least partially at fault and that makes me sick at heart. But worse still is the fact that you were completely right, Cat. I am certainly responsible for Elidor's death. I can't face his family.

I've paid Captain Shirrah for your passage to the Ergothian Empire and back. May luck see you through every trouble your bravery brings down on your heads.

Goodbye,<br>Davyn

"That's all?" Sindri said, finally breaking the silence.

"Of course that's all," Cat snapped. "What else would he say? Why would he give us any more thought than that? Isn't that what he has always done? Should we not expect him to take part in planning our next step and then just wander off to follow whatever path he fancies?"

"It's not really like that," said Sindri.

"And isn't that how things always go wrong?" continued Cat, cutting Sindri off before the kender could finish. "We talk about our situation, weigh our options, and make a plan. Then someone gets a burr under his saddle and goes off in some other direction, following some other plan, and the rest of us are left to follow in his wake so that he doesn't get his fool head handed to him."

"Cat," Sindri said. "Maybe you should just take a breath and calm down for a minute."

"I'm tired of being calm," she said. "I'm tired of being patient, and I'm tired of being ignored. But most of all, I'm tired of having to protect my friends from their own foolhardiness."

Cat's body quivered with emotion. Her hands were clenched into fists. Her eyes were rimmed with tears. Her shoulders shook with barely controlled anguish.

"If I have to tie your hands behind your back and use a pack of herding dogs to get you where you're supposed to be," she said with clipped, military precision, "I'll make sure that the next plan we make is followed to the letter."

"Gee, with an attitude like that, I don't understand how Davyn could ever have wanted to leave us," Sindri said under his breath.

"What was that?" demanded Cat.

Instead of backing down, however, Sindri stood up as tall as he could and answered.

"It sounds to me like maybe you were a little too hard on Davyn," Sindri said. "Did you really tell him that Elidor's death was his fault?"

"Not in so many words," said Cat. Then she shook her head and lowered her eyes. "Actually, yes, I did say that in exactly those words."

"And you think it's any wonder that Davyn didn't want to spend a week sailing around the Sirrion Sea with you? Cat, you're lucky he didn't try to kill *you* for saying such a mean thing. You know what good friends he and Elidor had become."

"I know," said Cat.

"What kind of leadership do you call that?" Sindri asked. "Trust has to be earned, Cat. What have you done to deserve our trust?"

That evening Catriona stood at the ship's railing and stared out across the water. The sea was choppy due to the heavy weather that still hung along the horizon. Every few moments Cat could see lightning arc from one cloud to another or leap down to strike the sea. Distant peals of thunder mixed with the constant sound of the waves and sails flapping in the wind. Although it was certainly noisier than in their cabin, where she and Sindri had sat silently for several hours, at least there was a greater sense of peace here on the deck.

"Beautiful, isn't it?" said a voice directly behind Cat. She let out a mild yelp of surprise and turned to see Captain Shirrah standing a respectful distance away.

"I did not mean to startle you," he said.

"No, Captain," Cat answered. "I was merely lost in thought."

"Trouble between friends is like a storm at sea," he said. "It always seems small and unimportant until you are in the middle of it."

Cat looked at him with wide eyes.

"How did you know?"

Captain Shirrah laughed.

"An old sea dog knows many things," he said. "The look on your friend's face when he gave me the note told me a great deal. Your expression upon receiving it said a great deal more. But the most informative source is the fact that a ship's walls are quite thin and your cabin shares a wall with mine."

Cat blushed.

"I apologize," she said. "We seem to have run out of things to say to one another though, so we won't keep you awake with our arguing."

The captain chuckled and stepped up to the rail. Cat was struck again with how charismatic the man was, what a good leader he seemed to be—the kind of leader she used to dream of being.

"There is nothing quite so painful as having your friends scoff at your heart's desire," he said.

Cat was even more impressed. It was almost as if he were able to read her mind.

"Some dreams are unattainable," she said.

Shirrah watched the horizon for a moment before saying, "In my experience, the only unattainable things are those that one is afraid to reach for."

"But doesn't it hurt even more to reach for a dream and fail?" asked Cat.

"Perhaps," the captain answered. "But even if you never gain your heart's desire, you may find something more valuable in the trying."

By the time Cat came back to the cabin, Sindri was clearing off the desk and pulling on the hinge to flip it back into a bunk. He had the tired, bleary-eyed look of someone who had spent too many hours reading.

"Sindri," Cat said and waited for the kender's reply. There was no use trying to start a conversation if he was still offended. Much to her relief though, Sindri's anger seemed to have lifted the same way that Cat's melancholy had—not completely, but enough so that it was no longer sharp and unavoidable.

"Yes?"

"I'm sorry about earlier," said Cat.

Sindri smiled. "Me, too," he said.

"And I wanted to give you this." She pulled a dagger from her belt and handed it to him. It was surprisingly light, made of a burnished metal, and had patterns of thorns etched along its blade. The handle was wrapped with a leather grip, and the pommel was shaped like a stylized rosebud.

"What's this for?" asked Sindri.

Cat smiled down at him as though he were a child who asked why the sky is blue. "Most people use it for cutting things," she said playfully. Despite the improvement of his mood, Sindri did not seem to feel playful. In fact, he seemed rather suspicious of the gift. "My aunt bought it for me in Palanthas when I was her squire. She said it was her way of watching out for me when she was not around."

"Thank you," Sindri said. "What a nice gesture. Are you sure you want to give up your good luck charm now?"

Cat laughed. "It's not a good luck charm," she said. "It's a dagger. Use it in times of trouble. It has saved me on a number of occasions, and I hope it will do the same for you."

"Oh," said Sindri, his voice flat and emotionless. "Thank you for the thought, Cat, but I think I'll just stick with my spells. That's what we wizards do best."

"For Paladine's sake, Sindri, you can't rely on your magic." In spite of her good intentions, Cat could not fight her exasperation at Sindri's refusal to admit the truth. "Half of your spells come from a ring, and the other half never do what you intend them to."

The kender's expression grew stony.

"Sindri, I've known you longer than anyone else in our group," Cat continued. "You are my friend, and I want nothing but your happiness, but you are not a wizard. So far you have benefited from extraordinary good luck and the fact that nearly everyone under the sun underestimates what your people are capable of. But you cannot trust your life to dumb kender luck. It cannot last."

"Gee, Cat," said Sindri, his normally cheerful voice filled with as much hurt as Cat had ever heard. "I can't imagine why Davyn thought that you wouldn't be supportive of him. You're nothing but the soul of encouragement."

Catriona had no idea what to say. She hadn't meant to insult any of her friends but that's exactly what she had done and kept doing. Thinking over the past few days she wasn't sure if she'd uttered a single sentence that wasn't hurtful to someone.

"I-I didn't mean. . ." she said.

"Actually," Sindri said, "I think you did mean every word you said. You just didn't think about how they'd make us feel. You don't seem to care."

Cat flinched at the kender's words.

"No, Sindri," she said. "I do care—"

"Of course you do," he interrupted. "You care about beating Asvoria. You care about saving Nearra's life. You care about a lot of things. But the thing you care about most is that bizarre, twisted mess of rules you call your 'Code of Honor.' It's more important to you than anything anyone else says or feels."

The tears were in Cat's eyes again, but she bravely held them at bay.

"You do not understand," she said. Her voice was weak. "That code is everything. It tells me what is important in life, how to act in any situation, and where to draw inspiration. Without it, I am nothing."

"If that's true," said Sindri, "then you really are nothing."

Cat stood there mute. Her jaw hung open and her eyes felt like they wouldn't close. She felt as though she had just been punched in the stomach. Her whole body felt numb and like it might collapse at any moment. She wanted to tell Sindri how wrong he was. She wanted to pummel the kender for even suggesting such a thing. She wanted to run. She wanted to cry. She wanted to apologize. She wanted to scream. Most of all she wanted to think of something to say, but no matter how hard she tried nothing came to her mind. Nothing but the same nagging thought that plagued her after the last conversation she'd had with Davyn: What if he's right?

Bitter, hard-edged silence returned to the cabin, and as they climbed into hammock and bed respectively, neither Cat nor Sindri said another word.

Cat woke from a sound sleep to a nearly deafening explosive noise. Her hammock swung violently back and forth as the floor pitched and rolled wildly. Sindri at first was tossed to the far side of his bunk, landing with his back and feet pressed flat against the cabin wall. Then, when the ship rolled the other way, the kender literally tumbled out of bed and all the way across the room.

"That was fun," Sindri said. "Let's do it again!"

"Are we under attack?" asked Cat. "How could Asvoria have found us so quickly?"

Another explosion sounded above. This time, though, the two were awake enough to recognize it as thunder, but thunder the way it sounds when the tree next to you is struck by lightning.

Cat moved slowly to keep her balance while getting out of the hammock as the ship began to pitch the other way. By the time she was at the cabin door the floor was in its usual orientation, but she could tell it wouldn't stay there for long.

Meanwhile, Sindri curled himself into a ball and let the tilting floor roll him back and forth across the room.

"Where are you going?" called Sindri as he rolled past the doorway.

"Up on deck," Cat said. "The crew might need some help."

She stepped into the hall, arms outstretched so that she could lean on both walls for support. Just when it seemed to be settling into a rhythm, the vessel took a sudden lurch to one side (usually to the right) before falling back into the previous rhythm. As Cat reached the door to the main deck she saw why.

The seas were wild. Waves taller than the *Miller's Dream*'s main mast rose all around them. As the crew tied off the main sails and worked to keep the rigging from becoming tangled or worse, broken in the wind, the ship crawled along the sides of the swells sailing from one wave to the next to avoid being caught in any crest. Every once in a while the sea or the wind did not cooperate and a wall of water smacked into the midship sending sailors sprawling and causing the whole vessel to tip dangerously to the side.

Lightning flashed almost constantly, but Cat heard only a few cracks of thunder. Those, however, were monstrous sounds, rumbling so deep that it gave Cat a weightless feeling in the pit of her stomach.

The wind and waves had torn ropes and tarps free from where they had been secured. Several heavy barrels rolled across the deck threatening to crush any sailor who wasn't alert enough to sense its presence. One hit the wall near the door where Cat stood watching.

"Wow!" said Sindri as he tumbled down the hall. He might have spun out onto the deck if Cat weren't there to bar his way. "Who knew thunderstorms could be this much fun?"

As the sea pitched, the barrel slowly started to roll straight down the deck toward a group of sailors who were trying to secure a corner of the main sail whose rigging had torn loose. They couldn't know it was coming and it would build up quite a head of steam by the time it reached the far end of the deck. Cat imagined the sailors flying here and there like pins in a gnomish bowling game.

Cat leaped from the relative safety of the doorway, landing directly on top of the barrel. It was full of something heavy and even though it was moving slowly, it had a good deal of power.

"What are you doing?" Sindri cried.

"Saving those sailors!" Cat said. "They're fighting to protect us. Honor demands that I do no less for them."

"This is what I was talking about," said Sindri, rushing across the deck after her. "You have no clue what to do on a ship in a

DRAGON DAY

storm. What do you think is more dangerous to the crew, a barrel that rolls just the way every other barrel on the ship rolls or a crazy woman with a sword who runs onto the deck in the middle of a storm?"

Together they managed to wrestle the barrel to a stop.

Cat wanted to argue with Sindri, to tell him he was wrong, that the sailors would thank her for the help. Then she thought about how she felt whenever Nearra got involved in a battle. No matter how badly they were outnumbered, Cat always felt better if the untrained Nearra would simply stay on the sidelines. Every time she grabbed a weapon and tried to help, it only gave Cat one more thing to worry about.

"You're right," Cat said.

"Of course I am," said Sindri.

"A wise warrior knows which battles to fight."

"And when to run away," Sindri added with a smile.

Suddenly a tremendous wave crashed over the rail swamping the deck. Cat found herself tumbling weightless through the water. Wherever she reached out she found nothing solid. There was no trace of the deck or the barrel or even Sindri.

"I've gone overboard," she thought to herself. "Sindri was right, and now I'm going to be lost at sea because I was too stubborn."

She tried to call out for help, but only took a mouthful of seawater into her lungs.

"This is it," she thought as she started to choke. "The sin of pride will be my downfall."

Then, as suddenly as it had come, the water receded leaving Cat lying on the deck. She was safe—wet, bruised, coughing, and sore, but safe.

"Help!"

It was Sindri.

Cat rolled to her feet and looked around, but she couldn't see the kender anywhere.

"Cat!" came Sindri's voice again. "Help me!"

Then she saw him. Sindri was on the wrong side of the railing, dangling over the raging sea. He held onto the wooden rail with both hands.

"Sindri!"

Cat took a single step toward her friend and then once again was knocked down by a crashing wave. The feeling was just as disorienting as before, but this time Cat did not panic. She held her breath and let the water take her where it wanted—toward the rail and Sindri.

She opened her eyes and through the murky water she saw Sindri still hanging on for dear life. Cat reached a hand out between the railing's posts, stretching to grab her friend's arm or sleeve or even a good handful of hair. Sindri let go with one hand and stretched it toward Cat's. Their fingers just brushed against one another when the wave crested and the water began to recede.

Suddenly, instead of floating in the churning water, Sindri was hanging from a slick wooden railing by only one tiny hand. He gasped once and his eyes went wide as his fingers gave way.

Cat tried to grab him, but she couldn't move fast enough. As she watched, Sindri tumbled through the air toward the roiling water below. She cried out his name, but the sound was lost as a bolt of lightning crackled overhead and thunder filled the air. By the time Cat's vision cleared from the flash, Sindri was gone, lost somewhere beneath the waves.

CHAPTER

5     LOST AT SEA

T hat's a shame," Sindri thought while tumbling headlong away from the railing.
"Things had been going so well, too."

Sindri wasn't certain what had happened, though he felt pretty
sure that he'd been knocked overboard by a wave—either that or
a giant octopus. Whichever it was, the kender wished he'd been
looking the right way when it happened. Not that he would have
been able to get out of the way, in fact he probably wouldn't have
even tried, he just would have loved to see either one of those
things close up. The chances of him getting hit by another giant
wave (or giant octopus) were remote at best. But Sindri was more
bothered by another nagging thought.

"I can't swim."

And with the sea rushing up toward him so quickly, that was
sure to be his biggest problem very soon. Cat had just finished
telling Sindri that she was tired of rescuing her friends. And he'd
just finished telling her that a wise warrior needs to know when
to run away. Why did she have to pick this time to listen to him?
She'd ignored him so many times in the past.

44     But Sindri was almost out of time. The wave below was rising

just as quickly as he was falling. It looked so angry. The sea had always seemed a peaceful thing to Sindri in the past, but this wave seemed to be reaching up for him, trying to grab him the way so many merchants and constables had, angry and accusatory.

If it was a merchant, I'd be able to slip away, he thought. I'd find a quiet spot to sit until he'd calmed down. That's what I need, a quiet spot of water until things blow over.

As if in answer to Sindri's thoughts, the patch of water directly below him grew calm and still.

Perfect, he thought as he hit the water headfirst. Sindri didn't notice that the water was not only calmer, it was also bluer and it seemed to be glowing slightly. He also didn't notice that instead of a splash he broke the surface with a bright white flash like a lightning bolt.

However, as he looked around the surrounding water hoping to see a giant octopus, Sindri did notice that there was no trace of the ship, whose hull should have been bobbing in the water nearby.

"Now this is interesting!"

"Help!" Cat called, in hopes that one or more of the sailors had seen Sindri's fall. But they were too busy trying to keep the ship afloat, never thinking the passengers would be foolish enough to come out on deck in such a storm. By the time she got their attention and explained what had happened it would be too late. There would be no hope of rescuing Sindri. In truth, there was only one hope for the kender and Cat was it.

Catriona climbed onto the railing. She took a long careful look along the ship's waterline and saw no sign of the missing kender, then dived headlong into the stormy sea.

She expected things to be calmer underwater away from the wind and rain and thunder. But the truth was it was just as chaotic here. Cat could still hear the storm raging above, but it sounded faraway and slow, as though the clouds and thunder were wrapped in thick blankets.

With a strong series of kicks, Catriona broke the surface. As she breathed deeply to fill her lungs as much as possible, she looked all around for signs of Sindri—his robe or belt or even a few random items from one of his pockets—but there was nothing. There didn't seem to be any current that would have pulled Sindri away from the general area. Where could the kender have gone?

Cat took another quick series of deep breaths, held the last one, and dived back below the waves. The water was dark, and although the lighting above provided flashes of illumination, she couldn't see more than a dozen feet in any direction. If Sindri was unconscious, sinking, or in any other sort of trouble that had carried him away from the surface the only way Cat would find out was by diving deeper.

Cat tried to swim straight down, but she could feel that the water was lifting her up. Then, although she stopped swimming and just floated scanning the area for signs of her missing friend, she could feel the wave crest and start pulling her down. This was the sort of motion she had feared—the kind that, if Sindri had been caught in it, there would be no way to predict where he'd been carried.

Cat could feel her chest starting to ache. It was time to go back up for another lungful of air. She kicked toward the surface, but instead felt the swell suddenly and quickly pull her downward.

She found herself tumbling so wildly that she lost all sense of direction. Even if she could free herself, Cat no longer had any idea which way was up. The current sped up, changed direction, then changed direction again and sped up even more. She still had no idea of which way she was being pulled, but she was going there in a hurry.

Cat could feel her heart beating powerful, slow beats. Each one used more of the oxygen in her lungs. When at last, there seemed to be none left, her heart began to beat very quickly. Her lips started to quiver as her chest shuddered with the urge to cough, but Cat knew that the moment she did her lungs would fill with water and that would be the end of her.

Finally, she could hold it back no longer. Her stomach clenched in a body-wracking cough at the same moment that Cat broke the water's surface and returned to the stormy night air. As she drew in a series of ragged, desperate breaths, thanking Paladine for what she presumed was divine intervention, Cat realized that she was still moving upward—that the wave was cresting. It would crash again at any moment.

She looked over her shoulder to see how long she had to refill her lungs. Instead of seeing the raging sea, though, Cat's eyes were filled by a massive wall made of curved wooden planks.

The wave broke against *Miller's Dream*, smashing Catriona headlong into the hull. When the water pulled back, it took Cat's unconscious body with it. The ship sailed on, and the waves carried their new toy away into the night.

"Aha!" Sindri yelled out loud as he burst through the surface of the water. He wanted to think about how he'd gone from swimming down to jumping up, how the wild churning sea had turned into a shallow pool of chilly brackish liquid, and what the horrible little creatures were who crawled on the floor outside the pool. Sindri wanted to think about all these things, but right now he was too busy taking heaving gasps to refill his empty lungs.

When his head stopped spinning, Sindri stood and looked around. The room was small and dark, but some light came from under a door in the wall directly in front of him. There were dozens, perhaps hundreds of the misshapen creatures scurrying about the room and swimming in the pool, each with a few recognizable body parts—eyes or claws or mouths—arranged in a completely different unnatural and disgusting form. They made quiet chittering and whining sounds, but did not pay any particular attention to the kender or one another.

Sindri raised one leg over the stone lip that surrounded the pool, careful not to step on any of the bizarre creatures. Before his foot could touch the floor, though, a hand grasped the back of his collar and pulled him abruptly into the air (a sensation that every kender eventually becomes accustomed to). He found himself face-to-face with a man wearing black robes. The dimness of the room and the depth of the robes left the man's face completely hidden in shadow except for his eyes—golden eyes that seemed to Sindri to be shaped like hourglasses.

"What are you doing in my home?"

# 6     Kindness from a Stranger

By and large, the Solamnian coast is as rocky and inhospitable a shore as any in Ansalon. The water is generally deep, which is good for merchant vessels weighed down with cargo, but there are precious few places where the waves lap up to welcoming beaches. More often they crash into sheer cliff faces or pound relentlessly over shoals that could snap the spine of even the sturdiest Ergothian ship.

The beaches that are to be found are covered with stones and broken seashells rather than soft golden sand, and twice per day the incoming tide deposits all sorts of flotsam and jetsam on their shores. Walking along these beaches was difficult and uncomfortable. Sleeping on them was even worse.

Adyn Thinreed managed to get only a few fitful hours of sleep on the rocky beach and had eaten a few handfuls of dried rations when he felt safe enough to stop and dig them out of his pack. Despite the fact that he'd been able to heal all his major wounds through the gift of Paladine's divine power, Adyn was still bruised and sore. But no matter how fast he moved, the wind still carried to his ears the voice of Fostben yelling "burn the heretic" and "death to the god worshipper" telling him that **49** he had to somehow find a way to move even faster.

He couldn't let the Bursurs or anyone from the town of Tidesafe catch him, so he pressed on along the beach as fast as his bruised legs would carry him. He passed all manner of items scattered across his path by the morning tide—strips of seaweed, the carcasses of fish and squid, shards of broken bottles, driftwood, and coins from seemingly every realm in Ansalon. There was nothing, Adyn thought, nothing that could be so interesting that he would make him slow his pace by even a single stride.

Then he saw the girl.

Certainly she was a girl—or, more correctly, a young woman— and even with seaweed tangled in her red hair, cuts and scrapes covering her face and arms, she was quite a pretty girl, Adyn thought. But neither her gender nor her looks were what struck him at first glance. When he initially saw her lying at the surf's edge, there was something in her posture and lithe frame that told him this young woman was a warrior.

Upon closer inspection he noticed that she wore chain mail under her tunic. That she had managed not to drown dressed this way was additional proof that the gods were watching over her. And on the beach near her unconscious body were a sword and helmet of the type used by Solamnic nobles and knights.

Adyn bent down and shook her gently by the shoulders.

"Milady," he said. "Are you all right?"

The young woman did not answer. What's more, Adyn realized how cold her skin was and how shallowly she was breathing. If he left her here, she would certainly die of exposure.

At first he thought that she was a gift from Paladine—that if he simply left her here, the Bursurs would have to stop their pursuit of him to help this poor shipwrecked soul. But immediately he realized that they would do no such thing. In fact, if they picked up on the clues that she had ties to the Solamnic knights, the Bursurs might well kill her for being associated with a "god worshipping cult" like the knighthood.

No, it was clear that Adyn had no choice but to stop his flight and tend this lost sheep. Yet another challenge on his pilgrimage, he realized. He must somehow find a way to tend her wounds and nurse her back to health without being caught by the fanatical Bursur family.

The question remained, how to do it.

As Adyn made a quick assessment of the damage the girl had suffered then cleaned the cuts on her face and neck—certainly the result of being washed unceremoniously onto a rocky shore—he thought about his options. There had been no time for him to meditate and pray for Paladine to renew his magical reservoir. Without those devotions, Adyn had no healing power and that meant he would have to carry the unconscious girl wherever they were going to go.

The beach was a few hundred feet wide now as low tide approached. It was covered in smooth, rounded stones and sea-shells. There were patches of scrub brush scattered here and there as the beach led up the steep hill to the Solamnic plains.

After a few moments' consideration, Adyn decided that the hill was their best option. It might be slow going, but he doubted the muscle-bound Bursurs would be able to do it much faster. In fact, they seemed clumsy enough that Adyn thought, even carrying the unconscious girl, he might be able to climb faster than they would. After a while the might just give up and go home.

The acolyte hoisted the girl across his back, picked up her helmet and sword (for he was sure if he didn't she would just come back for them the moment she awoke) and marched to the hill. The first few steps up the slope were tricky. Adyn felt as though his feet might fly out from under him at any moment. But once he got six feet up the hill the footing became more stable and he was able to proceed at a more reasonable pace.

At his best guess, the Bursur family was an hour or so behind him, perhaps more as they were not moving with the same sense of emergency that Adyn was. He'd spent a good fifteen minutes examining and treating the unconscious girl, and another five or more deciding what course of action to follow. So, at a conservative estimate, he would be able to climb for about half an hour before the Bursurs came into view, and about forty-five minutes before they could begin climbing after him. If he kept up his current climbing pace, he'd be almost halfway to the top by then. That might actually be enough of a lead to convince his tormentors that following just wasn't worth the effort.

Things were beginning to look better than they had since before Adyn walked into the town of Tidesafe.

That's when his foot came down on a loose piece of shale. His weight dislodged the sliver of stone and about a square foot of loose dirt that surrounded it. Before he was even sure what had happened, Adyn and his charge were tumbling down the hillside on a tiny avalanche of scree and dust. They slid off a small ledge and fell the final few feet to the rocky beach, landing with a teeth-clattering jolt.

Once Adyn made sure that neither he nor the unconscious girl had more than a few extra scratches to mark their wild ride, the acolyte stood up and dusted himself off. This complicated things considerably. Now he would only have time to climb a few hundred yards up the hill before the Bursurs arrived, not nearly enough to discourage them from climbing after him. In fact, he was worried that they would still be within range of the Bursurs's spells.

As he bent to lift the young woman again, something caught Adyn's eye. For several moments he stood there staring. The ledge from which they'd just fallen hid beneath it a small, dark passage that seemed to lead into a tidal cave. Obscured by the overhang and scrub brush and set low on the hill, the cave had been completely invisible to him when he stood on the beach.

"And that means it'll be invisible to the Bursurs, too," he said to himself, hoping that he was actually correct in that assumption. For all he knew, the cave was well known to the people of Tidesafe. But it was the best chance he and the young woman had to escape his pursuers.

Adyn lifted the girl in his arms the way a parent might lift a sleeping child. Her body was shivering and her forehead was covered with beaded sweat. Carefully he hunkered down low and carried her into the dark space beneath the ledge.

It took a minute or so for his eyes to adjust, but Adyn could soon see that this was indeed a tidal cave. The floor was covered with rocks, shells, and flotsam just like on the beach. Clearly the tide reached here during its high phase. That was good in that it would provide a period of protection when no one could enter the cave, so Adyn could safely sleep or pray. On the other hand, unless he could find a ledge that remained above the waterline, there would be nowhere for him or the girl to rest. They would have to spend all of the high tide floating or treading water.

Thankfully, after a few feet or so, the cave opened up. The walls were layered and stratified—like natural steps—and there were literally dozens of ledges above the apparent water line. Looking up, Adyn saw that although the cave walls narrowed about forty feet over his head, the space continued for quite a ways afterward. Judging by the diffuse light that seemed to be coming from the ceiling and the cool breeze that came in the cave mouth, he guessed that the space went all the way to the top of the hill.

Climbing to a safe perch, Adyn gently lay the unconscious girl down and made her as comfortable as possible. He used his pack as a pillow, and covered her with his own blanket, but still she shivered as though she were stranded in a blizzard. He knew that her body was in shock because of the trauma it had suffered. It was important to keep her as warm as possible. To do that, Adyn would have to build a fire, but he wasn't sure that was safe.

Even though the opening at the top of the cave gave them a natural chimney to keep the air clear, that was actually a problem. Smoke in the middle of the wilderness was sure to tip off even the reasonably dull-witted Bursar family.

Still, it was a risk he'd have to take. The young woman's life could depend on it. With any luck, the Bursurs would continue their mindless pursuit through most of the day, and once night fell it would be nearly impossible to trace the smoke back to its origin. After a good rest, Adyn would have the strength of body and mind to renew his contact with Paladine, and a relatively small dose of healing magic would certainly put the girl to right. All they had to do was make it through the night.

# CHAPTER

# 7    The Master of the Tower

"Hello!" Sindri called out. He was glad that the man in the black robes had taken him out of the room with the pool. After only a few minutes in there, Sindri had begun to feel disturbed by the labored breathing and unearthly noises the creatures made. Sindri had hoped the man was going to take him to a nice parlor with a fire and something warm to eat and drink.

Instead, the stranger had taken Sindri a few doors down the hall, ushered him into what seemed like a dungeon cell, and then mysteriously disappeared. Sindri didn't hear him go. He didn't even hear him close the cell door, but by the time the kender turned around the stranger had vanished. The cell was too small to pace around, the walls were too slick with mold and slime for him to climb, and the only furnishing was a hard wooden pallet that was bolted to the wall. With nothing else to do, Sindri simply sat there and tried desperately not panic, or worse, get bored.

"Helloooooo!"

For a while he had watched faint, flickering torchlight play against the small patch of wall visible through the cell door's 55 single tiny, barred window. But the torch was too far down the hall to cast any interesting shadows.

Then Sindri put all his effort into listening. He concentrated so hard that he felt as though his ears were actually stretching away from the sides of his head. But try as he might, he didn't hear anything but the occasional gurgling, whining sounds of those horrible creatures in the other room.

Finally, Sindri thought up a game to occupy his mind. The game was called "What If I Hadn't Lost All My Spell Components and That Strange Man Hadn't Taken My Ring?" Although the name was rather long and complicated, Sindri thought the game itself was quite fun. He imagined all sorts of magical solutions he could come up with to solve his current predicament. One minute he pictured himself blowing the door off the hinges with great bolts of lightning. The next he imagined himself summoning a griffin that would tear down the cell door or maybe even part of the wall then fly away carrying Sindri on its back. Of course, the fact that he'd never performed any of these spells wasn't part of the game. What fun would that be?

The kender had been playing his new game long enough to imagine no fewer than one hundred and fifty-seven different ways to escape (several of them having up to a dozen minor variations on color, sound, and the amount of collateral damage) when he heard the sound of footsteps descending a stone staircase. He sprung from his seat and leaped at the door, grasping onto the window bars with both hands. Even though this took up almost the entire space of the tiny window, Sindri tried to squeeze his nose and eyes through the bars for a better look.

He could see a shadow blot out the faint torchlight as the footsteps drew closer. And closer. Soon they were only a few feet away, practically right outside the door. Then they stopped.

Sindri waited to see what the feet would do next, but they

didn't do anything. Try as he might, Sindri could not see anyone or anything in the hall. Complete and utter silence returned. Finally, he could take it no longer.

"Helllllooooooo!" Sindri called out as though he were in a valley trying to get the attention of a friend standing on a nearby hill. The sound echoed in the hallway in a way that usually the kender would have found so interesting that he'd repeat it several times. Right now, though, he was frustrated because whatever had caused the sound of footsteps (and in a strange place like this, you could never be sure that anything was what it sounded like) was gone.

Sindri let go of the bars and dropped dejectedly to the cell floor. Turning around to return to the pallet, he was shocked to see someone standing in the corner of the cell.

"Greetings," said the same golden-eyed man who had pulled Sindri from the pool and put him in this cell.

"Oh! Hello," Sindri said in a more reasonable tone. "I was wondering where you'd gone off to."

"I was simply taking the precaution of making sure that you were the only kender that managed to find his way into my home," the stranger replied.

"Oh yes," said Sindri.

"One can never be too certain," the stranger said. His tone was casual, but he seemed to be watching Sindri very closely. Of course, it was difficult to tell exactly where he was looking because of the hourglass shape of his eyes. "It is my experience that when one kender finds his way into a place, dozens more are sure to follow."

Sindri laughed. "I'm not an ordinary kender," he said.

"Apparently not," said the stranger. "But the question remains how did you get past the Shoikan Grove and all the Tower's defenses? And why did you decide to go for a swim with the Live Ones?"

Sindri's eyes opened wide. "Am I in a tower?" he asked, his voice bright and cheerful. "That would explain the dungeon. Very few houses have dungeons, but I think that most towers do. Is this your tower? Can I go all the way to the top? I'd love to look around and see where—"

The stranger leaned forward and fixed Sindri with his strange golden eyes. Sindri felt the blood chill in his veins. When the stranger spoke it was barely a whisper, but the sound echoed like thunder.

"I *am* the Master of the Tower, but I have very little patience for distractions," the man said. "And even less for nuisances. Tell me how you got here so that I can make sure that you are not followed by other kender or other pests."

Sindri laughed. "No other kender is going to be able to follow where I went," he said cheerfully, hoping that the good news would calm the Master down. But still the golden eyes held him in their icy glare, so he added, "I came here by magic."

This seemed to amuse the Master, who stood up straight again. A half-smile formed on his face. Others might call it a smirk, but Sindri liked to look on the bright side of things.

"By magic, you say?" said the Master. "Someone used a spell to send you here? I must be attracting a more droll brand of enemies these days."

"Oh, no one sent me here," Sindri said. "I cast the spell. I sent myself here, although I'm still not exactly sure where here is."

"Preposterous! Kender cannot perform magic," said the Master.

"Most kender can't," Sindri said proudly. "But I'm not most kender. I'm Sindri Suncatcher, the greatest kender wizard ever."

The Master of the Tower scrutinized Sindri even closer. He poked and prodded the kender, sprinkled Sindri's head with green dust, and had him hold his little arm straight out while the Master waved his fingers over it. "There is an aura around you," he said finally.

"See?" said Sindri. "I told you I'm a wizard. If only it was this easy to convince everyone. I mean, even my friends still don't really believe me. Could you maybe write a note saying that I'm a wizard? That would be really helpful when—"

"Where are your friends? Why have you come to visit my lonely tower by yourself?"

The kender's shoulders slumped as he lowered his gaze to the ground.

"I just needed some time to myself," he said. "To think. You know how it is for us wizards, we need to brood and ponder all by ourselves or our magic turns sour."

The Master cocked his head. Even behind the cloak's shadow and with his strange, unreadable eyes, Sindri knew this was a look of disbelief.

"We had a fight," Sindri said dejectedly.

The Master's look softened.

"I wouldn't worry about it if I were you," he said. "All friends have fights. It's only then that you can tell who is truly your friend. If they cannot accept you for who you really are, then they were never your friends to begin with."

Now it was Sindri's turn to smile.

"That's what I always say."

"So, you had a fight with your friends," said the Master. "That explains—at least in a round about way—why you're here. But I still don't know how you managed to breach my defenses. Tell me everything about how you came to be here."

"Well, a few months ago I was traveling alone when I met a dwarf," Sindri said.

"And the dwarf is one of your friends?" asked the Master.

"No," Sindri said. "But he was on a quest—"

The Master put his hand on top of Sindri's head.

"Let me rephrase my request," he said. "Tell me what happened earlier today that directly led to your arriving here."

"Oh, okay," said Sindri. "That's a much shorter story."

Since he wasn't sure exactly what details might be important to a man who was the master of a tower and obviously didn't go out in the sun very much, Sindri told the gold-skinned stranger about everything that had happened since he'd gotten up this morning. Every now and then the Master would stop the tale to ask a question, but before Sindri could give the whole complete answer he would instruct the kender to continue with the original story again. Sindri realized he was clearly one of those addle-brained wizards who could not concentrate on any one thing for very long.

It was less than two hours later when Sindri finished the tale by saying, "And that's the basic story. But I left out some really interesting facts. I could go over them if—"

"No," said the Master. "I believe I have enough information for the moment."

"So you believe that I'm a wizard."

"I believe," said the Master, "that, unique among all kender of my acquaintance—and I have known quite a few unique kinder—you seem to have a natural aptitude for tapping into arcane forces."

"So I'm a wizard," Sindri said proudly.

"You are a kender," said the Master. "And given the right training—and enough time—you could develop into a gifted spellcaster."

"I accept!" said Sindri proudly.

"Pardon me?"

"You're right," said Sindri. "I do need training. I was getting some from Maddoc, but I don't know where he is now. I think that he might be dead. It's awfully nice of you to volunteer to become my new teacher."

The Master's golden skin began to turn ashen. He made a little coughing sound in the back of his throat that built until he was doubled over, though Sindri soon became unsure whether he was coughing or laughing.

"You misunderstand, little one," the Master said when the fit had passed. "I will not teach you. Indeed, I'm not even sure it is safe to let you free on the off chance that someone else will take you as an apprentice."

For once, Sindri did not know what to say.

"Kender are not spellcasters," the Master continued. "They never have been, and I dare say that in this world they never will be. That you have this ability is a mistake, an accident of nature or an error by the gods."

Sindri eyes opened wide and then blinked three times in succession.

"Do the gods make mistakes?"

"All the time," said the Master. "And one of these days someone is going to take them to task for it."

Sindri blinked a few more times as he tried to imagine that day.

"In any case," said the Master, "I am not in the habit of propagating others' mistakes."

Then Sindri Suncatcher, the greatest kender wizard of all time, did something he almost never did. He got angry.

"You're just like everybody else!" he cried. "Everyone seems to walk around with their heads filled with neat ideas about how the world works. Only one plan or scheme can possibly work to save the day. People have to act thus and such a way in order to be called honorable. Kender cannot ever be wizards no matter what. I thought that spellcasters would be different. I thought that dealing with magic all the time would have shown you all the possibilities in the world, all the ways it can be different if you simply put your mind to it. But all you seem to have learned are new, sterner rules to go on top of the old ones."

The kender stood up and walked until his nose was pressed against the door. He closed his eyes and pounded his fist on the wood.

"Well, I don't care!" Sindri shouted. "Ever since I was a lad people have been telling me that I can't be a wizard. No one believed in me. No one but me. I knew that it was my destiny to be a great wizard. I knew it as sure as I knew my name. Do you know how difficult that is, when no one believes in your dream but you? And now you tell me that I was right—that I have it in me to be everything I've always dreamed—but that I can't. You say that it's all a mistake. Well, I don't care. I don't care if it's a mistake or an accident or whatever it is—it's my dream. And you can't take that away from me. So lock me in this cell for as long as you like, tell me everyday what a fool I am, and promise me nothing but pain and sorrow. I don't care. I'll find a way out and I'll find someone who will teach me. You just watch me—I will!"

He turned around, his hands still balled into fists to show the golden-eyed stranger his determination, but the cell was empty. Where the Master had been sitting was a bowl of porridge.

"I believe you, Sindri Suncatcher."

The voice came from the other side of the door.

Sindri looked up and saw a dark silhouette with golden, hourglass eyes.

"You remind me of someone I once knew," the Master said, his voice sounding far away in memory. "You remind me of a boy who was too small and sickly to do much of anything. He was so frail that his brother had to protect him from the other children. But the boy swore that he would grow up to be more powerful than anyone in his town. He swore that he would never be afraid again."

Sindri sat on the ground and put his chin in his hands. He stared up through the window at the man on the far side of the door.

"Did it work?" the kender asked. "Did he grow up to be strong? Did he beat up all his enemies and show them that he wasn't afraid?"

The Master started suddenly, as though he'd forgotten that Sindri was there. He looked down with his strange eyes and they seemed kindlier than they were before.

"In a fashion," said the Master. "But he also learned an important lesson."

"What is it?"

"That everything comes at a price," said the Master. "You cannot have everything you want without giving up something in return."

Sindri thought about this for a few moments.

"That's okay with me," he said.

"Be careful what you say, my little friend," said the Master. "Some offers, once accepted, cannot be abandoned."

"I don't have anything I'm not willing to give up."

"Not even your friends?"

Sindri thought again.

"My friends have already given up on me," he said.

"Then I think I know a place where you can go to study magic," said the Master. "I will speak with the headmaster and encourage him to accept you as a probationary student."

Sindri leaped to his feet. "Really?" he cried. "You'll get me into a magic school?"

"Yes, but with the following proviso," said the Master. "If I hear of you shirking your studies or, worse, pulling any kender tricks with the equipment or the other students' belongings, I will

63

come there myself, pull you out of whatever hole you're hiding in, and toss you back into the pool with the Live Ones. Do I make myself clear?"

Sindri nodded his head so hard that he could hear his brain rattling around inside his skull.

"Very well," said the Master. "Wait here. I must gather a few items before we leave."

"Can't I come out with you?" asked Sindri.

"No," answered the Master. "As good as your intentions are, it is safer for you to wait here. Many things in my home do not react well to being inspected by unfamiliar hands."

As the Master ascended the stairs he could hear Sindri humming happily as he ate the porridge that had been left in the cell. Halfway up the stairs the Master turned to his left and walked straight through the wall and into a room beyond.

The room was brighter than the stairwell or the dungeon below. Lamps burned along the walls and another one sat on top of a large worktable in the center of the room. The table was bare but showed stains and burns of many different shades. Such was the fate of tables in the Tower of High Sorcery. Either the Master or one of the students was always performing some sort of experiment on them, and those experiments often had unexpected side effects.

The far wall of the room was covered with shelves bearing powders, liquids, and crystals of every color of the rainbow. Other jars held feathers, fur, and talons of various animals. Cages with live specimens occupied any open shelf space.

A man stooped with age and wearing a black cloak stood with his back to the entrance, examining the shelves and their contents.

"Did you hear everything?" asked the Master.

The old man said nothing.

The Master stepped up to the old man and removed a jar labeled "Bramble Root" from the man's hands—hands that, while withered with age, had a firm and steady grip.

"Answer me! Is that the kender of which you spoke?" asked the Master, his voice taking on the distant echo of thunder.

The old man pulled back his hood revealing a face that would have been all too familiar to Sindri if he could see it.

"Yes," said Maddoc. "That is the kender."

# 8   END OF THE CHASE

Adyn sat bolt upright and his eyes shot open. Something was different. How long had he been asleep? What time was it? Was the girl all right?

He took deep breaths and forced his mind to slow down.

The cave was completely dark except for the meager light coming off the dying fire, but the air was still filled with the sharp, salty smell of burned seaweed. It had obviously been hours since Adyn had nodded off—all the light was gone from the sky (at least it seemed that way by the lack of illumination coming from the top of the cave) and the fire had almost burned down to embers.

But there was something else that was different and it took Adyn a few moments to realize what it was. The cave was as quiet as a church. The sound of the waves had once again retreated to a distant rhythmic roar. The tide had gone out. The cave mouth was no longer flooded.

What little relaxation he'd managed in the last few minutes dissipated again. The cave mouth was open and anyone could come in. Still, clearly no one had. There were no sounds other than the slow, deep breathing of the young woman, which seemed to be more labored and raspy than when Adyn had fallen asleep.

"The fire," he said out loud. His voice echoed in the darkness.

The girl was still suffering from the effects of being tossed about on the stormy sea and needed the warmth of the fire. But what if the Bursurs came back now that the tide was out? What if they spotted the plume of smoke rising from the top of the cliffs and were even now scouring the beach for the entrance to this very cave?

Adyn decided that he would just have to risk it. He wasn't sure what time it was, but it would be at least another hour until he could perform his morning ablutions as the sun rose. Until then he had to keep the girl warm and safe.

He tossed the last few pieces of driftwood he'd gathered earlier onto the fire. The flames began smoldering to life filling the air with salty smoke.

"I'll be right back," he whispered to the sleeping form. "I've got to gather more seaweed and wood for the fire. You should be safe until I get back."

The young woman crinkled her nose and fidgeted in the bedroll, almost as if she was responding to Adyn's voice. Perhaps she was closer to recovery than he thought. Still, he decided the fire could only do her good, so he climbed down from the ledge as quietly as he could.

The cave floor was covered with fresh clumps of seaweed, left there by the tide. Adyn would have to dry them before he could add them to the fire. He picked up a bundle and spread it out on one of the cave's lower ledges. It would start to dry on its own as he scoured the beach outside for small pieces of driftwood.

Solinari bathed the sea and rocky shore in her white light giving the whole scene a dreamlike quality. The red moon,

Lunitari, was nowhere to be seen, and that told Adyn that dawn was about an hour away.

The tide had left behind even more driftwood and seaweed than earlier in the day thanks, no doubt, to the storms of the night before. There were also bits of cloth and other detritus scattered here and there. Perhaps, Adyn mused, there had been a shipwreck. Perhaps that is where the unconscious girl had come from. Perhaps there were more survivors.

He picked up more wood and then moved closer to the water. There was enough light that he'd be able to see anyone lying in the surf. But other than the bodies of a few dead fish and the crabs scuttling about the carcasses, there was nothing else in the water.

There were, however, three men walking north along the beach.

"There he is!" cried out a voice Adyn immediately recognized as Galdon Bursur's. The hulking man began sprinting toward the surprised acolyte. "Let's get 'im!" After a moment's hesitation, his brothers followed close behind.

Adyn stood frozen. What should he do? Go back into the cave? Try to climb the hill? Run up the beach and lead the Bursurs away?

Before he could make up his mind, though, Fostben Bursur took matters into his own wrinkled hands. As it had the night before, the ground underneath Adyn's feet exploded in a great fireball, sending the acolyte flying through the air. His flight ended with a bone-jarring crash onto the rocky beach that made stars flash before his eyes.

Adyn lay there uncertain of which way was up, but knowing for sure that he tasted blood on his tongue. He heard a crunching sound in his left ear and thought for a moment that the fall must have shattered his teeth and they were rattling around in his mouth. But when he realized that the sound was getting louder despite the fact that he wasn't moving his head, he knew he was in real trouble.

Through bleary eyes Adyn saw someone sprinting into view. By the time the person stopped, mere inches from his head, all Adyn could see was a massive pair of leather boots.

"He ain't dead!" called a thick, deep voice.

The acolyte tried to lift his head, or crawl away, or roll over—anything to get a little farther away from the feet that he knew were attached to Galdon Bursur's legs. But his body wouldn't respond.

Two more hulking figures came into view and took up positions at the top and other side of his head.

"Are all god worsh'pers this dumb?" asked Jandor Bursur.

Galdon leaned over and looked Adyn in the eyes. "Don't you even know when Paladine's calling you home?"

Hannod giggled evilly, and before long his brothers joined him. It was a chilling sound.

"Don't just stand there laughing your fool heads off," called Fostben. "We just wasted a whole day and night chasing this heretic up and down the beach. Crush his skull and let's get on home."

With a dreadful certainty Adyn realized that his time was up. The Bursurs were going to kill him and there was nothing he or anyone else could do about it. At least he'd managed to save the young woman.

Adyn saw one of Galdon's massive feet raise in the air, and knew it was being positioned over his head. He closed his eyes, held his breath, and waited for the end. Instead of a bone-shattering crunch, though, Adyn heard the sharp click of a stone dropping onto the rocks near his head. He opened his eyes and saw a stone very much like all the other stones on the beach only bigger than most. Half the stone was wet, but not with water. Rather, it was covered in a thick, red liquid.

At the very moment that Adyn realized the wetness on the stone was blood, Galdon Bursur's boot fell back to its original spot. Then, an instant later, the tremendous man collapsed in a heap next to the acolyte. Galdon's eyes rolled back and there was a large, bleeding wound on his forehead.

Suddenly there was noise and shouting all around Adyn. The feet on the other side of his head ran off in different directions. Both the remaining Bursur brothers screamed at the tops of their lungs as they went. Further down the beach he could hear Fostben Bursur cursing and starting to cast another spell. But the most amazing sound of all was a voice he'd never heard before—at once both sweet and vicious.

With every ounce of concentration he could muster Adyn managed to raise his head and look toward the new voice, coming from the direction of the hillside. He saw the young woman, the one he had left asleep in the cave, red hair wild about her head as she held her sword in one hand and a large rock in the other.

"Beautiful," Adyn thought as he began to lose consciousness. He laid his head back down on the rocks and let his eyes close. "Beautiful and terrible."

"Villains!" shouted Catriona.

Reaching down, she grabbed another rock.

One of the men lost his nerve and ran away down the beach screaming incoherently like a frightened child. The other one, however, yelled something inane like "You can't do tha'!" and charged straight at her.

Again Cat shouted, "Villains!" and moved to meet his charge.

The man had no weapon other than his fists, so Cat kept her sword in its sheath. She did not need its cutting edge to strike down this ungainly foe. She ducked under his first wild swing and smacked him in the midsection with the broadside of her sword.

The wind escaped from him in a gushing breath, and he dropped to his knees.

Cat still wasn't sure exactly where she was or what was happening. It had only been a few minutes since she woke up on a ledge inside a tidal cave surrounded by the smell of burning seaweed. The gear near her seemed to belong to a Paladinean priest named Adyn Thinreed. Before she could find any more answers than that, Cat had heard the sound of a fireball—the sound of battle. Still slightly dizzy, she'd used the sword to steady herself as she descended the to the cave floor and stepped out onto the moonlit beach. But the second Cat saw the three brutish men looming over a fallen body she could only assume was her benefactor, she'd stood straight and shifted her sword to a ready position.

"Fool!" called a voice from farther down the beach. Then the voice began what she recognized as a spell—another fireball.

Cat cursed herself for overconfidence. She had been so focused on striking down these bungling brutes that she hadn't even considered that they might have a more competent ally. Looking up, she saw a shriveled old man making furious gestures in the air and continuing to intone phrases of arcane power.

Just as the chanting reached its crescendo, Cat took three running steps then threw herself in the air toward the spellcaster. Behind her the fireball exploded. Her ears were filled with the screams of the man she had just taken down mixed with the rushing whoosh of flames consuming the air around her. Next the blast from the magical explosion hit Cat in the back, pushing her toward the old man at an even greater speed. Unfortunately, it also knocked her off kilter—rather than landing on her feet and being able to confront the man face to face, she was going to land sprawled on the beach, and her opponent was already poised to take advantage of her disadvantage.

Even as she cartwheeled through the air, Cat could see the old man performing arcane gestures and mouthing words of power. If she guessed correctly, he was calling down a column of flame to incinerate Cat before she could move to threaten him—and in her wounded state, she doubted that she could survive such an attack. Only one option came to her mind.

In one fluid motion, Catriona unsheathed her sword and threw it like a steel spear.

The old man'e eyes went wide. He stopped chanting and turned to run. Cat could not see more than that as she spun uncontrollably in mid-air.

Before her rotation brought the man into sight again, Cat crashed into the beach. She landed face-up, feeling each stone dig into her back. She lay there for a moment feeling dizzy and disoriented. But she knew that if she didn't get up right away all her efforts would be wasted—the old man would easily be able to target her with a spell.

It seemed to Cat that she got to her feet just in time. The old man looked to be just regaining his balance from avoiding her sword. Now the fight would be joined in earnest.

Her sword!

Although throwing it had saved her life, Cat had given up her only weapon. She doubted that thrown stones would work against a trained spellcaster. She had to find her sword if she was going to beat this opponent, but where was it? Cat scanned the beach, but did not see her blade anywhere.

Then she noticed that the old man wasn't getting up. In fact, he wasn't moving at all. She looked at him more carefully and saw the reason why.

The old man had been too slow—or perhaps too indecisive—to move out of the way of Cat's thrown weapon. The sword had gone straight through his chest and stuck into the rocky beach, skewering the man in place. His lifeless body stood at an unnatural angle, like some sort of grizzly mannequin.

Cat walked up and saw the panic of the last few moments of life etched on the old man's face. The hilt of her sword was flush against his chest—she'd thrown the blade hard enough to push it all the way through his torso. She watched as his blood ran down the length of her sword and stained the stony beach red.

Suddenly Cat found herself thinking about the poor man's family. Did he have a wife? Children? Grandchildren? Would they ever know what happened to him? Certainly the man himself had been dangerous and his actions earned him this end, but in her mind the old man became linked with Elidor. The pain, remorse, and sorrow that Cat felt for her fallen friend was inappropriately transferred to this old man that she had killed with her own hands. In her mind it was as if she had killed Elidor.

Cat began to cry, then to sob, then to wail piteously. She didn't know where she was. What's more, she no longer cared. In her mind's eye she saw the face of everyone she'd beaten in battle—of every person she'd killed. The fact that all these people had meant to kill her never entered Cat's brain—she was not thinking rationally. As she thought of this her wail became a scream and then, mercifully, she fell unconscious once more.

Galdon Bursur sat up and gingerly touched his head.

"Ow!" he said and pulled his hand away to examine the blood from the wound. Someone had hit him in the head, but he clearly had no idea who. Galdon looked around the beach. Nearby lay the body of his brother Jandor. Hannod was nowhere to be seen. And his father stood a little way down the beach.

No. That was wrong.

Fostben wasn't standing at all—he had been stabbed through the chest. His father was dead. And kneeling on the rocks next to the body, still screaming her victory shout was a girl wearing armor.

Suddenly her shout ended and the girl fell to the beach, apparently unconscious. Fostben must have gone down fighting, but that was no surprise. He was a Bursur.

Was.

Galdon's face contorted into a grimace. He picked up the biggest, heaviest rock that he could find. Ironically, it was the same rock that had hit him in the head a few minutes earlier. He rose unsteadily to his feet and walked over to where the girl lay.

"You killed my pa," Galdon said raising the rock over his head. "Now I'm gonna kill you!"

Before the giant of a man could bring the rock down though, another voice said, "No, I don't think so."

Galdon Bursur turned to see who was there. He laughed uproariously when he saw that the god worshipper that had started all this trouble was standing right next to him. Galdon had to look down to stare the little cleric in the eye. "And you're next!" he said.

"I don't think so," said Adyn Thinreed. And without any other warning he swung both his fists toward Galdon Bursur's head.

The bigger man was about to laugh when he noticed that Adyn held a large rock in each hand. He tried to raise his hands to block the attack but he was too late.

With a sickening sound, Adyn landed two blows at the same time, sandwiching Galdon's head between two rocks. Blood flowed freely from the big man's nose, ears, and mouth. He teetered there for a second and Adyn prepared to swing again, but that proved unnecessary. Galdon Bursur fell to the beach as lifeless as his father.

# 9     SCHOOL DAYS

That was Raistlin?" Sindri asked for the fourth time.

"Yes," said Willabon Greeves, headmaster of the Greeves Academy for Thaumaturgical Studies.

"*The* Raistlin?" Sindri's voice was so strained with excitement that he practically squeaked the words. "Raistlin the Hero of the Lance? Raistlin, the Master of Palanthas' Tower of High Sorcery? Raistlin the greatest—"

"Yes," snapped Headmaster Greeves. "*That* Raistlin. What other Raistlin would it be?"

Unlike Sindri, Headmaster Greeves was not at all excited. In fact one might even say that he looked positively fretful as they walked toward the dormitory. Although he had one hand on top of the kender's head and held a stack of books in the other, he still had the air of a man who was wringing his hands or biting his nails or compulsively cracking his knuckles. His upper lip was covered in tiny beads of sweat and every few moments he ran his tongue across it to wipe them away. It looked unnervingly like he was trying to swallow his own nose.

Sindri couldn't think of anyone else named Raistlin, so he

couldn't answer the question.

"I wish he'd told me," Sindri said. "I mean I knew I was in a tower, but I had no idea I was in one of *the* Towers of High Sorcery."

"Yes, well now you're here," said Headmaster Greeves. "If you want to remain here you'd do well to concentrate on what lies ahead of you rather than where you've just been."

As they walked the headmaster continued to talk aloud to himself almost as if Sindri wasn't there at all. "Raistlin or no, I can't believe we're taking a kender into the academy," he grumbled.

The Greeves Academy was the most exclusive magical training facility in Palanthas and, by extension, all of Ansalon. Graduates from the school had a ninety-four percent chance of passing the Test of High Sorcery on their first attempt, and no alumnus had ever perished while taking the Test. The finest noble families in the land had to sign up and pay tuition years in advance to ensure that their children got into the academy. No one simply walked in off the street and was accepted on a whim unless that person had Raistlin Majere as a patron. After all, it would be unwise for any wizard to reject a request from the Master of a Tower of High Sorcery.

"Kender are completely incapable of learning wizardry," Greeves muttered, still seemingly oblivious to Sindri's presence or feelings. "They're nothing but tiny, lying thieves with absolutely no self-restraint and the attention span of a three year-old child."

Sindri could not argue with the fact that most kender could not learn magic. In fact, he'd never met a kender who was able to cast spells, except, of course, himself. He was what Aunt Freedinner used to call "the exception that breaks the rule"—a phrase that all non-kender seemed to find quaintly amusing.

But it was patently untrue that kender didn't have self-restraint or attention spans. It was just that humans, elves, and dwarves—not to mention centaurs, gnomes, and especially minotaurs—weren't able to understand a kender's frame of mind.

The thing that made kender so inscrutable to other races was their uncanny ability to focus their whole mind, their every thought both conscious and subconscious, on whatever idea or item had their immediate attention. Kender focused so intently on the one thing right in front them that they forgot about any other concerns or cares. For example, a kender examining an engraved spoon would be so captivated that he would not notice ten other similar utensils sitting nearby. However, if a kettle on the boil suddenly made a particularly interesting noise, the kender would switch focus to it, forgetting the spoon entirely. Of course, since the spoon was in his hand and he had to get rid of it in order to examine the kettle, the kender would put the spoon in the most convenient place possible, which more often than not would be one of his own pockets. When asked later where the spoon was, the kender would invariably and honestly answer that he had no idea. And when his pockets were turned out to reveal the missing spoon, the kender would show great and sincere surprise.

"Why not just take in a trained ape?" Greeves continued. "It wouldn't be any more disruptive and it would have a decidedly better chance of success."

"Do I get robes?" asked Sindri.

"Excuse me?" said the headmaster, roused from his thoughts of impending disaster.

"If I'm going to be studying magic, I think I should get robes," said Sindri.

"Of course you'll get robes," Greeves said. "They're in your cubby."

"Oh," said Sindri. Then after a pause he continued. "How do you know what color to make them?"

"Pardon me?"

"The robes," said Sindri. "How do you know what color to make them? I've been studying with a black-robe wizard—well, a black-robe wizard who can't actually cast spells anymore—but does that mean that I have to wear black robes, too? I mean, I'm just starting to learn about magic, I'd hate to start off on the wrong foot by having the wrong color robes. Maybe I should just wear different color robes on different days until we find out which ones suit me best."

The headmaster shook his head ruefully. "Your robes will be brown," he said. "Just like all the other first year students. Eventually, if you are diligent about your studies, you may advance enough that the faculty can judge which order is best suited to your skills and temperament. Only then will you get robes of a meaningful color."

"Oh," said Sindri. "What's a cubby?"

Headmaster Greeves grunted and led Sindri out of the Administrative Hall and across the campus.

Greeves Acadamy for Thaumaturgical Studies was located in the heart of Palanthas, the capital of Solamnia. In fact, the campus—a group of four modest buildings arranged in a square around a central courtyard—was built in the shadow of the Tower of High Sorcery. Headmaster Greeves' great grandfather, the academy's founder, designed the grounds so that students could see the Tower from just about every window. He had a replica of the Tower built in the center of the courtyard so that students would never forget their single, common goal—to pass the Test of High Sorcery and become an officially recognized and sanctioned wizard.

The Shoikan Grove was a haunted forest that surrounded the

Tower and protected it. The building nearest the grove was the faculty hall, where the academy's instructors had their rooms, offices, and work areas. Also relatively near the grove was the administrative hall, which sat off the east side of the faculty hall. This was where new students were tested, public demonstrations were held, and large-scale magical experiments were occasionally undertaken.

Directly across the courtyard from the administrative hall was the Lectorum—the building where all the academy's classes took place. The Lectorum had one large auditorium that could seat the entire staff and student body at once. It also had about two dozen classrooms of varying sizes, some of which looked like laboratories while others could have been mistaken for libraries.

Finally, on the side of the campus farthest from the Tower of High Sorce was Tazo Hall, the school's dormitory. This was where the students ate, slept, studied, and whiled away the odd hour that wasn't taken up by the taxing curriculum. The students varied widely in age, extraordinarily widely considering that a human first-year student might be as young as twelve and an elf upper-classman might be nearing two hundred years old. And since progression depended entirely on an individual's magical abilities rather than simply age or amount of time at the school, it was impossible to organize them by class or year. So instead, the academy grouped the students into "troupes" of individuals of varying ability levels, races, ethnic backgrounds, and ages. Troupes ranged in size from five to fifteen individuals.

Students in a troupe were responsible both to and for one another. Any infraction performed by one reflected badly on them all. This did not mean that individuals in a troupe were pressured to advance their magical skills at the same speed—there was no way to tell which students would pick up the arcane arts quickly and which would have to work for years to master even the most basic spells. Rather, the troupe was simply held accountable for all its members studying and performing to the best of their individual capabilities.

Headmaster Greeves explained all this to Sindri as they walked from the administration hall—a fairly dull-looking structure in the kender's estimation—to Tazo Hall, an ivy-covered building that seemed even from the outside to be filled with interesting nooks and hiding places.

"You mean that a 'troupe' is like a family," Sindri said.

"In a way," said the headmaster. "But it is not necessarily expected that the ties formed in a troupe will last any longer than your time here at the academy. Once you go out into the world your connections will fade unless you work at maintaining them."

"Yes," said Sindri. "Like a family. My Uncle Fussbuckle went wandering for ten years and never wrote home once. When he finally came home he had to work awfully hard to feel like he belonged again."

"Well," the headmaster said. "We like to think of troupes as friendships. You get out of them what you put in."

"But they aren't like friendships at all," said Sindri.

The headmaster looked puzzled. "And why is that?"

"Because you get to choose your friends," said Sindri. "Families are the people you have to care about, but friends are the people you choose to care about."

Headmaster Greeves cleared his throat. "Yes," he said, "That's very sentimental and all, but—"

"What if my troupe doesn't want to care about me?" said Sindri. "What if they don't like me?"

"That won't matter in the least," said the headmaster. "Once you are a member of the troupe they will be responsible for your behavior and you for theirs, whether you like one another or not."

"Just like a family," Sindri said.

"You met Raistlin?" the question came from Hasia, an elf girl who stood twice as tall as the kender but only weighed half as much. Her almond-shaped eyes seemed to take up half her face, giving her an expression that seemed half astonished and half terrified.

"Yes," said Sindri proudly. He was standing on his bed in the dormitory room shared by all the members of his new troupe. Along three of the walls stood a series of beds, cubbies, and nightstands—enough so that each member of the troupe had a personal set, but placed so close together that it was difficult at first to tell which bed went with which cubby.

Sindri didn't have anything to unpack. Although the journey here had technically been a long one, it wasn't one for which he had planned. So he immediately changed into his new brown robes, which did not look especially nice (he would have to remember to suggest to Headmaster Greeves that they switch to purple—*that* would be a good color), and began to introduce himself to his troupe-mates. Before long, the entire troupe was gathered around his bed asking questions.

"*The* Raistlin?" Hasia asked incredulously.

"What other Raistlin would it be?" the kender said in his best imitation of Headmaster Greeves.

"I-I've never h-heard of any o-other Raistlins before," stammered Bolli, a scrawny human boy with a head covered in wild, unkempt black hair. He stood at the back of the group, apparently not because he wanted to but because no one would let him get any closer.

"Exactly," Sindri said. "Neither have I."

"Raistlin is a common enough name in Abasinia," said Grigg, a human boy with wavy blonde hair. He was the tallest in the group and seemed to use his height to great advantage, looking down his nose or looming over anyone he wanted to intimidate. He had been doing both to Sindri since the moment that Headmaster Greeves left the room.

"Common among the commoners," chimed in Modaar, an elf as different from Hasia as night from day. Where she was tall and thin with a healthy golden glow to her skin, Modaar was short—barely taller than Sindri—had a round stomach, and was pale as a fish's underbelly. The odd thing was, the only time he seemed to speak was immediately after Grigg, and then only to agree with the taller boy.

"Anyway," Grigg said with a wave of his hand. "There is no way that Raistlin Majere sponsored your entry into the academy. The Master of the Tower has more important things to occupy his time than watching over a lowly kender."

"Yeah," echoed Modaar. "A lowly kender. He must be lying. I hear that they lie all the time. If a kender tells you it's morning, don't believe it until you see the sun in the sky. That's what my valet used to say."

"Or perhaps you're delusional," Grigg said. "I've heard that your people have a hard time telling fantasy from reality."

Sindri didn't mind the insults. He'd heard them every day since he left his village. Although he thought they came less frequently when he was traveling with Cat and Davyn. Like every kender, he expected people who had never actually met a kender to believe the stories about his race that were repeated so often. In fact, one of the most important responsibilities of his position as the world's greatest kender wizard was to serve as an ambassador between his people and spellcasters everywhere.

"Maybe you're right," Sindri said. "Maybe I am only a 'lowly kender.' I probably never did meet Raistlin Majere, and maybe I'm just plain crazy."

Grigg and Modaar nodded sagely.

Oddly enough, all the other members of the troupe seemed disappointed, especially Hasia. It would have been exciting for them to say that one of the members of their troupe had met Raistlin—in a way it would almost be as if they had met the Master of the Tower themselves. But they didn't send unhappy glares the kender's way. Indeed, they seemed to be looking at Sindri with a mixture of sympathy and pity. They reserved their frustrated glares for Grigg and Modaar.

"But then why in the world would Headmaster Greeves have accepted me into the academy?" Sindri asked.

The two boys immediately stopped grinning.

"Y-yeah," said Bolli. "W-why w-would he take in any kender?"

"And a delusional one at that?" added Hasia.

"It could be a joke," said Modaar.

"A joke on you," Hasia said.

The whole troupe laughed—well, all of them except Grigg and Modaar—even though it wasn't much of an insult. Sindri knew that if he did nothing else during his time at the Greeves Academy, he was going to have to teach his new friends how to taunt better.

"Come on," said Hasia. "I'll show you where we usually study."

"A-and d-dinner will b-be soon," said Bolli.

There were dozens of rooms in Tazo Hall—lounges, libraries, small laboratories, dens, closets, and of course dormitory rooms for each of the academy's troupes. Hasia, Bolli and the others showed Sindri which rooms their group usually used and which were claimed by other groups. All the while they laughed about Sindri's confrontation with Grigg.

"N-no one's ever s-stood up to him like that b-before," Bolli told him.

"Just because he's the top student in the troupe doesn't mean that he's always right about everything," said Hasia. "He doesn't treat me that way."

"Well, he was certainly wrong about me," Sindri said.

"Yes, but be careful," said Hasia. "He doesn't like you at all."

"Maybe I can change his mind," Sindri mused. "We'll see. But right now, did Bolli say something about dinner? Because I'm really hungry."

"I h-heard th-that kender were always h-hungry," said Bolli.

Sindri thought about it for a moment then said, "Take me to the dining hall and I'll show you how true that is."

They all laughed and headed to the first floor where the students took their meals. And, good to his word, Sindri impressed them all with the amount of food he ate. After four helpings of everything, and five of dessert, he finally admitted that he'd had enough.

By the time they got back to the dorm room Sindri could barely keep his eyes open. Even with all the adventures he'd been on recently, he'd never had a day quite as action-packed as today. While the others washed their faces and changed into their nightclothes, he simply dived beneath the covers of his bed—a real bed! He hugged the pillow and pulled the blanket tight around his shoulders.

Sindri was halfway into his first dream when he heard Hasia shout his name.

"What?" the kender said, sitting bolt upright in his bed. Traveling from one adventure to another had taught Sindri the ability to wake from the deepest sleep and be immediately ready for just about anything. But one thing Sindri was not prepared for was to look down and see that his hands had somehow turned purple.

He shrieked, half with surprise and half with delight. He'd never been purple before.

"W-what happened?" said Bolli.

"Is this what you'd call a 'kender trick'?" asked Hasia.

In the far corner of the room Grigg and Modaar exploded with laughter.

"No," Hasia said. "It's a distinctly unfunny joke. How could you two? It's his first day."

"Oh, but he's no beginner," said Grigg. "He was sponsored by Raistlin Majere."

"Raistlin Majere," Modaar echoed.

"Well this proves what a liar he is," Grigg continued. "That was just a simple cantrip—barely strong enough to be called a spell. For Nuitari's sake, anyone who looked at the pillow would have seen it planted there, but he just dived right in."

"Oh," said Sindri, who was only half listening because he was too intrigued watching his skin slowly change color to blue and then to orange.

Grigg stared down his nose at the ridiculous looking kender. "I don't care what the headmaster says," Grigg said. "You don't belong at the academy. It's an insult to those of us who worked so hard to get here."

Hasia stepped beside the Grigg. "As I recall," she said. "All you did was allow your parents to pay your tuition."

Grigg glowered as the rest of the troupe chuckled under their breaths. "Take his side if you want," the boy said. "But maybe the next time he isn't paying attention it will be in summoning class. I sure hope you aren't the one whose protective circle he accidentally erases."

"There's a difference," said Hasia, "between negligence and failing to notice that one of your so-called friends has decided to make you look like a fool for no good reason."

"There is not," said Modaar.

"Semantics," Grigg said waving his hand dismissively. "Say whatever you like, but I am going to prove beyond a shadow of a doubt that this kender is not one of us. He doesn't belong here and I'm going to make sure he gets tossed out on his thieving, lying little ear."

# CHAPTER

# 10 ECHOES OF THE PAST

**W**hat are you looking at?" said Cat. "Leave! Get going before I stick my sword through you, too."

Adyn had carried the unconscious Catriona into the sea cave to recover after their battle with the Bursurs. But Adyn made the mistake of laughing at Cat's words. Even though she had no intention of killing the young man, Cat was not going to allow him to laugh at her expense. She *could* kill him. Grabbing a handful of his robes, she backed him violently against the wall of the sea cave.

"Okay," he said cautiously. "You weren't joking."

"What about our very short series of interactions led you to believe that I'm even capable of joking?" asked Cat.

Adyn almost laughed again but the deadly serious glint in Cat's eyes stopped him. "Everyone is capable of joking," he said. "And although I hear that Solamnic Knights aren't especially good at it, I do know that you like drinking songs with ribald puns."

Fury flared in Cat's eyes. She tightened her grip on the acolyte's robes and lifted him until his feet dangled off the ground.

"I am *not* a knight!" she said. "Who *told* you such a thing?"

"No one," Adyn croaked. "With your armor and helmet and skill with the sword I just presumed—"

"Well you're wrong," said Cat. "I'm not a knight, and I never will be."

With that she let go and Adyn fell to the cave floor.

"That's a shame," he said, getting up and dusting himself off. "From what I've seen, you'd make a fine one."

"And what would you know about such things?" snapped Cat.

"About sword play and strategy and riding a warhorse? Precious little," Adyn said. Then he smiled his most disarming smile. "About living life by a strict code and dedicating all my actions to Paladin's name?" He pointed to his robes. "I'd say I know a fair deal."

The Solamnic Knighthood was closely tied to the Temple of Paladine. Both groups honored Paladine above all the other gods and devoted themselves to protecting the people of Ansalon against the forces of evil. Both groups fell on hard times in the years following the Cataclysm three hundred years ago, but both had experienced strong revivals since the end of the War of the Lance.

"But most of all, I understand the way people think," continued Adyn. "I am an uncanny judge of character. It's Paladine's blessing to me. And I know that as hurt and lonely and insecure as you're feeling now, that's not who you really are."

Now it was Cat's turn to laugh. It was not a happy, jovial sound. Rather, it was bitter and dry, completely devoid of anything but scorn. "Perhaps you should reconsider your calling," said Cat. "I'm not that person any more. I quit."

Adyn waited until Cat stopped laughing. "Your inner nature is not as easily shed as a suit of armor," he said.

"Spare me your philosophy," said Cat. "You think my disillusionment is just a passing phase? Stay a while, and see how little the outside world means to me."

"I can't," Adyn said. "I'm on my way to Palanthas. In less than a fortnight I'm supposed to take my vows of ordination."

"Good for you," said Cat. "I hope you become Head Priest of the Temple of Paladine someday." She climbed back to the perch where Adyn had built the fire. "But I would leave now if I were you. The tide is about to come in, and it's a long journey to Palanthas."

Adyn looked up at her incredulously. "You're just going to send me out there alone?" he asked.

"Why not?" she answered, not bothering to look down. "You were traveling on your own before I washed up on shore. Besides, you'll be better off without me—there is less chance of you getting killed if I am not by your side."

"That's not true," cried Adyn. "Those maniacs last night were just one family. I have an entire town mad at me. Groups of townspeople could be anywhere between here and the Vingaard Pass. I need protection."

Cat turned her back on Adyn. She owed him a great deal for having saved her life twice in less than a day, but the last thing she wanted to do was get involved in another quest—even one as simple as hiking to Palanthas.

Cat had been to Palanthas several times both as a young girl and later as a Solamnic squire. It was an amazing city, filled with sights, sounds, and smells that could be found nowhere else in Ansalon. And given the fact that everyone she knew and cared about had either left or died—for if she barely survived a night in the stormy sea, what chance could poor Sindri have?—Palanthas seemed like a logical place for her to go. Once there she could get work in a caravan or on a merchant ship. It wouldn't be glamorous work, but she could lose her troubles and forget the past.

Palanthas was the best destination she could think of, but she didn't want to go there with Adyn. She did not want to take another person under her protection. She did not want to take a chance on failing again. That was the only thing she seemed to be any good at.

"I cannot protect you," she called down from her ledge.

"That's not true," Adyn called back. The young cleric was relentless. "You saved my life last night."

Last night! Cat cringed at the thought of her behavior. Since joining up with Sindri, Davyn, and Nearra there were many instances in which Cat had failed to live up to her training and expectations, but last night was the worst. In the middle of the battle she had completely frozen. Some might excuse her behavior by saying that she had not yet recovered from her ordeal during the storm. Others might say that such a reaction was not unusual when the last time Cat had swung a sword was the night Elidor died. But Catriona knew those were excuses.

The truth of the matter, Cat said to herself, was that she was not reliable in combat. She could not be trusted to stand her ground and fight—she just didn't have the constitution for it. No matter how hard she tried, she would always fail, so why bother even trying?

"You have put your faith in the wrong quarter," Cat shouted. "You are a cleric, or soon enough will be. Trust in Paladine to protect you."

"I do," said Adyn. "And he sent me you."

For several minutes the only sounds in the cave were the crackle of the fire and the rhythm of the incoming tide. Then Cat began to climb down the cave wall.

"Or perhaps," she said, "he sent you to me."

Adyn liked sleeping under the stars. In the wide, open skies above the Solamnic plains he could see the constellations dance their way through the night. All the gods were represented in the stars—each one had a home in a certain corner of the sky—and camping in the open made him feel acutely aware that nothing that happened on Krynn was beyond their notice. Even if they chose to do nothing, Adyn was comforted by the knowledge that the gods saw everything.

He was certain that Catriona did not share this appreciation.

She seemed uncomfortable under the open night sky. Despite the warmth of the late summer evenings, every night Cat insisted on building a roaring fire and always sat close staring into the flames. When it was time to go to sleep she pulled her blanket over her head. It was almost as if she was trying to hide herself from the gods' sight.

In the morning, she slept as late as possible. Adyn was sure that she was hoping that he would just become annoyed with her sluggish ways and leave without her. When she did get up, finished her morning meal, and packed her gear they invariably had the same conversation.

"Keep walking due east," she would say. "In a few days' time you will come to the King's High Road. Turn north and it will take you through the mountains and directly to Palanthas."

"You aren't leaving are you?" Adyn would ask, making sure to put an edge of panic in his voice.

"You will be fine," Cat always assured him. "We haven't seen anyone since we left the coast. No one could be so offended by your beliefs that they would chase you this far."

"How can you be sure?" he would say. "They're fanatics. They could still be chasing after me." Then Adyn would keep fretting and worrying until Cat agreed to travel with him just one more day.

In truth, Adyn knew for certain that he was no longer in any danger. On the very first night as he ran down the beach he'd heard the Bursurs arguing with other villagers who wanted to go home to bed. After that the only voices he heard belonged to Fostben or Galdon. But lying to Cat seemed to be the only way to keep her focused on the new mission he had set for her.

It had been easy for Adyn to see from the first time they talked that Cat was in emotional pain—something terrible had happened and she was at a complete loss. As they traveled and he was able to pry more of her story from her, he realized—even if she didn't—that Cat was at the lowest point of her young life.

People said that once you reach bottom there is only one way to go and that's up. But Adyn knew that it was entirely possible for Cat to wallow in self-pity for an interminable period of time. Nothing would get better until she tried to make it so. In order to restore her confidence Cat needed a success in her life, even one as simple as escorting a "helpless cleric" to Palanthas.

After a week hiking across the Solamnic plains, the pair turned to the north when their path intersected a heavily worn trading road. The road, covered in packed dirt and tiny pebbles, crunched under their feet as it led toward the mountains.

"Do you know what that structure is up ahead?" asked Adyn. He pointed to a fortress that completely blocked the road ahead. Anyone who wanted to continue into the mountains would have to pass through this structure first. The walls were thick and seemed to be carved from the living rock of the Vingaard Mountains, which they protected. Inside the compound rose a spire that towered a thousand feet above the roadway.

Catriona gave Adyn a scornful look. "It is the Tower of the High Clerist," she said. "You don't have to be a former Solamnic squire to know that."

"No, I suppose not," he replied. "It has a long and storied history."

"Indeed," said Cat. "It has been the site of many of the order's greatest triumphs and tragedies."

"Most recently thanks to the actions of a knight named Sturm Brightblade," Adyn said.

Cat shook her head ruefully. "I know the tale of what happened that day," she said. "If you are trying to show me proof of Paladine's divine plan, you have picked the wrong example. It does nothing to bolster my faith when you remind me of the meaningless, hollow death of the single greatest knight of our time."

"Really?" said Adyn. "That's odd, because the way I heard the tale, it's the story about how much inspiration and good can spring from a single death."

"What do you mean?"

"Well, according to my sources Sturm's fame came only posthumously. In his life he was, as I understand it, notorious but not at all glorified."

"It is true," Cat said. "For years he was thought of, by those who knew of him at all, as a renegade knight who believed too fervently in the old ways. They thought his adamant belief in honor above all else was obsessive in the extreme and his unshakable devotion to the gods bordered on madness."

"Indeed," said Adyn. "And when he came to this tower, the knights stationed here only really accepted his leadership because he stood beside the Qualinesti Princess Laurana. It was she who truly won their allegiance, even though she had never fought in a battle."

"Yes," Cat answered. "But the knights say that he provided her with wise counsel and advice. He taught her exactly what she needed to know to achieve victory. How much greater would her victories have been if he had stood by her side through them all?"

Adyn made a show of thinking about that question, but Cat could tell he had already prepared a reply.

"I doubt there would have been any other victories at all," he said. "In fact, I doubt that the High Clerist's Tower would have held back the Blue Dragon Army that day if Sturm had not died on that rampart."

"What?"

"The greatest gift that Sturm gave to Laurana was inspiration. She may have had noble blood and bearing, but she knew less than nothing about war—real war. As I hear it, when the first wave attacked, Laurana was frozen with dragonfear along with all the other untried knights."

At this, Cat's glare grew so intense that her eyes were nothing more than slits in her furrowed brow. Adyn could ridicule her all he wanted, he could believe in some strange interpretation of recent history, but she would not let him impugn the honor of even the most junior of Solamnic Knights. They deserved better than that.

He recognized the source of her anger. "I mean no insult to the knights," said Adyn. "It's well known that dragons have a supernatural effect on mortals that even the bravest heart may succumb to, especially when encountering it for the first time."

She relaxed slightly.

"My point was that alone among the tower's defenders, Sturm resisted this overwhelming dread and stood his ground. He battled the Blue Lady nearly to a standoff—a near-miraculous feat. But not nearly as amazing as the miracle he performed when he fell under the enemy's spear."

"And what was the incredible accomplishment Sturm Bright-blade achieved with his dying breath?" asked Cat, who was nearly ready to declare this conversation over.

"He freed Laurana from her torpor," said Adyn. "He gave her the jolt of fear and horror and inspiration she needed to lead the troops on to victory. He took a timid, uncertain, first-time commander and turned her into the 'Golden General.' And in doing so, he gave all of Solamnia—indeed, all the free lands of Ansalon—a hero, someone capable of winning the war against Darkness."

Cat had no reply.

Adyn continued, " Surely, if he had lived, Sturm would have done a great many things, won a great many battles. But by dying, he saved the world."

Cat remained mute. What could she say?

"It would have been easy for Laurana to give in to grief at the death of her friend." Adyn said. "But I think she knew something that most mortals don't—life can only be understood in hindsight. None of us will ever truly understand the things that are happening to us at any one moment. It is only through the perspective of time that we can gather enough information about the world, other people, and even ourselves to allow us to truly comprehend the impact of our actions—or inactions.

"I am not saying that your friends' deaths are the building blocks of great things. I could not possibly know such a thing to be true. However, you cannot possibly know that it is false. But either way, you have the power to make something from these tragedies. And for the rest of your life, your memories of these people and your time with them will be inextricably bound to whatever events grow in their wake."

A single tear rolled down Cat's cheek.

"But what about Davyn?" she said.

"Your friend has gone through much of the same things you have," Adyn said. "These events will shape each of your lives in different ways. From what you've told me, this Davyn has his own demons to confront. For now he has chosen to do that on

STAN BROWN

his own. One day, whether in this life or the next, you will meet up with him and all your friends again—there is no force in the world more powerful than friendship. Live your life so that your friends will be proud of the legacy you created from your time among them."

Cat wiped her face as they walked the final few yards to the gates of the High Clerist's Tower. A pair of Solamnic Knights stood on the ramparts watching merchants and other travelers come and go across the Knight's High Road.

"I was wrong," Cat said. "You do know this place better than I do."

They smiled waved to the Knights who waved back.

"Just a lucky guess," said Adyn.

# 11  PEER PRESSURE

$A$nd now let's see how young Apprentice Suncatcher did on this particular problem, shall we?"

At the sound of his name, Sindri looked up from the slate on which he was scribbling furiously. This afternoon's lesson was on the subject of spell components—knowing which powders, leaves, ores, and other items were used in the casting of which spells. As with all the classes at Greeves' Academy, this one included students of varying levels of magical accomplishment. The instructor, Master Dappleleaf, gave different assignments to different groups or persons based on their individual skills.

The senior students learned how to create "dragon's tears," a dangerous combination of alchemist's fire and rubber tree sap used in several high-level fire spells, while the majority of the class studied the differences between ordinary acorns and spider-web kernels, a rare nut used to keep the various grasses and leaves fresh in a wizard's spell component bag. Only two students, Sindri and his troupe-mate Bolli, were given an even more boring assignment. During the first half of class they were supposed to study a list of the one hundred most common spell components—rose quartz, a white feather, chameleon grass, and so on. In the second half of the class they were supposed to close their text and recreate the list from memory.

"Well, Apprentice Suncatcher," said Master Dappleleaf. "Let me see your slate."

Everyone else in the class wrote on paper—loose sheets of parchment, pads held together by string and glue, or leather-bound volumes. Sindri did not yet have any paper so he was forced to write his lessons in chalk on a slate tablet. Headmaster Greeves promised that if Sindri managed to stay focused enough to remain in the school for a full month, he would get a journal and textbooks of his own. For now the kender had to borrow all his supplies from his troupe-mates. Fortunately for him, everyone else was so much further along in their studies that they rarely needed the same materials. Well, everyone except Bolli, who seemed to struggle with spellcasting as much as kender were supposed to.

Sindri handed his slate to Master Dappleleaf, who was as odd-looking an elf as Sindri had ever seen. Like most elves, he was shorter than an average human and yet still managed to look down at everyone and everything. He was originally from Silvanost, and had the fair skin and blonde hair common among the elves of that region, but what Master Dappleleaf didn't have was a typical elven physique. Rather than being thin and willowy, Dappleleaf could most charitably be described as stocky—his chest and belly ballooned out directly under his chin and didn't seem to end until about where his knees should have been. Sindri would not have called him fat (especially not to his face), he seemed built that way naturally rather than having gained the frame from overindulgence. But Master Dappleleaf certainly did take up more space than most elves did. In fact, on the very first day of class Sindri remarked that the instructor looked remarkably similar to his troupe-mate Modaar, only to be told that they were father and son.

At first, Sindri hoped that this connection would make his own acceptance in the class easier. After all, if the instructor chastised him it would also reflect badly on the other members of the troupe. But he soon realized that Master Dappleleaf's distaste for kender outweighed his desire to see his son excel; the teacher made no effort to help Sindri pick up the curriculum or even feel welcome in the class. And while he called on the other members of the class to read their work aloud about once or twice per week, Master Dappleleaf made Sindri do so at least once per session.

Rather than make the kender feel overwhelmed or picked on, the attention made Sindri concentrate even harder than he already had planned to. After the first few days when he didn't seem to know anything at all, Sindri began to have the correct answers more and more frequently.

Master Dappleleaf ran a pudgy finger down the slate, mumbling to himself as he read. "Stink weed . . . rose quartz . . . pinch of salt . . . light a candle. . ." Finally he stopped and looked down at Sindri, his eyelids half closed, and his mouth pursed into a funny puckered shape.

"Correct," he said. Then, handing the slate back to Sindri he added, "You would do well to commit this information to your mind permanently. It is the basis of all future work in this course and I may decide to test you on it again."

Sindri looked at the slate. As the instructor checked the work, he had run his fingers over the chalk writing smudging it beyond recognition. Sindri would have to find a more permanent way of keeping the list. "Yes, Master Dappleleaf," he said.

At the Greeves Academy all the instructors were addressed as "Master" (with the exception of Willabon Greeves, who was called

"Headmaster") and all the students were called "Apprentice." This seemed painfully formal to Sindri, but he did his best to remember and follow the rule.

Master Dappleleaf checked a few other apprentices' lessons and, for the most part, told them how many things they'd gotten wrong. When he seemed satisfied that he had crushed his pupils' spirits enough for one day, the instructor returned to the front of the classroom.

"As you no doubt know Dragon Day is in less than a week," he said. "In anticipation of this celebration, our next few sessions together will be spent preparing the necessary spell components for the school's traditional role in the festivities."

"Dragon Day?" Sindri whispered to Bolli. "What's that?"

"Y-you've n-never heard of Dragon Day?"

"No," said Sindri. "How many dragons will there be?"

Before the boy could answer, Master Dappleleaf's pointing stick rapped them soundly on the tops of their heads.

"As I was saying," the instructor continued, fixing his gaze on the talkative pair of students. "Although we will be focusing on practical matters here in the classroom, this does not relieve you of the responsibility to keep up with your reading. On our first meeting after the holiday you each will be tested on the next three lessons in your study track."

Sindri jumped out of his seat waving his arms around wildly.

Master Dappleleaf sighed wearily. "Apprentice Suncatcher," he said as though the words were almost too painfully heavy to get out. "What are you doing?"

"I want to ask a question," said Sindri. In the world outside the school, jumping up and down was often the only way for him to get people's attention, they seemed to be unable to notice him otherwise. (Sindri guessed this was because kender were shorter than other races who weren't used to looking down to waist level for people who might have questions. He considered that thought confirmed when he noticed that gnomes tended to have the exact same problem.)

"And what did I say about jumping around like a . . . well . . . like a kender?" asked Master Dappleleaf.

Sindri thought for a moment.

"You said not to," he answered.

"And?"

"And that simply raising my hand above my head would 'do nicely,'" continued Sindri.

The instructor stared balefully at the kender, who still was hopping back and forth.

Sindri stopped jumping, sat down in his chair again, and raised his hand directly over his head.

Master Dappleleaf sighed again, pinched the bridge of his nose so tightly that it was a wonder his eyes didn't tear up, and then looked back toward Sindri. "Yes, Apprentice Suncatcher," he said finally. "What is it?"

"How am I supposed to know what my next three lessons are, Master Dappleleaf?" asked Sindri.

"The lessons are marked in the back of your text," answered the instructor.

"But I don't have a text."

Dappleleaf sighed one more time. "Then I suggest you borrow one from one of your troupe-mates," he said.

"But what if they're using theirs?" asked Sindri. "They have assignments, too."

"Be inventive," the instructor suggested. "Use different people's texts at different times."

"But wouldn't it be easier if I had a text of my own?" asked Sindri.

"If you ever hope to achieve this milestone, then you'd better do well on the upcoming test," Dappleleaf answered.

"Will you please be quiet!" yelled Modaar. Several other members of the troupe mumbled agreement with the sentiment, if not completely with the anger. Some of them were sitting at the reading table in the center of the dorm room while others were sitting or lying on their beds, but they all had books or scrolls open in front of them.

"I'm just studying," said Sindri. He was sitting cross-legged on his bed, robes pulled up to nearly his waist, saying the one hundred most common spell components out loud over and over and over again.

"Can't you study quietly from the text like everyone else?" Modaar demanded.

"Sure," said Sindri.

With a loud huff, Modaar picked up his book and tried to find his place.

"I could, but I don't have a textbook—so I can't," said Sindri.

The young elf buried his head in his book.

"If you're going to take a nap, can I use your book?"

"I am not going to take a nap," shouted Modaar. "I'm trying to gather my self-restraint before you make me lose my temper!" The elf's voice echoed in the chamber.

"Well, you aren't doing a very good job," said Sindri.

Before Modaar could respond, Hasia stood up and carried a book over to Sindri's bed. "I'm studying for potions and alchemy class now," she said. "You may use my book, Sindri."

The kender beamed from ear to ear. "Thank you, Hasia," he said. "That's very kind of you."

"Just be sure he doesn't 'accidentally' keep your book," muttered

Modaar. "He might want to give it to the dragon as a present on Dragon Day."

"Shut up!" said Hasia and kicked Modaar's chair for good measure.

Sindri, who was already flipping through the pages of the spell component text, stopped and looked up.

"Do we really give presents to a dragon?" he asked. "What kind of dragon? I killed a dragon once—I hope I won't have to give a present to one of its relatives."

"Y-you k-killed a dragon?" asked Bolli.

"He never did any such thing!" said Modaar.

"I did, too!" cried Sindri. "It was a green dragon named Slean."

"Well," said Grigg from a corner of the room. "You're a real hero, Sindri."

"I had help," the kender said. "My friends and I killed Slean together."

"Still, you must be very brave," said Grigg. "You sound like the perfect person to represent the troupe on a task for Dragon Day."

As nice as it was to have the senior member of the troupe complimenting him, Sindri was suspicious. Up to this point, the only times Grigg had spoken to him was to yell or say that Sindri would never succeed at becoming a wizard. Still, maybe he was impressed with the kender's spirit and effort.

Sindri had heard about some organizations that gave new members a very difficult time for the first few weeks—they made a new person do the worst jobs and work the longest hours just to test whether or not the person was truly dedicated. Then, once the person had proven his commitment, everyone stopped bothering him and he became part of the group. Perhaps that's what Grigg was doing. And maybe by doing this Dragon Day task Sindri would finally pass the test.

"Do you want me to talk to the dragon for our troupe?" asked

Sindri. "I'm sure that I could think of something suitably auspicious to say—"

"There's no need for that," said Grigg. "In fact, we've been having a little fun at your expense—there are no actual dragons involved in Dragon Day. It's purely metaphorical."

Grigg put his hand on Sindri's shoulder and gave it a friendly squeeze. However, rather than reassuring him, this gesture made Sindri's blood run cold. Looking around the room, the Hasia's and Bolli's faces spoke of similar feelings. Grigg was definitely up to something—something Sindri was sure he wouldn't like.

"Metaphorical?' said Sindri.

"Yes," Grigg said. "It means that it's not to be taken literally."

"I know what 'metaphorical' means," said Sindri. "I was hoping you'd give me more details like why is it I've never heard of this holiday before."

"That's easy," Grigg said, his face beaming with the most insincere smile that Sindri had ever seen. "Dragon Day is a Palanthan holiday. I don't think it's celebrated anywhere outside the city."

"Oh!" said Sindri. Despite the fact that he did not trust Grigg, he was still interested to learn about a local custom, especially one involving dragons (even metaphorical ones). And he trusted the friendlier members of the troupe to let him know if Grigg was leading him astray. "And is Dragon Day a holiday just for wizards or does everyone celebrate?"

"Actually, the holiday was started by Vinas Solamnus himself early in the city's history," Grigg said. "Since Palanthas took its name from Paladine, he thought it was important for the citizens to have a day when they paid homage to the leader of the gods. No one knows why he chose the exact day he did, some say it was to have a festive celebration that fell between Spring Dawning and Knights' Day. Like all great leaders, he knew that it was important to give people reasons to feast and celebrate on a regular basis."

"So why didn't he call it 'Paladine Day'?" Sindri asked.

"He wanted to," said Grigg. "But the clerics complained. They did not want Vinas to use their god's name in a purely secular or even politically motivated holiday. So instead he named the day after Paladine's chosen form. Originally the holiday was known as Platinum Dragon Day, and it was celebrated with huge banquets, fireworks, and a parade around the city ending at the Central Plaza. But then the priests complained again. They wanted to know how this celebration had anything to do with Paladine. Seeing that this was not a problem that was going to go away, Vinas said that this was a day to keep the Platinum Dragon in your heart and suggested that it would be the perfect day for acolytes in the Temple of Paladine to take their oaths. In fact, he offered to restructure the celebrations on the Central Plaza so they focused on the clerical ceremony."

"What a terrific idea!" exclaimed Sindri.

"It was," Grigg continued. "It satisfied the clerics' need for a religious aspect to the day yet maintained the festive atmosphere. And everything worked perfectly. Platinum Dragon Day became a touchstone of the city's calendar and remained that way for centuries. Then came the Cataclysm."

"What does that have to do with the holiday?" asked Sindri. "You just said that it was basically a made up holiday. Why couldn't it go on after the Cataclysm?"

"Because by that time the ordination ceremony had become a central part of the day. For many people, the feasts were in celebration that people had found their lives' pursuits. And when the gods withdrew from the world, the number of people who chose to devote themselves to the priesthood dwindled rapidly. Finally, one year Platinum Dragon Day approached but there were no acolytes left to take their vows. The clerics were at a complete loss. What should they do? Perhaps they themselves should retake their vows. Or perhaps they should simply cancel the holiday, just for one year."

"What did they do?" asked Sindri, sitting on the edge of his bed and leaning forward as though he could make the tale unfold more quickly.

"They didn't do anything," Grigg said. "But the wizards did."

Sindri almost fell onto the floor.

"But why would they do that?" the kender asked. "What did they care about the problems of the Temple of Paladine?"

"They didn't," said Grigg. "But they did care about the people of Palanthas. And they knew that although the people of Palanthas would mark the holiday, it would feel meaningless if no one got ordained. They also knew that if the holiday stayed hollow for too long people would stop celebrating altogether. And the only thing worse than having a hollow, meaningless holiday was to have no holiday at all. So for the sake of Palanthas—for the sake of the citizens—they found a new reason to celebrate.

"They shortened the name of the holiday to Dragon Day, and rededicated it as a day to honor the city's history. Instead of the ordination ceremony, the people gathered at the Central Plaza to see a magical display of amazing sights from the past—Vinas Solamnus first arriving on the spot that would be the Lord's Mansion, knights on dragonback fighting in the skies over the Vingaard Mountains, the raising of the Tower of High Sorcery— all created with arcane spells."

"Oh," said Sindri. "So it is our holiday now."

"Not if the priests have anything to say about it."

"What do you mean?"

Grigg's expression grew taut. "For more than three centuries the priests avoided the Dragon Day celebrations," he said. "For more than ten generations the Wizards of High Sorcery have kept the tradition, not to mention the morale of the people, alive. But this year the clerics are going to ruin Dragon Day."

Sindri was shocked. "What do you mean?" the kender asked.

"Now that their gods have returned, the priests want to take over their former place at the heart of the Dragon Day celebrations while the wizards are pushed aside."

"That doesn't seem right," Sindri said. Clearly Grigg was not telling the whole story, but Sindri figured it would be best to let him finish before asking what parts were being left out.

"No. No, it doesn't," agreed Grigg. "But there's something we can do about it."

Here it comes, Sindri realized. All of Grigg's friendly talk and helpful explanations were just a lead up to some bit of mischief that he wanted Sindri to perpetrate. But how bad could it be? And if doing it meant that Grigg would finally accept Sindri as a member of the troupe—as a fellow apprentice—wouldn't it be worth it, no matter what "it" was? After all, ever since he arrived at the academy Sindri had been saying that he would do *anything* to be accepted. Perhaps this was the moment to prove those words.

"What are you suggesting?" the kender asked.

"Well," Grigg said, dropping his voice to a conspiratorial whisper. "The ordination ceremony features the Crown of Paladine—a platinum circlet cast in the image of Paladine's draconic form. The head priest places it on the acolyte's brow and ushers him into the sight of Paladine—or some such religious nonsense. At all other times, the crown is on display in the new Temple of Paladine here in the city center." Grigg smiled, nodded, and winked at Sindri as if he'd just told the punch line of a racy joke.

"I don't understand," said Sindri.

"The crown is on display," said Grigg. "In the temple. Where it's not guarded."

Sindri cocked his head like a puppy hearing the word "sit" for the first time.

"If someone was to sneak into the Temple of Paladine and take the crown," Grigg said enunciating each word slowly and clearly, "then the clerics could not hold their ceremony."

"Who would do such a thing?" Sindri asked with all sincerity.

"You would!" shouted Grigg. "You would, you stupid kender!"

"I would not!" Sindri's voice was steeped in indignation.

Grigg's face turned pink, then red, then nearly to purple as he shook with fury and frustration. His hands were balled into fists and it seemed quite possible that he might use them to pummel the newest member of his troupe.

"By the ever-changing moons, I'm telling you to do it!" he yelled. "Get off your bed, sneak out of the building, go over to the temple, steal the crown, and bring it back here!"

"What? Why?"

"Because it will keep the priests from taking what is ours—the hearts of the people of Palanthas."

Sindri cocked his head again, this time to the other side. "So you want the people of Palanthas to continue to respect and admire wizards," said Sindri. "And in order to insure this you want to resort to subterfuge and thievery."

"Whose side are you on anyway?" demanded Grigg. "Do you want the clerics to be rewarded for three hundred years of neglect? Do you want them to make a mockery of High Sorcery and all that we wizards have done for Palanthas during that time?"

"No, of course not," Sindri said.

"We won't let anything happen to the crown," said Grigg. "And after Dragon Day we'll make sure it is 'found' in some suitably innocuous location. We don't want to harm a historical treasure, we just want to make sure that it is not used to rob us of our hard earned position of authority and prominence."

"But what if someone sees me?"

"You're a kender," said Grigg. "I thought sneaking quietly around came naturally to you."

Sindri gave an exasperated sigh. "It does, to a point," he said. "But a kender still has to work on it. And I, in case you hadn't noticed, have spent all my time working on my wizardly skills."

"Just don't get caught," said Grigg. "If someone sees you, so what? There are hundreds of kender in the city, the constables can't arrest them fast enough or keep them once they're caught. If someone sees you, they'll just think you're an ordinary, run-of-the-mill kender—and everyone expects them to be thieves."

This bothered Sindri as much as it would any kender, but he could not argue the point. For some inexplicable reason, people expected kender to be pickpockets, swindlers, and especially thieves.

"It's easy," said Grigg. "It's safe. It won't hurt anyone in the long run. And most of all, you will be the one to save Dragon Day for the wizards of Palanthas. You'll be a hero." The boy paused and looked deep into Sindri's eyes. "You'll be one of us."

The kender's expression quavered. Uncertainty filled his heart. He looked over to Hasia and Bolli. They didn't say anything, but their faces were masks of hopeful anticipation. Behind them Modaar stood giggling quietly to himself. Could it be that they agreed with Grigg that Sindri should strike a blow for wizardly honor by stealing the Crown of Paladine?

"Come on, Sindri," Grigg said, his voice jolly and alluring. "What do you say?"

# CHAPTER
# 12  THE JEWEL OF SOLAMNIA

When the poets write about Palanthas they describe arriving by ship. They tell how the white towers rise from the sea and the city covers the entire horizon, its white towers shining in the golden sunlight.

There is another way to come into the city, however. Those who approach overland descend from the Vingaard Mountains, gazing down onto the city from above. Rather than a panorama of rising spires, these travelers come around a bend in the pass to see the entire city laid out before them. It fills the bowl of the valley that leads down to Branchala Bay.

Palanthas is famous for its non-stop activity. Great merchant ships sail into the harbor, unload their cargo, and then sail out for ports around Ansalon. Workers load cargo onto wagons or carry it to shops and stalls throughout the city. Everywhere, there is motion—people, horses, and carriages move from here to there along the roads and thoroughfares. Sometimes there are even creatures flying across the skyline—griffins arriving from Qualinesti or silver dragons carrying Solamnic Knights to important meetings of state. The city's most famous structures are easily identifiable—the Lord's Mansion, the Tower of High

Sorcery, and the newly constructed Temple of Paladine.

"There it is," Adyn said pointing down at the city below. "There is the temple. It is even larger and more beautiful than I'd been told."

Catriona chuckled. "Wait until you see it up close," she said.

He turned and looked at her in awe. "You have seen the Temple of Paladine?" he asked.

Cat smiled as she readjusted the pack on her back. "Construction was not yet complete, but I got a sense of how grand the temple was going to be," she said. "When I was a Solamnic squire I went where my lady took me. She just happened to take me to very nice places."

Adyn had always dreamed of coming to Palanthas. He had lived his entire life on the peninsula that formed the western edge of Branchala Bay, but he had never been to the city. There was no easy way to get there. Surrounded as it was by mountains, the only overland approach to Palanthas was the one he and Cat had just taken—the Knight's High Road—and his parents would never let him make the trip alone. Though he and his family lived less than a hundred miles away, as far as Adyn was concerned the alabaster buildings and bustling society of Palanthas might as well have been on one of the moons.

Yet now here he was, walking down the last few miles of switchback trail that led to the South Gate and into Palanthas. He could barely contain the smile on his face as he picked out more of the details he had heard about for so long. Each and every one of them was even more spectacular than he'd ever guessed. Perhaps the most surprising of all, though, was the Old City Wall.

Palanthas had not always taken up the entire this valley. In fact, originally the city had been contained within a protective wall, but now that region was simply known as the Old City. This seemed simple and logical enough when Adyn heard about it, but it in no way prepared him to see a thirty-foot, double-walled structure encircling the heart of the city. Every gate through the wall was guarded by a pair of towers, three-hundred feet tall. Like everything about the city, it exceeded his expectations. Somehow, Palanthas seem even more a place of legend than when it had lived only in his imagination.

"It's all so . . . so. . ."

"Huge?" Cat suggested.

"I was going to say majestic," said Adyn, "but huge will do."

"When a city is built to be a monument the architects do not do things in little ways," Cat said.

"I knew that the city was laid out like a wheel," said Adyn. "But the curve of the streets is so perfect. It's amazing."

"And note how the roads actually match the cardinal and ordinal directions." Cat pointed to avenues that cut through the circular pattern like spokes. "Any map that shows Palanthas has no need for a compass. The streets serve that function perfectly."

"Amazing," said Adyn.

They walked in silence for a while, Adyn stifling oohs and aahs from time to time when he noticed something new. It was often said that Palanthas was the "Jewel of Solamnia," and even with his romanticized image of the city Adyn had always imagined that to be a fair bit of hyperbole. But looking at Palanthas in the late afternoon sun, the acolyte thought it did look like a milky white jewel.

He was not the first person that the city bedazzled, and he certainly would not be the last. In fact, Palanthas could just as easily be called the "Jewel of Ansalon," for it beckoned to men, women, and children from across the continent. Adyn knew that on the streets below he would meet people from all over the map—elves from Silvanesti and Qualinesti, dwarves from Thoradin and Thorbardin, minotaurs from Mithas, gnomes from

Mt. Nevermind, humans from Abanasinia, Nordmaar, Ergoth, and even centaurs and barbarians from the Plains of Dust. And despite the differences in race and culture, they lived side by side with tolerance.

There was no place else like Palanthas in the world.

"Adyn Thinreed," Cat said as they roundied another curve in the switchback, breaking her companion's train of thought. "Welcome to Palanthas!"

Just ahead the road straightened out, and Adyn saw a gatehouse made of white stone. The gatehouse was built into the walls of the switchback path so that it was impossible to go around it without climbing gear. The two towers, much smaller than those Adyn had spied at the gates of the Old City wall, had knights standing guard on the parapets. And although the gate was open, another pair of knights stood there as well.

When they saw the travelers approaching, the knights came to attention and presented their polearms in an imposing fashion. They seemed young to Adyn, not more than a year or two older than he was, and quite possibly even younger.

"They certainly don't look like war-hardened veterans," he whispered to Cat.

She gave him a hard stare. "Being in a war does not grant you courage or skill," Cat said. "Make no mistake, they are fully trained knights or they would not be entrusted with this post."

"State your business," called out one of the guards.

Adyn held his arms out wide in a welcoming gesture, as if the guards were the ones entering *his* hometown.

"I am here for the Dragon Day festivities," he said. "May Paladine shine his blessings on us all."

The guards lowered their spears.

"Welcome, cleric," said the first knight.

"I'm still just a struggling acolyte," Adyn said, "Though I hope to take my vows in a few days' time."

"You and a few hundred others," said the second knight. "We've had more holy pilgrims than merchants pass through the gates this week."

"Thank the gods they finished that new temple," said the first knight. "Or the only place you'd have to stay is in the kender cell at the city jail!"

It was widely known that the Palanthas City Jail was home to the largest kender community outside the borders of Kendermore. Of course the population constantly rotated as prisoners (usually accused of picking pockets or petty theft) were admitted and released.

"Don't listen to any of the innkeepers you pass on the road," said the second knight. "Go straight to the temple for your lodging. You'll save yourself the extra steel piece all the inns seem to be charging for their rooms now that there are so many hungry mouths in town."

"That's what you get when the Merchant's Council has as much say as the Lord Knight," said the first knight.

"Thank you for the advice," Cat said quickly. She'd heard too many knights ramble on at length about the corrupt nature of the merchants. "We'd best be taking your advice and get to the temple before the clerics all bed down for the night."

They'd intended to arrive in the city in time for the evening meal, but traveling across the mountains was more taxing than they'd anticipated. It had been more than an hour since sunset, and it would still take them at least another half-hour to get to the Old City.

"Thank you, indeed," said Adyn. As he stepped past the gate and put his foot onto the paved streets of Palanthas for the first time he looked up and added a quick prayer of thanks to Paladine.

The road no longer snaked back and forth, instead it became a straight avenue that ran down the hill toward the sparkling waters of Branchala Bay. The land on either side of the road was tiered creating flat planes that were covered with shops and residences. The wind carried scents of laundry drying and pots on the boil leaving no doubt that this was one of Palanthas's working class neighborhoods.

As Adyn had heard, the city was incredibly stratified—broken into distinct neighborhoods and quarters devoted to one specific endeavor or social stratum. Gazing across the valley he could clearly pick out several sections.

"Is that Nobles' Hill?" he asked, pointing to the northeast sector of the city which was segmented into large plots of land each one featuring a large, ornate home that was surrounded by a wall.

"Yes," said Cat. "And that is Purple Ridge, and over there is the Old Temple District."

Adyn's eyes followed where she pointed—the upper ridges of the western side of the bowl that was Palanthas. Rather than closely packed homes or expansive manors, that section of town featured street after street of monumental structures built in the classic style, each a house of worship to one or more of the gods.

In the days before the Cataclysm the Temple District was supposedly the busiest part of the New City with people coming and going at all hours, leaving sacrifices and donations or just stopping in a chapel to pray. Now even at a distance it seemed almost abandoned, the buildings dingy and in poor repair. Some were clearly under repair—now that their patron deities had returned, so had worshippers.

"I wish we'd arrived during the day," said Adyn. "I would very much have liked to visit the old temples."

"I am certain that there will be time for that," said Cat.

"Yes," he agreed. "There are still a few days to spare. I was worried that I might miss the festivities."

"I could have told you that we were still a few days early," said Cat.

"How would you have known?" asked Adyn.

Cat chuckled lightly. "When you spend as much time as I have traveling in the wilder parts of the world, you learn to tell time by the sun and keep track of the days by the moons. I would think that a farmer's son would know a few such tricks."

Adyn laughed. "Yes," he said. "Well, I suppose I spent more time studying the stars than the moons."

They approached a gate in the Old City Wall and Adyn realized that it was even more impressive than he'd thought. No guards patrolled this gate, but the minarets towering over head felt like guards themselves—giant sentries protecting the heart of Palanthas from unwanted visitors.

A few blocks later they came to Lord's Way, the closest thing Palanthas had to a main street. It was one of the innermost circular roads, but it was also the road on which most of the important buildings were built, including the new Temple of Paladine. After nearly a fortnight on the road, having faced dangers of both his own and others' creation, and at the side of a warrior whose life he had saved, and who had saved his life in return, Adyn finally stood in front of the Temple of Paladine.

The temple grounds were large enough to be a park or small hunting grounds. Only one structure was built on the land, a monumental building with three wings, all made of sparkling white marble. The central wing was a cathedral that could hold more than one thousand worshippers at a time. Adyn knew that one of the side wings contained living quarters for a veritable army of priests and acolytes while the other held study halls, libraries, and offices for the temple's day-to-day business.

Adyn was about to say a quick prayer of thanks when the air was split with a doleful wail. A young man in acolyte robes identical to Adyn's ran out of the Worship Hall, his hands balled into fists on either side of his head, and it was clear that he was tugging on his hair hard enough to pull tufts of it loose.

From all around the temple grounds acolytes and clerics were rushing to the young man. Cat and Adyn joined them.

"What is it, Trysdan?" asked a cleric. "Tell us what's wrong."

"It's gone," the acolyte cried over and over. "It's gone! It's gone!"

"Calm down, son, calm down!" The cleric took the young man's shoulders in his hands and gave the lad a good, hard shake. "Take a deep breath, and get hold of your senses."

Trysdan breathed deeply three or four times and his eyes lost their wild, glazed look. He suddenly realized that he was surrounded by dozens of people, all of them anxiously waiting to hear his report.

"Now," said the cleric. "Calmly and sanely, tell us what's gone."

"The crown, sir," the acolyte said. "The Crown of Paladine has been stolen."

# 13 COURAGE OF THE SCAPEGOAT

The floorboards of Tazo Hall creaked ever so slightly under Sindri's feet. It was tough to sneak through old buildings, they always had loose planks or rusty door hinges or some other defect that created unexpected noises. The sack he was carrying over his shoulder didn't make things any easier. He hadn't been kidding when he'd told Grigg that he'd never practiced sneaking around the way other kender children did—scaring parents, grandparents, and most of all any human neighbors as often as possible. From as early as Sindri could remember, he had wanted to be a wizard, and the focus and training required to achieve that goal meant that there were a lot of typical experiences that he'd missed.

Still, even though he never played the climbing, jumping, tumbling, and hiding games that his friends did, Sindri was good enough at these things to get past most guards when the quest for wizardly knowledge required it. His current mission obliged him twice to sneak past Mistress Overhill, the academy's instructor for classes on potions, poultices, and powders and the House Mother of Tazo Hall. She had a room at the base of the stairs that Sindri had to pass by to enter or leave the dormitory rooms, and although **119** she was human, Mistress Overhill's hearing was so sharp that the students sometimes speculated she was really an elf whose ears had been polymorphed.

Sindri made both passes by Mistress Overhill's room without making as much noise as a dormouse, but here in the hallway leading to his room he felt as though his every step sounded a wooden creak or groan loud enough to wake everyone sleeping in the Faculty Halls.

He was only a few feet from a study lounge near his troupe's dormitory room. Sindri tried to cover the ground in a single step as he reached for the doorknob, but the wooden floor emitted such a loud popping sound that he jerked his weight back. This proved to be a ghastly error as the added momentum caused by the weight of the bundle over his shoulder threw the kender off balance. He stood there balanced on a single toe, one free arm pin wheeling in a vain attempt to catch his balance.

"Sindri! Stop fooling around and get in here!"

The door to the room opened a crack. A willowy arm shot into the hall, grabbed the kender by the collar, and pulled him so hard he practically flew through the air into the room. Before he could shriek (or even land in a heap on the floor), the door closed and the hall was silent again.

"What were you doing out there?" Hasia said in a hoarse whisper, as close as she dared come to shouting this late at night.

"What do you think?" Sindri hissed back.

"D-did you g-get it?" asked Bolli who was seated at the table in the center of the room, a large towel spread out in front of him.

"Of course," answered Sindri, insulted that the question even needed to be asked.

"We knew we could count on you," said Hasia.

"P-put it here s-so we can s-see the p-prize."

Sindri brought the sack over to the table and spilled its contents onto the towel—a turkey leg, two wedges of cheese, three small apples, a large bunch of grapes, and half loaf of bread.

"Now that's what I call a late night snack!" Hasia said running her tongue broadly around her lips as though she was trying to clean off the remnants of dinner to make room for this feast.

"S-so much!" said Bolli. "Are you s-sure that the chefs won't notice?"

"I doubt they bother taking inventory of the pantry at night," Hasia said. "Besides, I've heard them talking to Headmaster Greeves—they say we eat more than a battalion of goblin raiders. I'm sure that having leftovers is more suspicious to them than a few missing tidbits."

"Stop talking and let's eat!" said Sindri grabbing a handful of grapes in one hand and breaking off a piece of cheese with the other. "The real danger is that Mistress Overhill will make a surprise inspection and notice that we're not in our beds."

"Who can sleep?" Hasia said as she bit into an apple. "I'm still too wound up after your little stand-off with Grigg."

"It was nothing," said Sindri.

"N-no it w-wasn't," said Bolli. "I m-mean, you didn't just t-tell him no, y-you laughed in his face."

"He deserved it," said Hasia between bites. "To think that Sindri would even consider doing such an underhanded thing as stealing the Crown of Paladine."

The kender blushed but said nothing. He was afraid that if he opened his mouth he'd tell her how close he came to agreeing to Grigg's larcenous plan. In fact, the thing that really kept him from giving in was the look in Hasia's and Bolli's eyes. At first Sindri had thought they agreed with Grigg, but at the last minute he noticed Modaar standing behind the pair watching Grigg with a sycophantic leer on his face, his hands clamped on their shoulders—clearly Grigg's little helper had been warning them against interfering in the discussion.

Suddenly Sindri had felt himself filled with self-confidence and the absolute certainty that he would not allow himself to be talked into doing something that anyone with an ounce of conscience would know was wrong. As much as he wanted to be accepted as a wizard, he realized that he didn't care what Grigg thought of him. In fact, Sindri realized that no matter what he did—no matter how many tasks he performed or tests he passed—people like Grigg and Modaar would never think of him as anything more than a joke or a stooge to boss around when it amused them to do so.

"The look on his face was priceless," said Hasia, her mouth half-stuffed with the last of the meat from the turkey leg. "I'd pay good steel to see that again."

Sindri chuckled. "Really?" he said. "What did it look like? I was too busy to notice."

"W-were you s-scared?" asked Bolli through a mouthful of cheese.

"Oh no, not scared," said Sindri. "I was trying to think of as many ways as I could to say 'no.'"

They all laughed.

"Let's get back to our room," Hasia said after a while. "We're making enough noise to wake the dead."

"I'm n-not afraid of the d-dead," said Bolli. "B-but all their sh-shuffling and m-moaning might wake up Mistress Overhill, and sh-she scares the rose quartz out of me."

They laughed again, but more quietly than before.

After gobbling down the few remaining grapes and bits of bread and cheese, Bolli folded up his towel and brushed away the crumbs that remained on the table.

Sindri opened the door as quietly as he could and peeked out—

no one was there. He stepped carefully into the hallway, avoiding the loose floorboards as best he could. The others followed behind, each trying to trace the kender's steps exactly. There were a few creaks, and even one deep moan from the floor, but nothing that would raise suspicions.

They entered their room quietly, not wanting to wake Grigg or Modaar, both of whom had been soundly sleeping when the group had left. To their surprise, however, both of their troupe-mates were awake, out of bed, and leaning as far out one of the room's windows as they could safely balance.

"What's going on?" asked Hasia.

"Ask our little kender friend," said Modaar.

"It seems he's not as virtuous as he'd have us believe," said Grigg.

The others looked confusedly back and forth among themselves.

"What are you talking about?" said Hasia, more a demand than a question this time.

"The city guard is swarming along the Lord's Way," Grigg answered. "It seems someone has broken into the temple and stolen the Crown of Paladine. They say that the thief was seen running from the building, and he was wearing an apprentice's robes."

"What?" the three friends said in unison.

"But Sindri didn't—" said Hasia.

"H-he c-couldn't—" said Bolli.

"I wouldn't—" said Sindri.

"He was with us the whole time," Hasia said.

Grigg and Modaar leaned back into the room. They looked at one another and shrugged. "Well, if he was with you the whole time," said Grigg, "he has nothing to worry about."

"Yeah," said Modaar. "Thank goodness he took you all with him when he snuck off to the pantry."

The three friends stared at the fat little elf with equal parts disbelief and disdain.

"Oh, you didn't really think we weren't aware of what you were doing," said Grigg. "We may not be fashionable enough to merit invitations to your late night soirees, but that doesn't mean we're blind and deaf to them."

"It doesn't matter," said Hasia. "Even if he did go off on his own for a little while, we still know he wasn't away long enough to go to the temple and back."

"Perhaps," Grigg said, "But do you want to tell Headmaster Greeves that you were out of our room after curfew and eating stolen food?"

"Yeah," said Modaar. "And I don't know about Grigg, but I never noticed that any of *you* were out of your beds—just the kender." He said the final word as if it were a curse.

"M-maybe we're w-willing to get into a little t-trouble for a friend," said Bolli.

Grigg stared wide-eyed. It was as though he'd never seen Bolli express a conviction before, let alone a noble one.

"Maybe," said Grigg. "But are you willing to get thrown out of school for him? Because that's what they do to apprentices who are behind in their studies and then get caught breaking curfew and stealing school property."

Bolli's shoulders slumped and his eyes rolled in his head. He looked for like a fish that had leaped from a lake and landed in the bottom of a fisherman's boat.

"But I didn't do it!" insisted Sindri. "Doesn't that count for anything?"

Everyone in the room stopped and turned to look at him.

"Not really," said Grigg.

"As much as I hate to admit it, he's right," said Hasia. "All they really need to do is prove that you did *anything* wrong. The rest will just be assumed."

STAN BROWN

"Of course it will," said Modaar. "A kender is sneaking around where he shouldn't go and at the same time a valuable item goes missing, who wouldn't be willing to just accept on faith that the thieving little beggar took it?"

"I wouldn't," grumbled Sindri.

"And neither would anyone who's taken the time to get to know you," Hasia said casting a hateful gaze at Modaar. "But the fact of the matter is that the city constables will be more than willing to jump to exactly the same conclusions that your 'friend' Modaar has."

"Some friend," muttered Sindri.

"Well, maybe your true friends will stand by your side," said Grigg. "And maybe they will swear that they were with you tonight. And maybe they'll even risk ruining their own lives by lying and saying that you never left their sides. But there's one piece of evidence you're going to have a very hard time talking your way out of."

He pointed to Sindri's bed. The blankets were still tucked in tight, but there was a small bulge in the center of the mattress.

"When the constables' shouting woke us up, we thought that Sindri was the only one who hadn't sneaked out after curfew. But now I'd just like to know what it is that you've got tucked away in your bed."

Sindri walked slowly to his cot. He moved like a sleepwalker. This whole situation was absurd but he knew it was also deadly serious, and he was terrified of what he would find under the covers. Pulling back the blankets he saw his worst fears materialize. Resting on his bed, shining in the candlelight, was a circlet of silver metal crafted into the shape of a majestic dragon. The beast's wings, horns, and claws swept up creating a series of sharp peaks around the ring. The dragon's eyes, teeth, and scales were inlaid with gold to accentuate its regal manner.

Sindri's breath was so shallow that he could only speak in a whisper. "The Crown of Paladine," was all he could say.

"Well," said Grigg. "It would appear that you are a liar as well as a thief."

"As if there was ever any doubt," said Modaar

"He didn't take it," Hasia said stepping up so she faced her fellow elf nose-to-nose. "And what's more, you *know* he didn't take it."

"How would I know such a thing," Modaar said. He backed away from the seething Hasia, but for every step he took, she took one forward. Soon she had him backed against a wall. "I've been here in my bed the whole time, unlike some other people I can mention. All I know is that Sindri snuck out of the room, while he was out someone apparently stole the Crown of Paladine from the temple down the street, and now here it is in the kender's bed."

"The evidence does seem clear," said Grigg.

"But I didn't do it!" Sindri said again.

"Yes, well, be that as it may," said Grigg. "The heart of the matter is that the missing item is in your possession, and there are now five witnesses who can swear to this fact, whether they like it or not."

Sindri saw looks of despair cross his friends' faces as they realized Grigg was right. Even though they completely believed in the kender's innocence, they would have to tell the authorities that the crown had been discovered hidden in Sindri's bed. That would be all the evidence necessary to seal his fate.

"The question now becomes, what are you going to do about it?" Grigg asked

Sindri glared at the boy, anger practically leaping from his eyes in electric arcs. He balled his hands into fists and took a menacing step forward. Grigg raised his hands in front of his face presumably to ward off blows (although Sindri would have had to leap a full foot in the air to hit Grigg on the chin).

With a quick snap of his wrist, Sindri's arm shot out. Rather than throwing a punch, though, he simply snapped the Crown of Paladine off his bed and wrapped it in the sack that had so recently carried their late night snack.

"What I'm going to do is take the bloody thing back!"

# CHAPTER

# 14    LOST AND FOUND

The Temple of Paladine was in utter chaos. From all over the grounds acolytes came running to the steps of the Worship Hall bleating questions as they arrived. The air was filled with the buzz of dozens of conversations and the front of the temple was a constant whirl of activity.

The largest crowd of acolytes gathered at the top of the temple stairs around a middle-aged woman called Lady Brightfall. She seemed to be doing her best to answer and reassure while still questioning the acolyte who had discovered the supposed theft. Lady Brightfall's long, straw-colored hair was tied in two intricate braids that snapped back and forth around her head as she tried to give her full attention to no fewer than six different people at a time.

Cat watched as a strange cycle of events repeated itself about once every three minutes—acolytes arriving, asking the same dozen or so questions, then leaving.

Was it true? Had the Crown of Paladine been stolen? What would they do? What should they do? Who would do such a thing? Had the constables been summoned? Could the ordination ceremony go on without the crown? Could they use a replacement crown as a stand in? Could the Head Priest bless another circlet so it could serve the same purpose? If a priest were ordained with a different crown would he or she really be sanctified in the eyes of Paladine?

After determining that there were more questions than answers at this point, acolytes would pull themselves free of the crowd and rush off to spread what they knew to the far sides of the temple grounds and beyond. It wouldn't be long, Cat realized, before all of Old City knew about the missing crown. That sort of notoriety could be good or bad.

If everyone in town knew that the Crown of Paladine had been stolen and that the full forces of the Temple of Paladine and the Palanthas Constable's Office were working to find it, the thief would have a very hard time finding a buyer for his or her prize or smuggling it out of the city. Eventually the fear of being caught with the crown could lead the thief to return it or leave it where it would be found by the authorities.

On the other hand, the same forces could lead the thief to stick the crown in a secure holding spot and leave it there for a number of years or, worse still, destroy it so and eliminate all evidence of the crime. If either of these possibilities came to pass, the only way the clerics would ever know what happened to their crown would be through the use of arcane magic. However, since the thief was reported to have been wearing the robes of a student mage, it seemed unlikely that the Wizards of High Sorcery would be inclined to help publicly vilify one of their own.

All in all, Cat estimated that if the Crown of Paladine wasn't secured by daybreak, it would not be found before the Dragon Day ceremony. And that, judging by the panicked tone of the acolytes when that suggestion arose in nearby conversations, would cause a major upheaval in the Temple of Paladine.

"What difference does it make what crown you use in the ordination ceremony?" Cat asked Adyn.

"What?" said Adyn. In the tumult he seemed to have forgotten she was there.

"The crown does not have any special magical powers," she said. "Its importance is based on its history, not any divine gifts, correct?"

"Yes," he answered. "But what has that got to do with it?"

"With the need to find the crown and return it to its proper place?" said Cat. "Nothing. But it eliminates several possible motives for the robbery. For example, we can fairly conclusively say that the crown was not taken to abuse or to deny the Temple of Paladine access to its powers. We can likewise presume that it wasn't taken to disrupt the Dragon Day ceremonies."

"Why do you say that?"

"Because the ordinations will go on no matter what."

"Well, that's just not true," said an acolyte named Fallstorm, a tall, broad shouldered man whose wild hair and tanned skin were evidence of his southern plains origins.

"Aye," added Tarrok, a black bearded dwarf, wearing robes that had been cinched up so he wouldn't trip over them. "We might be able to take our vows, but without the crown we won't be doing it on Dragon Day."

"Why not?" Cat asked.

"You wouldn't understand," said Fallstorm.

"I wouldn't?" Cat made no effort to hide how offensive she found that comment.

"Nay," said Tarrok. "It's a complicated thing, steeped in tradition. Best not to worry your pretty head over it."

"My 'pretty head' generally worries about whatever I think is important," Cat said, her voice dropping in both tone and volume. "And what makes you think that I would not understand? I may not be ready to take a priestly vow, but I have given a good deal of sweat and blood in the service of the Platinum Lord and I understand a great many things. I especially understand when I am being insulted."

"That was not their intent, dear lady," said a deep voice from behind Cat. "Indeed, I dare say that the only insult on their minds was the one they hope the temple will be spared by this embarrassing situation being rectified quickly."

Cat turned to see an old man coming toward them from the administration wing of the temple. He was leaning on a cane and assessing the acolytes through cloudy eyes.

The old man addressed the acolytes directly, "Still, in the future, I would be happier if the representatives of this temple and the Platinum Lord chose their words with more care."

"Yes, Revered Son," all the acolytes, including Adyn, said with one voice, then they bowed their heads in deference.

It took Cat a moment to realize that she was standing in the presence of Elistan, Head Priest of the Temple of Paladine and spiritual leader to all who worshipped the Platinum Lord.

"Your Eminence," Cat said and sank to one knee.

"Rise, child," said Elistan. "And please call me 'Revered Son' if 'Father Elistan' is not formal enough for you—it always has been for me. 'Eminence' is a title for nobility, and I am merely a simple shepherd of humanity."

"I am Catriona Goodlund," she said as she stood. "It is a great honor to meet you, Revered Son."

"And I you, Catriona," said Elistan. "Such poise and manners are a rare thing these days."

Elistan used his hand to excuse himself from the conversation, then turned his head and began to cough. The sound was rough, and the action caused his whole frame to shudder. When the fit had passed, he looked even older and unsteady on his feet than before. His lips were moist with flecks of phlegm and spots of blood.

During her time as a squire, Cat heard a great deal about Elistan, the man who was returning Paladine to Palanthas by overseeing construction of the new temple. The knights spoke of him with the awe and reverence they reserved only for Huma, Vinas Solamnus, the Lord Knights, and the gods themselves. Elistan had spent a long time as a captive of the Red Dragonarmy during the War of the Lance, but worked with Tanis Half-Elf and the Golden General to free his people. Along the way he underwent an epiphany becoming, together with the barbarian princess Goldmoon, a steadfast herald of the gods' return. When the war ended, he single handedly raised the money, garnered commitments from the artisans, and secured land in the heart of Palanthas to build the new temple. It was no understatement to say that without Elistan, the site on which Cat now stood would not exist.

But Cat had always heard Elistan described as a burly man with flowing hair and a massive, gray-streaked beard. His voice, they said, could fill a canyon and he had more energy than ten men half his age. Practically none of those things could be said about the man Cat was looking at now. He certainly had once been strong and healthy, but now his large frame was bent over and he used a cane. He still had a prodigious amount of hair, but it had lost any color other than gray. By the way the younger clerics rushed to his side inquiring whether or not he needed assistance, Cat guessed his cough was a chronic condition.

Elistan showed, with a great shrug of his shoulders, that he was not some invalid who needed tending from a flock of fawning priests. He resumed his former stance and returned his attention to Cat.

"Are you well, sir?" she asked.

"Well enough," he said. "Wisdom may come with age, but so do a number of less welcome developments. Still, I am as Paladine would have me, and in that I find comfort." Elistan flashed her a smile that was among the most comforting things that Cat had ever seen.

"Now then, Miss Catriona," the old cleric continued. "How is it that you find your way to the Temple of Paladine in its very hour of need?"

"I have been traveling with one of your acolytes," Cat answered. "He encountered some difficulties on the road and enlisted my assistance for the remainder of his journey to Palanthas. We only just arrived when the alarm was raised."

"I see," said Elistan. "And which likely lad is it that has been your companion on this harrowing journey?"

"Adyn Thinreed," she said, pointing Adyn out of the crowd of robed figures.

The Revered Son called him forward and studied Adyn with a practiced eye. Despite the confidence and commitment Adyn had shown thus far, Cat noticed that he seemed shy and uncertain now that he stood in the presence of Elistan.

"Can you, Adyn Thinreed, without impugning Miss Catriona's intelligence, explain why it is that without the Crown of Paladine we will cancel the Dragon Day celebrations?"

"Pride, sir," said Adyn.

The assembled clerics and acolytes were shocked, and a murmur of disapproval ran through the crowd.

"Here now," said Elistan, a stern look on his face. "What do you mean by this?"

Adyn swallowed hard, trying to clear the lump that suddenly formed in his throat. "I mean, sir, that Cat was right." Despite having every eye and ear bent his way, including the Revered Son's, Adyn's voice was strong and his words were spoken with a measured confidence. "The Crown of Paladine, as great a treasure as it was, is merely a symbol. There is no reason that it is *necessary* for the Dragon Day ceremony other than a simple tradition."

The crowd's murmur grew into a rumbling growl, like a wild animal warning passersby not to step too close.

"A simple tradition?" said Elistan, his face becoming a mask of stone. "But you will admit that many of the things we do in the service of Paladine can be reduced to nothing 'other than a simple tradition'?"

Adyn swallowed hard again. "Y-yes, sir."

"And you will allow that there are times when a 'simple tradition' can have significant power or bring great peace to a believer?"

"Yes, sir."

Elistan's expression relaxed and he gave Adyn a wink and a smile. "Good then," he said. Then looking to Cat he added, "This Mr. Thinreed of yours has good deal of promise. I thank you for seeing him safely to our door."

Cat smiled back at Elistan. No matter his age or physical condition, she thought, he certainly is every inch the man the knights spoke of.

"Now," Elistan said to the crowd. "Something unfortunate has happened here this evening, but it is hardly a tragedy and it will have no impact on our plans for Dragon Day. So those of you who hope to participate in this year's ordination had best return to your prayers lest Paladine find you wanting."

Half the throng scattered, many of them heading to either their cells or to one of the study halls. Elistan looked with a rueful eye at the crowd that remained on the temple stairs.

"So sure of yourselves are you?" he asked. "Perhaps pride *is* something we're going to have to work on."

Cat smiled, but Adyn blushed.

"If we're going to get any useful information about this incident," Elistan continued, "we can't have half of Paladine's faithful tromping around the cathedral at the same time." He pulled a handful of people to his side—Trysdan, the acolyte who had discovered the robbery, Lady Brightfall, Adyn, and Catriona. As they entered the chapel, Elistan turned to the others in the crowd and said, "The rest of you find some other way to get into trouble."

"Yes," said Elistan, "it certainly is gone." His booming voice echoed in the cathedral. Cat imagined it would seem even more powerful when he spoke from the pulpit.

Trysdan nodded his head vigorously.

"Did you check under the pews?" Cat asked. When Lady Brightfall looked scornfully at her she added, "It has been my experience that the simple explanations are often overlooked. The crown might have been accidentally knocked from its pedestal. I simply think it's wise to be certain that it was actually stolen and isn't merely missing."

"A fair point," said Elistan. "Did you check the floor, Trysdan?"

"Yes, Revered Son," said the young man. "It was nowhere to be seen. But I did find this."

The acolyte pulled what looked like a metallic stick from the seat of a nearby pew.

"It's a dagger," Trysdan said.

"May I see that?" Cat asked, and the acolyte handed her the blade. She turned it over in her grasp. The dagger was made of burnished metal with thorns etched along its blade and a pommel like a stylized rosebud.

"Is something wrong?" asked Elistan.

"No, nothing wrong," said Cat. "It's just that I used to have a dagger just like this one."

"Perhaps our thief is the same person who stole your dagger."

"That would be a fine theory," said Cat. "Except that my dagger was not stolen. I gave it to my friend Sindri."

The priests and acolytes looked at Cat waiting for further explanation. None was forthcoming.

"How well do you know this 'Sindri'?" Elistan asked.

"I knew him very well," Cat said casting her eyes to the floor and lowering her chin to her chest. "But he can't be responsible for this—he's dead."

A high-pitched voice called from the back of the cathedral, echoing all the way. "I guess you don't know me as well as you think!" it said.

"Sindri!" cried Cat.

The kender raced down the chapel's central aisle, launched himself into the air, and wrapped his arms around Catriona's neck.

"Cat!" he shouted.

They hugged one another with all the strength in their bodies. Finally, Sindri released his hold, leaned back in Cat's grip and said, "What are you doing here?"

"Me?" she said suspiciously. "What are you doing here? You're supposed to be dead."

"I am?" said Sindri. "No one told me that. How am I supposed to know these things unless someone tells me? Since I am alive, though, you'll let me stay that way, right?"

Cat laughed like she hadn't since before Elidor was killed.

"I saw you get struck by lightning," Cat finally managed to say, still laughing despite the seriousness of the thought. "I saw you die."

Sindri thought about it.

"No," he said. "No, I never got hit by lightning, though it sounds like an interesting experience. But I did teleport myself from the middle of the Sirrion Sea into a pool of water in the dungeon of a tower, and you'll never guess where that tower was—"

"Wait. Slow down. If you went to some tower, how did your dagger come here?"

"My what went where?"

"Your dagger," said Cat. "The one I gave you on the ship before you di- . . . before you disappeared."

"My dagger didn't come here," Sindri said. "Well, it has now, but only because I came here." He reached inside his robes and pulled out a dagger that was practically identical to the one Cat held.

Her mouth hung open as she looked at the daggers. "How is that possible?"

Lady Brightfall stepped forward. She examined the knife that Cat held, then leaned forward and squinted at the one Sindri offered.

"There's a merchant in the Trade Exchange who sells decorative weapons," she said. "I believe that is one of his most popular designs. It looks nice, but don't try to do much with it—I hear that they break more easily than a gnomish clock."

"Well, that explains that," said Sindri.

"I *think* that's him," Trysdan said quietly pointing at Sindri. He had been standing toward the back of the group peering suspiciously at the kender.

Elistan turned a serious gaze at Trysdan. "What did you say?" he asked.

"I think that's him," Trysdan said again, only more confidently. "I think that's the person I saw running from the temple."

"But it wasn't," said Sindri.

"Are you sure, son?" asked Elistan.

"I think that's *him*," Trystan nearly shouted this time. "He's the right size, he's carrying the right kind of dagger, and he's wearing apprentice's robes. Maybe that's what he does, he steals something and leaves a dagger in its place. Kender do all sorts of crazy things."

"Trust me," said Cat. "For all the crazy things Sindri might do, this isn't one of them."

"Yeah," said the kender. "What sort of crazy things might I do?"

"Steal a wizard's robes, for one thing," said Cat. "Where did you find such a short wizard, anyway?"

"So he would steal some robes," said Lady Brightfall. "But he wouldn't steal the Crown of Paladine."

"No," said Sindri.

"No," said Cat.

"I think that's *him!*" insisted Trysdan.

"I didn't steal the robes," said Sindri. "I joined a magic school."

"You joined a what?" asked Cat.

"I believe we can trust young Catriona's judgment," Elistan said to Trysdan. "If she says that Sindri did not steal the crown then I, for one, believe her."

"I joined a magic school," repeated Sindri. "Actually, it's called the Greeves' Academy for Thaumaturgical Studies."

"You joined a magic school?" Cat said. "You actually got accepted at a magic school."

"It's an academy," said Sindri. "And it's great. They gave me robes and they've been teaching me about spells and potions and everything. Here, let me show you."

The kender pushed free of Catriona's grasp and leaped to the ground intending to show her some of the interesting things he'd learned in his classes. Unfortunately for him, as he hit the ground the sack tucked into his belt slipped loose and fell to the ground with a loud, metallic clang. The sack bounced once and then through the mouth rolled a silver colored ring about the size of a man's head. It wobbled around for a few moments and rolled to a stop at Elistan's feet where everyone could see it plainly—a platinum circlet crafted in the shape of a great dragon.

"The Crown of Paladine," said Elistan.

"Oh yeah," said Sindri. "I found your crown."

# CHAPTER

# 15    The Master and the Manipulator

Maddoc worked like a man possessed. For nearly a fortnight he stayed in the same small workroom he had been in since arriving at the Tower of High Sorcery feverishly putting his plans into action. The room contained everything he required—spell components and alchemical ingredients, a fireplace, a cot, even a washroom. Food and drink appeared three times daily, always while Maddoc was otherwise engaged. He just looked up to find a tray filled with exactly what he craved at that particular moment. Likewise, the water and linen in the washroom were always clean whenever he entered the room.

As puzzling as these events might be, Maddoc gave them very little thought. The food arrived and it was not poisoned, that was all that really mattered. He knew enough not to waste his mental energy on idle speculations. Rather, his concentration was bent toward a goal that continued to elude him. Laid out on the table were the shattered remains of Asvoria's Aegis.

When he first poured the pieces onto the worktable, it was practically impossible to recognize that they had once been a shining, silver sword. What once had been a sterling blade

140

covered with glittering emerald shards now was merely hundreds of metallic slivers dotted with green stones. The hilt that had once been formed from a single malachite stone now was a pile of small, rough-hewn rocks. It took Maddoc nearly three days and nights just to put all the pieces in order.

For the next few days, all the old man did was stare at the ruined sword. One by one he would pick up pairs of shards, hold them together in the correct orientation, then examine the spots where they touched checking the seam to be sure that there weren't any cracks or divots that would indicate that another sliver of metal or stone was needed to make the union complete. Sometimes he would look at a particular pair for only a few seconds, other times he would gaze at them for hours on end, squinting bringing them so close that you might think he meant to put them in his eye.

After he had tested every piece with all the other pieces it came in contact with, Maddoc began assembling whole sections of the Aegis. Using only hand-held pressure, he would shake each piece vigorously watching to see if any of the smaller pieces came loose and listening to hear if there was a loose fitting anywhere within the structure. When Maddoc was satisfied that a section was intact, he then disassembled it and placed the pieces back on the table.

During these first two phases, Maddoc slept and ate sparingly. His face grew sallow and his skin took on an unhealthy jaundiced tone. Anyone who saw Maddoc in this condition would certainly conclude that the old man did not have long to live. However, since Maddoc never left the room and no one ever came to visit, he was saved from having to listen to well-meaning suggestions for rest, not that he would have listened anyway.

Because the room had no windows, it was difficult for Maddoc to track the passage of time. He was completely unaware that six and a half days had passed by the time he set the last of the pieces of the Aegis back in place. Rising from his seat, Maddoc stood over the serving tray and ate the mushroom broth and rich, grainy bread that it held. He then walked into the washroom and splashed water on his face. The sunken bags under his eyes were so heavy he could feel them with his wrinkled fingers.

Maddoc didn't even look at the Aegis as he crossed the room to the cot, lay down, and crossed his hands over his chest. From a distance an observer might think that the old man had passed away, so shallow was his breathing. But anyone who got closer would see that Maddoc's eyes were open and darting back and forth as though he was reading an important document.

For two more days Maddoc simply lay there in lonely silence reading pages that were not there. On the third day he sat up suddenly, as though he'd had a brilliant insight or awakened from an intense dream. Neither of these things had happened. He was merely ready to begin phase three of his work.

Unlike his previous efforts, Maddoc's next task was quick and relatively painless. He stood over the segmented Aegis, held his arms straight out from his body his palms facing down over the shattered item, closed his eyes, and began to chant in a deep, hoarse whisper. Slowly his voice rose in both pitch and power until the entire room was filled with a howling wail. Maddoc closed his hands into fists, squeezing them tighter and tighter until drops of blood oozed between his fingers. The blood pooled along his closed knuckles until it sagged, a red bead hanging heavy, waiting for gravity to pull it free.

When the first drop of blood fell on the Aegis, Maddoc ceased his chanting.

Silence reigned in the room as the pieces of the Aegis began to glow. Maddoc shut his eyes, but the light was so intense that he could see his hand even through his closed eyelids. Still the pieces glowed brighter. Soon he could see nothing, just a field of white light.

Then, just as suddenly as it had begun, the display ended. Indeed, all the lights in the room went out at once.

Maddoc stood in the dark, wavering on his feet. After taking a deep breath he opened his eyes and intoned a magical phrase causing the lamps to flair to life. Compared to the previous radiance, their light seemed feeble and uncertain.

As his eyes adjusted to the illumination, Maddoc looked down at the table. Before him, glistening with beads of the purest water was the Aegis—whole again.

Maddoc smiled.

He took his prize in his bony hands and lifted it up to eye level, searching its surface for the slightest crack or imperfection. There were none.

"Perfect," he said to himself.

"Well begun, perhaps," said a voice. "But that is only half the process. The more difficult portion yet remains."

Maddoc looked up. The voice came from a frail figure dressed in black robes and standing in the shadow of a doorway that wasn't there the last time Maddoc had looked at that wall.

"Master Raistlin," Maddoc said. "How gracious of you to share this moment with me."

"It seemed the prudent thing to do," answered Raistlin. "What you hold was once the receptacle for an ancient power."

"Yes, Master." Maddoc disliked having to be so fawningly subservient, but he dared not risk angering the Master of the Tower. He might have successfully concealed from Catriona and the others the fact that he had magical power at his command, but he could not hide from Raistlin that he was still far from at his peak. Even at his strongest Maddoc doubted he would have been a match for Raistlin—frail though the mage's body was, every fiber of his being seemed infused with arcane energy.

"Until recently the Aegis was the key to my future," said Maddoc.

"Yes," said Raistlin, coughing slightly as he did. "The future is not what it used to be."

"Excuse me, Master?"

Raistlin coughed one more time, but refused to say any more.

"It is vexing," Maddoc said, bringing the subject back to his personal topic of choice. "For months the only thing that stood between me and my goals were a handful of whelps—my own among them. They were young, inexperienced, and without means or any source of real power, and yet they managed time and again to thwart my will and delay my success."

Raistlin gave a single, mirthless chuckle. "Such is the power of fools and kender," he said.

Kender. Maddoc almost inquired about Sindri, but decided against it. It had been important to him to get Sindri out of the Tower of High Sorcery—he couldn't concentrate on the work he'd been doing if his mind was constantly distracted by the possibility that the little pest would somehow happen into the laboratory and, knowing how kender were, he almost certainly would have. Exactly where Raistlin had taken Sindri and what became of him afterward was none of Maddoc's concern. And yet, he wondered.

"Just when I finally clear my path of that obstacle," Maddoc said. "Just when my adversaries succumb to their own emotions and lack of experience, the one tool I need to complete my efforts is destroyed in a twist of fate. It is as though Nuitari has decreed that I should suffer."

Beneath his hood, Raistlin's golden eyes smoldered at the mention of the god of black magic. "When the gods want to mock us, they give us exactly what we want."

Maddoc looked down at the Aegis in his hands. The sword was whole. Every emerald chip was in place. The blade was as smooth and pure as the day it was forged. It lacked the magical aura it once had, but otherwise there was no way to tell it had ever been broken.

"Now I have only to finish my work and everything I desire will fall directly into my lap," said Maddoc.

"Perhaps," Raistlin said. "But no mortal knows what fate holds in store. And nothing in this world happens except at its appointed hour."

"What do you mean, Master?" asked Maddoc, though his eyes continued to caress the mended Aegis.

Raistlin did not answer.

"Master?" Maddoc said, looking up, but there was nothing to see other than a bare wall. Both Raistlin and the doorway in which he stood were gone as if they had never been there.

# 16  Friends and Enemies

"I didn't steal it!" Sindri said for what he thought must have been the hundredth time that night. He was used to having to repeat himself in order to be heard, but this was ridiculous.

He looked to Cat for support, but for the first time that he could remember, didn't find it. Instead her face was a mixture of confusion and disappointment.

"A likely story," said Lady Brightfall. "Give it here, kender!"

Sindri held the Crown of Paladine out at arm's length.

"That's what I came here to do," he said, but he knew that already the woman was no longer listening to him.

"I told you it was him," said Trysdan.

"I didn't st—"

"That's enough, Trysdan," said Elistan, cutting off both the acolyte and the kender before they could renew their game of accusation and denial. "May I please see the crown?"

Lady Brightfall handed the silver circlet to the Revered Son, bowing her head slightly as she did.

"Th-this is it," Elistan said, his breath coming in short wheezes. "Th-thank goodness you re-retur-returned this to us."

The last few words were almost completely incomprehensible because the old man began to cough. It was an ugly sound, wet and harsh, and his whole body shook with the effort. What's more, there seemed to be no end to the fit in sight. Elistan's pale skin flushed, first pink, then red, then to purple and still he continued to cough.

Finally, with a supreme assertion of willpower and a final deep, raspy breath, Elistan willed the coughing jag to cease.

"Praise Paladine," he said weakly, smiled, and then collapsed in a dead faint.

"Revered Son!" cried Lady Brightfall and Trysdan.

"Father Elistan!" cried Adyn and Cat.

And they all rushed in to catch him before he could fall to the ground.

Sindri stood as still as a kender can as the cathedral suddenly swarmed with activity. At least ten men and women rushed in at the cries of alarm. They supported Elistan's fragile, unconscious body. His breathing was so labored that Sindri could clearly hear it even over the cacophony of voices shouting orders and mumbling prayers.

Sindri, Cat, and Adyn followed the procession out of the chapel, but remained on the temple stairs as the others rushed Elistan to his chambers where, it was hoped, skilled healers would give him assistance. Half the clerics went with the Revered Son to his rooms while the other half moved as a vigilant group carrying the Crown of Paladine into a room hidden deeper inside the Worship Hall.

Before long, the only ones remaining on the stairs were Sindri, Cat, and a few dozen acolytes.

"This is your fault, kender!" said Fallstorm.

"I don't see how it could be," Sindri said. "First of all, I feel fine—I don't have a cough at all. But even if I did, I don't think someone can catch a cold that quickly—even someone as old as that."

"Are you implying that Revered Son Elistan is too frail to perform his duties?" asked Tarrok with a frightful scowl.

"No! Of course not. I would never do such a thing," said Sindri. "Who is Revered Son Elistan?"

"Who is—?" stammered a dwarf in loose-fitting robes. "Are you saying that Elistan is not worthy of his lofty role?"

"Absolutely not!" said Sindri. "How lofty is—?"

Before things could degenerate even further, Catriona stepped between Sindri and the crowd.

"We must not let our worry for the safety of Revered Son Elistan move us to actions we'll regret when things calm down," Cat said.

"Who are you?" several of the newly arrived acolytes asked.

Adyn moved next to Cat. "She is here at Elistan's invitation," he said. "Right on these stairs he praised her sense of propriety and ability to judge a person's merits. I think if her counsel was good enough for the Revered Son, it should be good enough for us."

"Besides," Sindri said poking his head through the space between Adyn and Cat. "I returned your crown thing."

"Only because you stole it in the first place!" Trydsan.

"I didn't steal it!"

"You probably heard all the commotion and knew that Paladine was about to reap righteous revenge upon your wicked brow," said Fallstorm.

"What was going to go where?"

"Sindri did not steal anything," said Cat. Then she added, "from this temple . . . tonight."

A groan rose from the surrounding acolytes.

"How can you know that?" asked Trysdan. "You weren't here

when the Crown of Paladine was taken. All we know is that the kender had it when he arrived."

"That is not all I know," Cat said. "I know this kender. And I tell you with every ounce of certainty I have that he is not the thief."

Sindri was stunned. The way she'd looked at him earlier, he wasn't entirely sure that he would be able to count on Cat's help. "Thank you, Cat," he said.

"Where did you find the crown, Sindri?" Adyn asked. He clearly wanted to get the conversation going on a more positive, helpful track.

"In my bed," answered Sindri. "In the students' wing of the Greeves Academy."

"You mean he really is a magic student?" said Marta, a pretty, red-haired acolyte.

"In your bed?" said Cat.

"I thought he just stole the robes," said Tarrok.

"He's a kender and he studies at the academy?" said Fallstorm. "Why haven't we tied a rope around his wrists and turned him over to the authorities already?"

The crowd murmured its support for this idea.

"Because he is not dumb enough to steal your crown or to try to return with a cock and bull story like that unless it is actually true," said Cat.

The crowd did not seem convinced.

"But he is dumb enough to fall in with a crowd that would keep him around as nothing but a scapegoat," Cat continued.

"Hey!" cried Sindri.

"Come on now, Sindri," said Cat. "Who stole the crown and put it in your bed? Who would want to see you blamed for such a thing?"

Sindri thought for a moment. Grigg sure seemed happy enough

to blame him for the crime, but there was no real proof that the boy had anything to do with the crime itself. Besides, he was much too tall to be mistaken for a kender even in the dead of night. As much as he wanted to point the finger of blame at Grigg, there wasn't enough proof. And since Sindri hated being blamed for things he didn't do, he refused to put anyone else, even Grigg, through the same ordeal.

"I don't know," he said.

"Sindri," Cat said, dropping her voice to little more than a whisper. "This is not the time to develop some twisted version of kender honor. You are doing nothing but hurting yourself by withholding the information."

"Twisted?" sputtered Sindri. "You really haven't learned anything, have you Cat? You're still arrogant and self-righteous. Well, I have news for you. Real friends stand by one another no matter what. Real friends are like a family. And if someone in your family does something wrong, you still support him anyway."

"So you do know who did it," said Fallstorm.

"I have a suspicion," Sindri answered.

"And you're protecting his identity," said Tarrok.

"So that makes you an accomplice," said Marta.

"And just as foolish as ever," said Cat. "For goodness sake, Sindri, hasn't our time together taught you anything about how important it is to choose your friends carefully?"

"I'm not sure I'd say you've done much better, Catriona," Sindri snapped.

"What's that supposed to mean?" she demanded.

"Oh, nothing," said Sindri. "Just that surrounding yourself with people who are even more judgmental and closed-minded than you are doesn't actually make you any less stubborn or rude."

"Judgmental? Closed-minded?" The acolytes were livid.

"Rude and stubborn?" exclaimed Cat.

"And insulting!" Sindri said. "Or is that the same thing as rude?"

"How can you say that to me after I stood up for you?" said Cat.

"Is that what you call standing up for a friend?" Sindri asked. "Excuse me, but I don't think that proclaiming me 'innocent because of idiocy' really counts as standing up for me."

"I didn't mean it like that," said Cat. "Sindri, you know I don't think of you that way."

The kender put his fists on his hips and tried to meet Cat nose-to-nose. "Then why do you speak about me that way?" he said.

For a moment Cat's face softened. Perhaps she was sorry, perhaps she was insulted, or perhaps she was just surprised to see Sindri standing up for himself so effectively. Whatever the reason, the look turned back into a steely glare the moment she noticed that the entire crowd was waiting for her reply. The last thing she could ever do, Sindri knew, was back down from a fight.

"Would you rather I just get out of the way and let you deal with this angry mob by yourself?" Cat said through gritted teeth.

"He won't be alone," cried a voice from the street.

Everyone turned their eyes to the bottom of the stairs leading up to the Temple of Paladine. It was Hasia, Bolli, and even Grigg and Modaar along with twenty more individuals wearing wizard's robes—a few, like Grigg, wore colors that showed allegiance to one or another of the orders of High Sorcery, but most were dull brown like Sindri's robes.

The wizards in training marched up the steps and clustered around Sindri in a semi-circle.

"Are you here to proclaim the kender's innocence as well?" asked Marta.

Before Hasia could proudly and loudly say yes, Grigg stepped forward.

"We're saying that the kender is one of us." He spoke as though he was making a speech or teaching a lesson. "And we support and defend one another no matter what."

"So you admit that the kender stole the Crown of Paladine," said Tarrok.

"No," cried Hasia and Bolli.

"I didn't steal anything!" said Sindri.

But the acolytes paid no attention to them. Their eyes and ears were focused on Grigg.

"What does it matter?" Grigg said. "You have your crown back. Let us deal with the kender in our own way."

"Isn't that just like a wizard," said Fallstorm. "Seeing everything in black and white. There's more to this than who has the Crown of Paladine. We still haven't had satisfaction."

"Spoken like a true holy man," someone yelled from the back of the wizards group. Sindri recognized Modaar's voice, but he couldn't see him. "Where is your spirit of forgiveness and charity? Or is that only for use in situations that have no personal meaning for you?"

The acolytes grumbled loudly.

"In order to receive forgiveness, you must first ask for it," Marta said. "And charity is not granted to those who have already taken more than their fair share."

"So you're saying that all wizards are thieves?" said Grigg. "Three hundred years ago we saved the meaning of a holiday that you abandoned, and you think that makes us thieves? We took nothing that you did not first throw away."

"Holiday?" said Sindri.

"Who said this has anything to do with—" Cat began to say, but she was cut off.

"Dragon Day is traditionally celebrated with a holy ceremony," said Tarrok.

"Perhaps it is 'traditional' for your long-lived people," Grigg said. "But there are precious few people in Palanthas who even know that a religious rite used to happen on Dragon Day."

"The gods have returned," said Fallstorm. "Is this not a cause for celebration? Why are you so threatened by that possibility?"

"Why does your order insist on performing your ceremony on the one day that the people of Palanthas choose to show honor to the practitioners of High Sorcery?" Grigg asked. "I'll tell you why. It's because you are jealous. Our patrons never left us. We have had three hundred years of adulation from the populous and that drives you crazy. You don't want anyone or anything getting praise other than your inconstant Paladine."

"Wait," said Adyn feeling as though he had been in this argument before. "That's not what is being said here at all."

"Paladine is the Lord of Lords, first among the gods," said Tarrok. "No one should come before him."

"I think you've forgotten your point," Sindri said to Grigg. "You were insulting me, not Paladine."

Grigg and Tarrok stepped forward until they were chest-to-chest and screaming directly into one another's faces.

"If you have a problem with wizards just say so," yelled Grigg. "Don't use a simple kender to cover up your jealousy of our place in Palanthan society."

"Well, Black Robe, if you and your godless schemers want to keep the people of this city away from the powers of light and truth," shouted Tarrok, "you'll have to do more than send your kender spy to steal a holy relic."

"G-godless s-schemers?" said Bolli.

"Jealous of you arcanists are we?" demanded Fallstorm.

"All we've ever done is serve the people," yelled Hasia. "We've sure as day never led them into three hundred years of godlessness."

"Usurpers!" called out the acolytes.

"Charlatans!" howled the apprentices.

"I think perhaps we should calm down," Cat said to the acolytes.

"Why don't we just agree that everyone hates me and go home," Sindri said to the apprentices.

But their voices were lost on the rising wind of anger and resentment. Hasia opened a spell component pouch on her belt and began to pull out dried stinkweed. Marta gripped her holy symbol tightly and began to pray. Bolli started to make conjuring motions with his hands. Fallstorm cursed and balled his hands into fists. Both sides stood poised on an emotional precipice ready to throw aside rational discussion and dive headlong into an all out war between arcane and divine spellcasters.

# 17    TEMPLE OF THE DRAGON

"Enough!"

No one was more surprised to hear Adyn's voice than Adyn himself. He was even more surprised to find that he had stepped between the leaders of the two factions and placed the palm of one hand on each of their chests, separating them like an official at a brawling tournament.

Now, rather than the two sides staring each other down, all eyes turned Adyn's way. And although he had managed to redirect their attention, he had done nothing to assuage their anger.

"Look at us all," he said, very aware of the fact that he was wearing acolyte robes. He had to choose his words carefully or the wizards would simply lump his words in with those of the crowd. "Is this the amity and compassion preached by the Revered Son? Is this the dispassion and measured action your masters have taught you?"

Hasia grumbled loudly. How dare this acolyte presume to understand the practice of High Sorcery?

Marta bristled. Adyn had only just arrived at the temple—who was he to lecture to people who had been here for months?

And yet, they both had to admit that Adyn made complete

sense. They relaxed their posturing, and so did all their counterparts—the apprentices cinched their bags of spell components, and the acolytes let their holy items dangle from their necks and belts.

"We have our differences," Adyn continued. "Of that there can be no doubt. But we are not without similarities as well. We all want what is best for the city and people of Palanthas, although we have honest disagreements about what that may be. We all have devoted our lives to particular principles and ideals—given up other opportunities and perhaps even gone against the hopes of our loved ones solely for the sake of what we believe. In our hearts each and every one of us wants our actions to add to the glory and honor of our cause and our order."

Even Grigg and Tarrok were shamed into calming down. Like all those around them, their scowls softened until no anger remained, only expressions of regret and contrition.

"There's one thing I can tell you with absolute certainty," said Adyn. "Whether you are acolyte or apprentice, whether you craft arcane forces or channel divine might, if this confrontation comes to blows there will be nothing but shame on all our houses."

The steps of the Temple of Paladine, where angry shouts and spiteful threats filled the air just moments earlier, stood in complete silence.

"We have the Crown of Paladine," Adyn said after a few moments. "It was graciously returned by a member of your school. Perhaps it is best if we part now and simply agree that we will never be certain how the crown went missing or what forces brought us to this point."

Still no one spoke or moved.

At the center of the crowd, Cat and Sindri stood side by side simply staring at one another with looks filled with doubt. The silence became deeper and more uncomfortable when they realized that all the apprentices and acolytes were staring at them, waiting to see how they resolved their argument.

Finally, Sindri made a big show of yawning loudly and stretching like a kitten in the sun.

"I don't know about the rest of you," he said turning his back toward Cat and talking to his fellow apprentices, "but I sure am tired."

"And we have yet to be shown where we are to stay," Cat said as she took Adyn by the arm and stepped back to join the acolytes. "We've been traveling all day, and missed our evening meal because of all this excitement."

"Oh, I'm hungry, too," Sindri said as he took Grigg by the sleeve and led him down the stairs. "Do you think we could stop by the larder on the way back to our rooms?"

A few hours and a good meal later, Catriona lay on a cot trying not to listen to the conversation going on in the next room. At Father Elistan's insistence, one of the highest-ranking clerics personally offered Cat a cot in the residence wing for as long as she cared to be a guest at the Temple of Paladine.

The chamber was about fifty feet on each side and was filled with simple cots and cabinets. The acolytes at the temple were not supposed to have many luxuries, and they all had to share living quarters. Elistan had underestimated the number of faithful souls who would come to seek ordination, so some of the acolytes had to sleep on the floor.

Cat insisted that there was no need to give her preferential treatment. "Your stables would be a step up from some of the places I have stayed in the past few months," she told the priest. But he said that they would be shamed in Paladine's sight if they did not provide the best possible accommodations for such an honored guest. Cat was certain that the priest was repeating Father Elistan's instructions, because he did not seem to hold her in particular esteem.

The cot was comfortable enough, and she was so tired from the day's activities that Cat had expected to drift immediately and deeply to sleep. She likewise expected the same for Adyn, who had been given the neighboring cot. (Apparently being associated with Cat earned him similar treatment, at least during her stay at the temple.) However, before her head even touched the pillow, she could hear a group of four acolytes arrive and begin talking to Adyn about the encounter on the temple stairs.

"You may think that what you did was very clever," said a voice that Cat was sure belonged to Tarrok. "But all you did was make things worse."

Cat could hear Adyn shift around on his cot.

"You mean that when I stopped you from engaging in a street brawl on the stairs of the newly consecrated Temple of Paladine, I actually was thwarting the Platinum Lord's will?" he said, his voice thick with exhaustion.

"Make jokes all you want," Tarrok said. "But believe me, this matter is not over."

"The apprentice wizards are a vengeful lot," said Trysdan. "We would have been better off if they had succeeded at taking the crown. As the Revered Son said, that would not have had any impact on our ordination ceremonies. But now the wizards will be looking for another way to disrupt our Dragon Day plans."

"And this time they may hit on a more effective scheme," said Fallstorm.

"And how would anything be better if things had come to blows on the stairs?" asked Adyn.

"In any number of ways," Tarrok said. "At the very least, the authorities would know that there is trouble brewing. It would be more difficult for the apprentices to get away with any mischief if they and their masters had an official warning from the constable's office."

"The same is true for the acolyte's," said Adyn. "So why don't we just pretend that we've had that warning and refrain from doing anything that might cause us grief later on."

"Who's talking about doing anything like that?" said Trysdan. "We just want to protect ourselves if the wizards try something else."

"And they will try something else," said Fallstorm.

"So what do you suggest?" asked Adyn. "Shall we make a raid on their school to draw the attention of the constables? Or maybe you want to pray that Paladine visits the entire student body of the Greeves Academy with cases of the goblin flu sometime between now and Dragon Day?"

"Of course not," Tarrok said. "What sort of servant of Paladine do you take me for?"

"At this point in the conversation, you probably don't want me to answer that question," said Adyn.

"All we are saying," Trysdan said, "is that we should be prepared to protect ourselves."

"So we should all attend our ordinations with prayers for searing light spells on our lips just in case the wizards decide to cause trouble?" Lack of sleep was making Adyn's tongue sharper than usual.

"No," Fallstorm said. "We don't want to spoil our day by even thinking about fighting. We just need to make sure the apprentices can't do anything to us during the ceremony."

There was a pause in the conversation. Cat could imagine the confused look on Adyn's face and the expectant grins on the others'.

"What are you talking about?" Adyn said at last.

"Go ahead," said Tarrok. "Tell him."

For the first time, Cat heard Marta's voice. It was hesitant as though she wasn't certain that she should be saying anything at all.

"I've heard of a holy relic—the Medallion of Sanctuary," she said. "It has the power to completely block all arcane spells, but it doesn't have any effect on divine powers."

Again there was silence.

"You mean," Adyn said eventually, "that if someone had this medallion in the area, the apprentices would not be able to cast any spells at all?"

"Not just the apprentices," said Tarrok. "All the wizards no matter how powerful."

"We would be completely safe from their interference, as long as we stayed within range of the relic," said Trysdan.

"And where is this Medallion of Sanctuary?" Adyn asked. "You said that you'd heard of it, Marta. How do we know it's even real, let alone where to find it?"

"Oh, it's real," Marta assured him. "My father told me about it. He saw it work once. He was a child of the streets and a Red Robe wizard caught him stealing fruit from a farmer's cart. He chased my father up the hill into the Old Temple District, and Father tried to hide in an abandoned building. When the wizard found him, Father thought he'd be turned into a statue or a frog or something worse. But as long as he stayed inside the temple, none of the wizard's spells had any effect. It was only later that he learned the reason—the medallion hung on the temple's altar."

"Well, where is this temple?"

There was more silence. Cat pictured Marta with her chin down and drawing imaginary lines on the floor with the toe of her boots.

"It was the Temple of the Dragon."

"The what?" said Adyn.

"The Temple of the Dragon was a small shrine on the grounds of the ancient Temple of Paladine in the Old Temple District," explained Tarrok.

"Was?" said Adyn. "What happened to it?"

"There was a tremendous earthquake about fifty years ago," Trysdan said. "It opened a fissure underneath parts of the Old Temple District. People at the time said that it was a sign that the gods were never coming back."

"Many temples and churches were destroyed," Tarrok said, "but others fell whole into the crevasse. You can see the Temple of the Dragon's steeple rising from the fissure."

Cat found it easy to forget that because of the length of a dwarf's life, although Tarrok looked about the same age she was, he really had been living since her grandfather's time. He had firsthand experience of things that seemed like ancient history to her.

"If this medallion is so powerful," said Adyn, "then why hasn't anyone else gone in after it?"

For a few moments Cat could hear the others murmuring among themselves. It seemed to her that they were deciding which one got to deliver the bad news.

"The Temple of the Dragon is haunted," said Marta.

There were some people who thought hauntings were just superstitious claptrap, but you would never find a cleric who said such things. They knew that a person's spirit lingered after death until the gods ushered it into the Gray. But there were some spirits that were unwelcome even in the land of the dead, and those remained in the mortal world to plague the living.

"How haunted is it?" asked Adyn.

"Haunted enough," said Fallstorm.

"Then how are we going to get it?" asked Adyn.

"We thought," said Tarrok, "that since you were the one responsible for putting us in this situation—"

"I will go," Cat cried out from her cot, interrupting the dwarf in mid-sentence. "I will go first thing tomorrow morning."

"This is none of your concern, warrior," said Fallstorm. "Sometimes Paladine puts these obstacles in our paths to test us. We will never learn the lessons he intends for us to if we allow others to face them."

"I am as responsible for the current situation as Adyn is," answered Cat. "Perhaps *more* since I am Sindri's friend. Besides, it will be worth every moment of danger if only you will stop talking about it and let me get some rest."

The acolytes muttered among themselves and eventually Tarrok said, "Very well. You will go. May Paladine guide you."

Cat grunted noncommittally as the group left as noisily as they'd arrived.

The next morning, while most acolytes were still performing their ablutions, Cat and Adyn stood staring at the spire of the Temple of the Dragon that did indeed rise from a crack in the ground. However, topped as it was by a weather vane in the shape of a platinum dragon, it would have been easy to mistake it as an obelisk or some other memorial or marker. When they got close enough to see the fissure, though, they could clearly see that the structure continued deep into the ground—deeper than either Cat or Adyn could see. Marta and Tarrok had neglected to mention that the building was so tall and the cavern so dark.

Otherwise, the fissure was just as Tarrok had described it—a sudden and very unexpected gouge through the Old Temple District. It did not cross any of the main roads, but rather cut through several connected church and temple grounds.

STAN BROWN

Climbing down was not especially difficult, at least not for Cat who was used to such activities. A path spiraled around the fissure's lip leading deeper and deeper into the crevasse. The slope was not especially steep, and the path itself was so regular and even that Cat suspected some intelligent hand in its creation. The thing that slowed her progress the most was waiting for Adyn to amble over rocks and step timidly around mounds of crumbled earth that occasionally blocked the way down.

"Are you sure you don't want to just wait here?" she asked as he slowly and gingerly stretched his leg across a gap in the path. It was only a couple of feet across, but below it the fissure dropped away so deeply that neither one of them could see where it ended. Despite the fact that Cat had already traversed the gap safely, Adyn was not taking any chances that might cause him to fall into a potentially bottomless chasm. "The temple entrance is just up ahead. I could run in, get the relic, and—"

"No," he snapped. To his credit, there was more confidence and conviction in his voice than in his step. "We started this mission as a team, and that's how we're going to finish it."

"Well, if one half of this team doesn't start moving a little faster," she teased, "we may not get the medallion back in time for the Dragon Day celebrations."

"You know, constantly jabbering at me will not get me across this rift any faster."

"It's hardly a rift," said Cat. "It's barely a crevice."

"What does it matter to you?" he asked. "You don't even care."

"About Dragon Day? You're right," she said. "But I do care that you do not break your neck on this fool's errand after you begged me to protect you all the way to Palanthas."

Adyn finally planted his left foot firmly on the far side of the crack and shifted his weight there. With one final, excruciatingly slow movement, he pivoted on his toes and swung his right foot over to join the rest of his body. Cat provided a brief, sarcastic applause for the less-than-acrobatic maneuver.

"What is so foolish about this plan?" Adyn demanded. "Of all the possible responses I could imagine the others taking, at least this one is purely defensive in nature."

"Yes," Cat agreed. "But there are times when taking a guarded posture merely serves to encourage an opponent to test the sturdiness of your defenses."

"Careful there," said Adyn. "You're starting to talk like a warrior again."

Cat cast him a warning look. She might have agreed to take him to Palanthas, and she might have been willing to defend Sindri from a mob, but she was definitely giving up her warrior ways.

"Are you saying that you think that having this holy relic will provoke an attack from the apprentices?" Adyn asked in an effort to change the subject.

She thought for a moment.

"No," Cat said. "They did not appear to need any provocation to do something dangerously stupid. They seemed quite capable of whipping themselves into a frenzy based solely on their own wild suppositions."

"So where is the harm in getting a holy relic to protect ourselves?" asked Adyn.

"The harm," said Cat, "is in all the things you acolytes will *not* do if you feel safely protected by an amulet."

This deep in the fissure, intermittent dim shafts of sunlight dappled the ledge. The pair could see only twenty or thirty feet ahead, and even then they could not make out any details, just vague shapes. The Temple of the Dragon was in front of them, but other than that they could tell nothing.

Cat, having some experience with trips into ancient buried

chambers, had brought her knapsack filled with all the usual traveling gear despite the fact that they were still less than two miles from the new Temple of Paladine. And although Fallstorm and Trysdan had mocked them as they left, Adyn was glad for her dogged preparedness when she reached into the pack and pulled out a torch, steel, and flint.

"What do you mean?" asked Adyn.

"I mean," said Cat, "that once we get the Medallion of Sanctuary, the acolytes will consider the matter dealt with. You will not press on to try other avenues to bring closure to this incident."

"Like what?" he demanded. "What avenues could we try?"

Cat pursed her lips and nodded her head back and forth, making a show of pondering the question.

"Oh, nothing terribly obvious," she said, her voice dripping with sarcasm. "But you might want to try something unorthodox such as talking to the apprentices directly and seeing if you can't come to some sort of accord."

Adyn made a rough sound at the back of his throat. "They seem to have no interest in talking!" he said.

"Of course not," she replied. "The acolytes have given them no reason to suspect you are interested in listening."

The torch flared to life and filled the fissure with soft orange light and flickering shadows. The space they were in looked like a large cave except that in the center of the floor was a yawning chasm.

The temple sat at an odd angle, the left side raised five feet higher than the right, but otherwise it was whole—ramshackle and decrepit with age, but whole. It was built in a style that had been popular about five centuries ago and constructed entirely of wood, something rare in Palanthas during any age. There were no windows visible, and the only entrance was a set of double doors in the center of the structure. One of the doors had fallen off but the other hung at an odd angle, attached by a single completely rusted hinge.

"Well," said Adyn," it's too late to turn back now."

Cat gave a single chuckle that might actually have been a grunt. "While that is not actually true," she said. "I agree that it would be a waste of effort for us to turn back now after having come so far."

The temple steps creaked loudly as they ascended, the sound echoing for a long time in the dark depths of the fissure. Stepping into the chapel felt like stepping into a cave or, worse, the den of an animal you hoped was either absent or slumbering deeply. The darkness was deeper here—thicker. The light of the torch barely seemed to penetrate it.

The Temple of the Dragon was indeed quite cave-like. It was a single room with neither windows nor seats, and the floor was covered with dirt, small rocks, and the dust of decades. There was also a musky smell to the place as though it had been home to various subterranean creatures over the years.

"S-so, you do this sort of thing all the time?" Adyn said more loudly than he'd planned.

Cat chuckled. She didn't blame him for his anxiety. In fact, she had entered into situations like this with alarming regularity since the day she met Nearra, Davyn, and the others. Even so, she still found this nerve wracking.

"Don't worry," she told him in a carefully modulated whisper. "You're doing fine. Just remember to breathe."

At the back of the temple a broad table was built into the wall. A collection of small items (perhaps more rocks) sat on the table.

"That must be the altar," said Adyn.

Cat shushed him as they moved slowly and carefully across the room, a process made more difficult because the whole temple was on a twenty-degree slant to the right. It was a house of worship, so there probably weren't any traps built into the floor, but the wood was ancient and had already been subjected to a violent earthquake and plunged several hundred feet below the surface. In other words, there was no reason to think that all the floorboards were safe to cross.

Every step brought a strange new series of groans, creaks, and pops from the floor, each echoing within the closed space. As a result, the room was soon filled with a horrific combination of noises that sounded unnervingly like living creatures crying out in torment.

Once they reached altar and stopped moving, the noise quickly faded away, but not completely. Just when silence seemed about to reign, an echo would return from the depths of the fissure.

Cat scanned the altar. It was not nearly as solid as it looked from a distance. Unlike the building, the altar was constructed of stone, and it had not weathered the fall or the years nearly as well. Its surface was covered with spider-web cracks and entire sections had crumbled away revealing that the structure was, in fact, hollow. What remained of the altar was covered with a combination of small items—figurines, coin purses, ceramic bowls, ornamental daggers, and the like. It was also covered with fist-sized rocks and a gritty layer of dirt.

"What does the medallion look like?" asked Cat.

"Marta said that it was a disk about this big," Adyn said holding his hands up with his fingers measuring a rough circle. "It's inscribed with the image of Paladine's draconic form—"

"And the field shows the stars that make up Paladine's constellation," Cat finished the description.

"You found it?"

"I found it!" she confirmed, but her voice said that the problem was not yet solved.

"What's wrong?" asked Adyn.

"Look," said Cat. Half of the medallion was clearly visible—a five-inch diameter disk with exactly the design they had just described. However, it was wedged in the middle of a pile of rocks. Normally that would not be a problem, but the medallion seemed to be made of a thin, brittle rock—slate or flint or a similarly fragile element. Cat was not sure how to remove the rocks while not breaking the relic.

"How will you get it out?" asked Adyn.

"This is a puzzle, to be certain," answered Cat. "But it is one that we will solve easily enough. Things could be much worse."

"How?" Adyn said looking at the conglomeration of stones pressing against the medallion from different angles. The real worry was that in loosening this pile, a greater instability in the altar itself might reveal itself. If the section supporting the Medallion of Sanctuary collapsed before they freed the disk from the surrounding rocks it would surely shatter before their eyes.

"The rumors about this place being haunted could have turned out to be true," said Cat.

"You think they were just local superstitions?"

"Yes, the kind you tell children so they won't play around a dangerous hole in the ground," said Cat. "Perhaps there were haunts here once. But even malevolent spirits eventually heed the call of the Gray."

"No, I do not believe we have anything to fear here," said Cat. Then cocking her head sideways and peering at the medallion from a new angle she added, "There! That's the rock. Move that one and we have it!"

Adyn began to reach for the rock, but Cat reached out and grabbed his wrist.

"Wait," she said.

If you asked her what made her do this, she would not have

been able to give you an answer. There were many subtle clues, but she was not consciously aware of any of them. The skin on the back of her neck had prickled, the temperature in the room dropped enough so that her and Adyn's breath came out in faint plumes of steam, a faint wind moved through the fissure where none should have been. Cat had instinctively sensed all of these things, but she did not actually think about them.

What she did think about was her absolute certainty that in the chapel behind her a small band of ghostly figures floated inches above the grimy floor and that, with a singularity of purpose, the specters were raising their claw-like hands and preparing to rip her and Adyn's flesh from their bones.

# CHAPTER

# 18    The Cave of Abomination

N ow the acolytes have brought in a mercenary," Modaar said the minute Sindri and
his troupe got back to their dormitory room. "They're certainly
going to send her to ruin our Dragon Day displays."

"Cat isn't a mercenary," Sindri said, but no one seemed to be
listening.

"We can handle their thug," Grigg said. "But we still need a
way to show the crowd that the return of the gods does not make
the priests better than us wizards."

"B-but how?" asked Bolli.

Grigg simply smiled and said, "The Cave of Abomination."

"What's that?" Sindri asked. It sounded awful, but also really
interesting. "What sort of abominations?"

"The cave is as unholy a place as you'll find in Ansalon. I hear
that ogres used to take captive humans and elves there and torture them for fun, trying to cause them as much pain as possible
before they died. The cave is an abomination in the sight of the
gods," said Grigg.

"What's in it?" Sindri asked, even more fascinated than
before.

"No one knows," said Modaar. "They say that a demon from the pits of the Abyss guards the cave and that everything inside it is cursed."

"And you," Grigg said to Sindri, "get to be the first person to go in there in hundreds of years!"

"Why would a demon stay in a cave outside Palanthas?" asked Sindri. As fascinating as the idea was, something about it seemed unlikely.

"There probably isn't really a demon there," said Grigg. "Maybe someone summoned one once, but it surely isn't lurking around anymore. You've started studying how summoning spells work. Even if someone did bring a demon into the cave, it would stay only as long as it needed to. Then it would return to the Abyss."

"So you think people just made up all those stories about the cave?" Sindri had asked.

"Not all of them," Grigg answered. "If I didn't think that the stories of torture were real, why would I send you out there looking for an unholy item?"

Sindri couldn't come up with a good answer, so he decided he would go to the Cave of Abomination. It was a rare opportunity that he couldn't pass up.

But the next day, hiking by himself along a rocky ridge searching for a hidden cave mouth—which supposedly looked like a giant mouth filled with rows of razor-sharp fangs—Sindri felt a little less enthusiastic. But only a little. Mostly he wished he had someone else to share the adventure with.

His troupe-mates were good friends—well, most of them were. And they were just as interested in magic and spellcasting as Sindri was. But beyond that he found them sort of dull. They never wanted to go off on adventures after class. The only thing they wanted to do was study. Sindri knew that studying was the only way he would ever become a full-fledged wizard, but did it have to be his whole life? Couldn't he fit other interesting activities into his life as well?

The answer, for today at least, was yes.

Sindri closed his eyes, listened to the sound of the waves crashing against rocks, and breathed in a deep, bracing lungful of salty air. There was nothing quite as relaxing as sitting by the seaside. The kender opened his eyes and saw choppy waves the color of midnight, topped with little caps of gray foam. The Bay of Branchala rarely got calmer than this. In the distance he saw a towering cliff rise above the water. To the south it dropped gradually in height until it simply merged into Palanthas' Old Temple District. To the north the cliff continued as far as Sindri could see, though he knew that after many miles the land simply ended where the bay fed into the Turbidus Ocean.

He'd been walking practically all morning, and his feet were sore. The rocky, uneven path he walked on was all that remained of a paved road that ran along the length of Palanthas Harbor. As he walked farther from the city, the path had grown rougher, until now he was climbing over rocks to continue following its course. Still, this was exactly what Grigg had told him to expect, so the kender was sure he was still on the right track.

"When the path turns up the cliff," Grigg told Sindri, "you're almost there. Climb until you see a large rock shaped like a fist, then go off the right side of the path. That's where you'll find the cave entrance."

As Sindri rose from his brief rest he wondered whether or not he would be able to recognize a rock that looked like a fist. He'd seen a lot of rocks during the last few hours, and quite frankly most of them just looked like rocks. There had been one that looked remarkably like his Great Aunt Weedplucker, but the family had always said she had a face like granite.

Following the path uphill, Sindri began calling out the shapes of the large rocks he passed. "Rock . . . rock . . . rock . . . potato . . . rock . . . tooth . . . rock . . . rock . . . oh my . . . fist!"

Indeed, he was staring at a rock that looked exactly as if some great elemental creature had stuck its hand up through the ground and curled it into a fist. It didn't have the smoothness or precision of a sculpture, so Sindri figured it must be natural, but what an unusual shape. He decided that he would pay more attention to the rocks he passed on his journeys from that point forward. Perhaps he could even get Cat to keep her eyes peeled for interesting rocks—she was always scouting the surrounding terrain, why not use all that attention for something fun?

Of course, it didn't seem likely that he would be traveling with Cat anymore. Things really got out of hand last night. Although she had seemed happy to see him at first, Cat had quickly made it clear that she did not actually value his companionship that much—in fact, she seemed to enjoy her new acolyte friends much more. And wasn't that why Sindri was out on this rocky path?

He wandered through the rocky scrub brush beside the path and, much to his own surprise, soon was standing at the mouth of the Cave of Abomination, which did indeed look like a demonic mouth. Rather than plunging right in, though, Sindri paused. He wondered whether bringing an unholy item to the Dragon Day ceremony was the right thing to do. It seemed dishonorable.

Just using that word—dishonorable—reminded Sindri of Cat, and that made him a little angry. What did he care whether or not Cat would approve of this course of action? Hasia and Bolli had agreed (with no pressure from Modaar) that Grigg's plan was a good way to defend the honor of wizards everywhere without having to actually start a feud with the clerics and acolytes. At the very least, it would do no real harm to anyone.

Taking a deep breath and pulling his shoulders back so that he stood as straight and tall as a kender could, Sindri marched between the fang-like rocks and into the cave.

He soon let his shoulders slump back to their normal position and stopped marching. The floor of the cave dropped away steeply making it difficult to march—he was better off moving quietly from rock to rock the way he usually did.

Before long he was actually climbing rather than walking. He could hear the sound of sloshinig water getting louder and he realized that this must also be a sea cave with an entrance was below the surface of the bay. The air was humid and thick, smelling sharply of salt and seaweed.

Although it was dark, Sindri could see clearly enough. Some light filtered down from the cave entrance and the kender had very sharp eyesight—too sharp, most people said. But there was another source of illumination. A strange, greenish light played over the walls of the cave below him. It wasn't steady, like the light from a lantern, it bobbed up and down the way sunlight did when it reflected off water.

Reaching the bottom of the cave, Sindri discovered why the light was so strange. Rather than coming from the sun or a flame, the light came from fungus growing and glowing along the cave wall. The pale green light reflected off the surface of a natural pool that filled the center of the cave.

Something about the scene sent a shiver down Sindri's spine.

He looked around. As Grigg had predicted, no demon seemed to be here.

The luminous fungus provided only a dim light making it difficult to see anything in detail. A thin layer of slime covered just about every surface in the cave, making all the surfaces glisten and difficult to tell their exact shapes. Sindri saw what he believed were the remnants of four different campfires, a pile of rubble stacked with such care that it must have been placed that way purposely, and a heap of something that could have been clothing or refuse in the far corner.

"Phoo!" said Sindri. His voice echoed in the small space, each time sounding deeper and more unnatural. Maybe he could find something that would be impressive in a slimy, disgusting way. Or one of the campfires might have some scorched bones from whatever was cooked in them. Sindri hoped they weren't human or, worse, kender bones. Or, since the rocks in this part of the world seemed to be more interesting than anywhere else he'd ever been, perhaps he could find one that looked vaguely like a demon's face.

Then Sindri remembered the very first lesson the instructors had taught him at the academy—how to see the aura generated by a magical item or spell. He closed his eyes, cleared his mind, and said a short series of arcane words. When he opened his eyes again the scene looked slightly different. Green glows pulsed at several places around the cave. There were faint, dull glows in one of the campfire pits and the refuse pile, but something buried within the pile of rubble shone with a strong, bright glow. Whatever was under there was enchanted with powerful magic.

Carefully, Sindri began to take measured steps across the slime-covered floor. He kept his fingers crossed that whatever was in the rubble was strange and eerie looking—if it was just a ring or a necklace, no one would believe that it was a cursed item from the Cave of Abomination.

Sindri's hopes for something horrific were answered, but not the way he anticipated. As he took his fourth step on the cave floor, the surface of the black pool exploded, spraying everything in the cave with a layer brackish water. A tremendous, purple tentacle burst from the water and swung itself in the kender's direction.

Sindri tried to jump out of the way, but the water in his eyes and the slime on the rocks conspired against him. Instead of launching himself in the opposite direction, he slipped and fell right into the tentacle, which closed around him with a vicious grip.

The very next instant, Sindri found himself hanging upside down in the tentacle's grasp looking straight down at the black waters.

He had just enough time to say, "Hey, an octopus!" before the tentacle retreated below the water carrying Sindri with it and leaving the Cave of Abomination glistening, wet, and silent once more.

# 19    Strength in Numbers

"Duck!" Cat shouted as she pulled the Medallion of Sanctuary free from its stony prison.

She pushed Adyn to the side, and then threw her body in the opposite direction.

The acolyte, taken completely unaware, fell to the ground and quickly rolled all the way to the far wall on the tipped floor.

Having dived uphill on the slanted floor, Cat did not get very far. Once she landed, the prodigious amount of dust on the floor caused her to slide back more or less to where she started.

Cat's sixth sense proved amazingly accurate. Eight specters surged forward with fangs and claws bared. In life they may have been humans or elves, but now their faces were twisted into hideous masks that belied any connection between them and their mortal heritage. All that was left to these creatures was hatred for the living, and right now they focused that rage on Cat.

She howled with icy pain as three sets of incorporeal claws passed through her chest and shoulders each seeming to carry with them a small piece of her life force.

Adyn sat dazed, moving slowly but with no sense of purpose. 177

"Move!" yelled Cat. She scrambled across the floor to his side. "We have to get going, Adyn. We have to get going now!"

"The medallion," he said groggily.

Cat shoved the disk into his hands.

"Here," she said drawing her sword. "You keep the medallion safe. I'll try to do the same for us."

She drew her sword and swung it in big swooping arcs. Against living foes, this maneuver would have bought them at least a few moments to assess the situation. However, the ghosts had no fear of the blade and continued moving exactly as they had before. Fortunately for Cat, some of them were still clawing at the spot where she had been moments before and the others, while unfazed by her weapon, appeared to be distracted or confused by it—rather than striking at her body again, they swung their claws at the steel of her blade.

"One, two . . . I count eight of them," she said to Adyn. "How about you?"

"What?" he answered, still disoriented. "Eight? Yes, I see eight of them. Give me a minute to get my—"

"We don't have a minute," she snapped. Alone she might have been able to fend off, or at least avoid, these spirits indefinitely. They did not seem especially bright. However, protecting Adyn was another matter. He was useless in a fight, and he seemed too dazed to defend himself. If he stayed in the temple, he would die, it was that simple.

"Get ready to run," she said. "When I give the signal, get out the door as quickly as you can and fly up the pathway like all the demons in the Abyss were at your heels."

"No," said Adyn. "Let me just—"

But Cat was not listening. All eight ghosts had finally realized where their opponents had gone. They also seemed to have realized that it was pointless for them to try to strike her sword—there was no life force there for them to drain.

Another spectral hand passed through Cat's chest, and three others missed by bare inches. Next to her, a pair of the ghosts were preparing to strike Adyn who, rather than paying attention to the fight, seemed to be fiddling with the collar of his robes. Cat was not about to allow another ally to die while she stood by unable to do anything about it.

"I said, we have no time," Cat yelled. "Now stop trying to look the part of a priest and run. Run!" As she shouted the last part, Cat grabbed the scruff of Adyn's collar and took five quick steps toward the temple door.

The spirits were not so easily fooled this time. Their hollow, empty eyes followed her step by step and they seemed poised to strike at any second. There was no way Cat was going to get both her and Adyn out the door before they did, so with the last of her strength she lifted Adyn's feet off the ground and literally threw him out the door.

"Run!" she called. "I'll hold them off for as long as I can. You make sure the Medallion of Sanctuary gets to the Temple of Paladine."

"No!" he shouted. "I can—" but that was all Cat could hear. Her blood was racing with the excitement of battle, and in her effort to ensure that he got away safely she'd thrown him a bit harder and farther than she'd intended. Still, at least now he was out of danger.

Cat turned to fight the ghosts, but she was too slow. They were already upon her and four of them plunged their hands through her body. This time she did not make a sound—not a howl or a cry or a whimper. The pain was so intense that she was unable to make even the slightest gurgle. Frozen to the depths of her soul, Catriona fought to keep hold of her consciousness and her sword. If she lost either, she was dead.

"No!" Adyn shouted as Catriona lifted him clear off his feet. He'd finally been able to calm his nerves enough to find the pendant that hung around his neck and pull it free from the folds of his robe. Now the tide of battle would turn. Now the ghosts or spirits or whatever they were would know the power of Paladine, first among the gods. "I can—"

Now Cat heaved him back and with a mighty effort flung Adyn through the air and out the door.

"— destroy them now that I've found my holy symbol," Adyn finished, even though he was certain that Cat could no longer hear him.

Catriona had the torch with her inside the Temple of the Dragon, and the cavern outside was lit only by dim shafts of light. The ground rushed at Adyn out of nowhere. The back of his skull and left shoulder felt as though some unseen assailant had struck him with an ax handle.

But Catriona's toss had been so strong that Adyn was still was tumbling. With a sinking feeling he realized he was rolling toward the pit at the heart of the fissure.

Adyn clawed the ground with his fingers. He moved his feet and legs as quickly as he could in a running motion. And most of all, he prayed.

"Paladine, protect your servant," he mumbled. "Protect me from the wild over reactions of your other servant!"

As much as he appreciated Cat's concern, Adyn was frustrated that she never even considered that he might actually be helpful in the fight. She never thought about the fact that the divine power that allowed clerics to cast magic spells also gave them the ability to overpower and even destroy undead creatures.

If she'd allowed Adyn to present his holy symbol, he would

have been able to force the ghosts to turn away. Instead she took all the responsibility on her own shoulders. And, as strong as she was, this task was more than she could handle.

For now all Adyn could do was roll helplessly across the cavern floor, watching as the yawning pit in the earth grew closer. His fingernails made a terrible scraping sound as he clawed against the stone floor. His feet kicked up dust and his ribs thumped across rocks strewn in his path. Somehow Adyn managed to stop his tumbling progress mere inches from the lip of the fissure.

"Paladine be praised!" he said. "Now to get back in there and—"

With a crack like the sound of lighting splitting a two-hundred-year-old oak in two, the ledge on which Adyn rested gave way. He was suddenly falling again.

Cat was so cold that her entire body was covered with goose-bumps. She'd lost count of how many times spectral hands had passed through her flesh. Nothing she tried affected the ghosts. She even considered sheathing her sword and rushing straight through them. But she knew that purposely touching the creatures would be just as painful as being attacked by them.

It was not the sharpness of the ghosts' claws that caused the pain and numbing cold, it was the very nature of their bodies. Ghosts were made of negative energy—the very opposite of life.

Six of the ghosts floated between Cat and the door, another was circling around to her right, and the final creature had disappeared below the temple's floor—not exactly what she would call an ideal arrangement. Still, there was room for hope. She was thankful that the spirits for the most part seemed to be completely unfamiliar with battlefield tactics. Judging by their spectral clothing, most of them were either priests or merchants in life, they had no reason to have ever learned such things.

The two exceptions were a spirit wearing what seemed to be ancient knightly armor, who was moving up on her flank, and another who wore beggar's rags but carried a curved dagger in its belt and had disappeared into the ground below. Their tactics were clear. These two wanted to arrange things so that Cat had to choose between focusing on the larger collection of ghosts or paying close attention to their particular activities. Either way she would leave herself open to some sort of devastating attack.

"If I allow them to set the rules of engagement," Cat said to herself, "then my hopes are as insubstantial as their bodies. There must be some advantage to having weight and form."

A slight smile formed on her face.

Instead of rushing for the door or turning to face the flanking ghost, Cat did something totally unexpected. Using her sword as a lever, she pole-vaulted over the spectral knight. It flew straight up trying to rake her with its claws, but she passed just beyond its reach and landed on the far side of the chapel—the place where the building was tilted highest.

The six clustered ghosts moved toward her, moving away from the door to attack en masse.

Cat waited two heartbeats, and then curled her body into a ball and dropped to the floor. Gravity and the slant of the floor sent her tumbling away from the group of ghosts, under the floating spectral knight, and right back to the spot she had just vacated only traveling at a much faster speed than before. She grabbed her sword as she passed it, landed with her feet flat against the wall of the structure, and was one muscle twitch away from using her momentum to springboard through the air and out the door.

Unfortunately for Cat, that was the moment that the remaining ghost, the one that had disappeared below the temple, chose to return. As she squatted, muscles tense, an incorporeal hand rose up through the floorboard and sunk its ghostly talons deep into her chest.

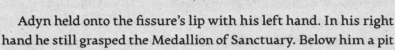

Adyn held onto the fissure's lip with his left hand. In his right hand he still grasped the Medallion of Sanctuary. Below him a pit as deep and dark as the Abyss waited hungrily. Above he could hear Catriona's tormented cries growing weaker and weaker.

Teamwork might have been the answer a few minutes earlier, but right now both their lives depended on him, only him. Somewhere deep within himself, Adyn Thinreed, farmer's son, wanderer, seeker after truth, and acolyte of Paladine had to find the physical strength to literally pull himself out of this predicament.

He could feel his toes brushing against the fissure's wall, so he knew he wouldn't have to perform this task through upper body strength alone, thank Paladine. He was no weakling—growing up on a farm had certainly forced him to develop physical strength along with his spiritual fortitude—but there was a difference between being fit and being capable of doing one-handed pull-ups with his off hand.

Adyn took a deep breath, said a silent prayer, and began scrambling up the precipice.

"Get up," Cat said to herself. "Get up. Move." But no matter how many times she repeated it, her legs did not seem to get the message. She remained in the same crouched posture, seemingly ready to escape if only she could summon the will to force her body into motion.

Thankfully, rather than attack again, the spectral hand had disappeared back below the floor. Apparently it did not recognize how serious a blow it had struck, so the ghostly rogue had opted to go back into hiding, the better to strike another blow when its victim least expected it. The fact that Cat could not actually do the creature any harm did not seem to affect its tactics. Or perhaps the ghost simply had no ability to deviate from the habits it had practiced during its life.

Cat could not spare the time or focus to wonder about such things. The most immediate threat might be gone, but seven more were already preparing to strike, and still her body would not respond.

"I guess this proves that I really am unworthy," she thought. "No true warrior would allow herself to die this way—frozen and unable to defend herself."

Her limbs remained completely uncooperative. She could neither bend her arm in defense nor stretch her leg in hope of escape. And although she already felt chilled through to the bone, Cat could feel the temperature drop even more as the ghosts approached.

Then despite the pain wracking her body, despite the desperation of her situation, despite the fact that she had failed at every other thing that was important in her life, Cat did a miraculous thing—she tried. She tried to fight for her life.

"Paladine, please," she whispered. "If it is time for me to leave this life at least let me go swinging my blade."

This, she knew, was the moment of truth. She summoned every ounce of will and cleared her mind of everything except the absolute and total belief that she could make herself move—and she did.

With a resounding "thunk" Catriona fell onto her side.

It wasn't much, but it was enough. Seven pairs of spectral claws slashed through the air where her heart had just been. But there was no time to celebrate the victory, for the ghosts now floated lazily in the air immediately above Cat's head, and she knew that she could not repeat her feat of determination.

"I only pray that Adyn made it safely out," she said. "Look after him, Paladine. Watch over Adyn and Sindri and all of the people I've let down in this life."

"The only person you've ever failed is yourself," said a voice from the doorway. "But that may be the greatest sin of all."

Adyn stood tall and proud at the temple entrance, His face was smudged with dirt as were his torn and frayed robes, but he seemed to shine with an inner light. In his hand he held a pendant carved in the image of a platinum dragon. He was wielding it like a deadly weapon.

"Creatures of darkness," he said, his voice deeper and stronger than usual. "Too long have you tarried in the mortal world. Now, by the power of Paladine, I release you!"

Adyn's pendant suddenly glowed with a light as bright as the sun. But rather than pass through the ghosts the way everything else had, the light struck them like a strong gust of wind. The ratty cloth of their ghostly clothing flapped, and their matted hair danced around their faces. They raised their clawed hands to block the light, but it did no good.

The pendant began to glow even brighter. Soon the ghosts were nothing but silhouettes frozen in the light the way Cat had been frozen by their claws. And as the light continued to increase, the silhouettes got thinner and thinner until they couldn't be seen at all.

Seven unholy screams filled the air, and Cat could hear an eighth coming through the cavern floor below the temple. The sound echoed in the chapel until it was impossible to tell the scream from the reverberation, and then they faded into silence. At the same time, the light from Adyn's pendant dimmed until he and Cat were once again alone in an ancient, decrepit, all-but-forgotten room.

"I didn't know you could do that," Cat said.

"People can surprise you, Cat," Adyn told her, still brandishing his holy symbol. "And they're generally more capable than you think, especially when there are lives on the line. I'm sure you consider that whenever you're facing an enemy. You should remember that it's true of your friends, too."

She thought of all the times she had ignored suggestions from Nearra, sneered at Davyn's ability to deal with a difficult problem, and insisted that there was no way in creation that Sindri would ever become a real wizard. She remembered every time she had insisted on supervising or performing a particular task because she did not trust that her friends would do it well enough.

In the cold dark of the Temple of the Dragon, Catriona's heart was filled with understanding that although her friends had suffered the brunt of her ego, the person she was failing in every single instance was herself. She failed to live up to her own principles, and she failed to put the needs of others before her own, and she constantly failed to treat others the way she would want to be treated.

"Paladine forgive me," she said.

"He already has," Adyn told her. "Now all you have to do is forgive yourself."

Cat smiled weakly. "And keep from making the same mistakes all over again in the future," she said.

Adyn laughed. "Don't worry," he told her. "You've got plenty of new mistakes ahead of you."

He extended his hand, offering to help her get up. And she accepted, even though the strength had returned to her limbs.

# 20  WET AGAIN

Sindri's life might have been passing before his eyes, he really wasn't sure. He was too busy trying not to get squished by the tentacle. He didn't have time to think about anything other than plans for escape.

A giant octopus, he thought, lives underwater. It probably hates heat and flame, so some sort of fire spell would probably be good. But since we're already underwater, I don't think that would work.

The tentacle thrashed back and forth trying to shake the life out of its prey before eating it. The water was too black and the luminous fungus in the cave was too weak for Sindri to be certain, but he thought he was still pretty close to the pool's surface.

Sindri belched out a mouthful of air. The tentacle was squeezing hard enough that he could feel his ribs bend under the pressure.

Electric spells are too dangerous, he reasoned frantically. Acid won't work because the water will dilute it. Cold might work, but freezing the octopus (or whatever it is) won't do any good if I freeze myself, too.

The tentacle squeezed again.

This time Sindri let out a scream along with the bubbles. When the pain from his ribs ceased being the only thing he could think about, the kender realized that his lungs were now burning for air. He had to do something, and he had to do it quickly.

I have to make it want to let go of me, just for a moment, he thought. I could tell it that I had a nasty rash, or that I don't taste very good. Well, I could do those things if I could speak while being held underwater and crushed. Now I know why Cat gets upset when I tell her all the things I can't do—

Wait a minute, Sindri thought. Cat! The dagger!

He moved his hand under the rubbery skin of the tentacle. The octopus (or whatever it was) must have thought that tickled because the tentacle loosened its grip for just a second. It was enough time for Sindri to find the dagger tucked in his belt and pull it free.

With a short punching motion, Sindri stabbed the iron dagger into the tentacle's rubbery flesh. Then he did it again and again.

The black, murky water of the pool filled with a horrible sound. It was something like a scream, but it was also very much like the sound lute strings make when they are tightened too far and almost snap.

The tentacle threw Sindri away. He broke the surface of the water and flew fifteen feet into the air.

That worked pretty well, he thought. He would have said it out loud but he was too busy filling his lungs with deep, gasping breaths. Sindri also realized that he was not out of danger yet. Even though the tentacle had let him go, gravity was bringing him right back to the pool. And he knew the tentacle would grab him again—only tighter this time.

Sindri could only just get his bearings thanks to the light from the fungus and the blackness of the pool. He was fairly close to the lip of the rock ledge, but not close enough to reach it with his fingers.

He stretched his right arm toward the ledge anyway, wiggling his fingers as if he was grabbing for it. In fact, he was using the ring on his middle finger—the ring that could magically push or pull a nearby object.

"I hope this works," he said to himself.

The magic of the ring focused on exactly the rock that Sindri had intended and pulled at it as strongly as the spell allowed but, the rock was simply too big, and it would not budge. Instead, Sindri felt himself being pulled through the air toward the rock.

With a loud cry of "Oof!" the air that Sindri had just sucked into his lungs came rushing out again as the kender landed stomach first across the rock ledge.

"Well," Sindri said hoarsely. "At least now I'm safe."

As he said the words, though, the tentacle, or another one that looked just like it, came out of the water. It waved about wildly in exactly the same way that some humans—and elves, and dwarves, and especially minotaurs—had shaken their fists at Sindri at one time or another. Then it grabbed for his legs.

This time Sindri knew it was coming. He might not have been the most agile and slippery kender in all of Ansalon, but he was more than able to avoid a giant tentacle that he knew was coming after him. He rolled onto the ledge and got as far away from the pool as he could.

Sindri rolled directly behind what earlier he thought was just a pile of rubble. Now that he was nose-to-rock with it, he could see it was a carefully made cairn. And based on the magical aura Sindri had seen earlier, some sort of enchanted item was buried inside the cairn.

The tentacle reached farther out of the pool, scraping along the cave floor searching for its lost prey. It felt around near where Sindri had landed and roughly along the path that he had tumbled, but then it seemed to become confused. Obviously, the kender realized, it cannot actually see into the cave. It must somehow be able to feel vibrations through the rocks.

"That's how it knew where to find me the first time," he thought.

Very quietly and carefully, Sindri took a rock from the top of the cairn and threw it into the far corner of the cave. The tentacle lashed out in that direction, but soon realized that there was nothing there. Sindri lifted another rock from the cairn and threw it in the opposite corner. Again the tentacle snapped to search that area but quickly gave up. One by one Sindri tossed the rocks into different parts of the cave. Before long, though, the creature realized that it was being tricked. The tentacle sank back over the ledge and into the pool.

Eventually Sindri removed enough of the cairn to uncover a small, black idol crafted roughly in the shape of a person with both arms raised. The top of the idol's head was flat, and its round body was covered with writing of a kind that Sindri had never seen. It looked vile and accursed—exactly what he was looking for.

"This may be creepy enough to scare the smug smile off Grigg's face," Sindri said.

Immediately the tentacle reappeared and curved in his direction. Obviously it could sense sound as well.

Sindri carefully picked up one last piece of the cairn. With a quick flick of his wrist he tossed the rock so that it skipped across the floor, bouncing six or seven times as it crossed the cave, like a pair of feet running over the floor. The stone landed with a sickly splat in the pile of refuse that seemed to be made of some horrible, squishy green material that Sindri was glad he couldn't identify.

The tentacle reacted immediately. It stretched all the way into the corner, quickly snatched up the filth, and pulled it below the black surface of the pool.

Sindri stood and, as softly and silently as he could, began making his escape. He had only taken a few steps before the slimy goop came flying out of water, very much the way Sindri had after stabbing the octopus (or whatever it was). The tentacle followed after it, returning to the far corner to search for its missing prey.

With a deep-but-quiet sigh of relief, Sindri returned to making his stealthy exit.

# 21    Dragon Day

"Are my robes on straight?" Adyn said for the eighth time since breakfast. He was beside himself with worry—were his robes clean, was his hair neat and combed, did he have any porridge smeared on his cheek, had the sun come out yet, did boots look more dignified than sandals. Fortunately for Adyn, all the acolytes were in exactly the same state, so he did not stand out.

As fortunate as the situation was for Adyn, it was just that unfortunate for Catriona. As the only person who was not fretting over looking appropriately clerical, remembering all the words to the oath of ordination, impressing relatives and friends in the crowd, or just being an effective representative for Paladine and his church, Cat was the one that each and every one of the acolytes came to with every little problem (real or imagined) that cropped up. On her best of days, Cat was not especially patient about nonsense worries and matters of pure vanity. This was not turning out to be one of her best days.

"As straight as they were when you asked me ten minutes ago," Cat said without actually raising her head.

"You didn't even look!" said Adyn. "What are you doing, anyway?"

"After traveling together for as long as we did," Cat said, a teasing edge in her voice, "I would think that you might recognize the sight of me packing my gear. Or are such worldly activities now beyond you?"

"What I meant was why are you packing?"

Cat kept her back to the acolyte so that he would not see the playful grin on her face.

"Well then, you should have said so," she said. "A cleric should be very careful with his words. Say what you mean and mean what you say. Remember, you are the Platinum Lord's representative on Krynn. Your ignorance and imprecision reflect badly on your superior."

"Catriona," he said with mock solemnity. "I think you may have found a new calling. You should set aside your sword and take up a musical instrument—the world is in dire need of entertainers with such rare wit."

Just then Trysdan stepped into the doorway, his face contorted by sheer panic. "Are my robes on straight?" he demanded.

"Yes," Cat answered. "However, you have them on inside out."

"What? I do not!" Trysdan said, but he looked down and patted the cloth just for added confirmation. When Adyn and Cat burst into laughter he let out a breath with a huff. "I don't see what's so funny about that. I just want to look my best for the occasion."

"What am I supposed to do?" asked Sindri for the tenth time in the past two minutes. Still Grigg seemed disinclined to answer him.

"Bolli, remember that you're responsible for the lightning not only during the night of the Great Storm but also when Huma's knights battle the wing of blue dragons." Grigg, as the most senior member of the troupe was in charge of their participation in the Dragon Day Pageant of History. Everyone seemed to know what he or she was supposed to do, everyone except Sindri, but Grigg appeared to enjoy ordering them about anyway. "And for Nuitari's sake, be sure you don't let your spells hit any of the spectators.

Bolli nodded his head vigorously.

"What am I supposed to do?" Sindri asked again.

"Hasia, you—"

"I know what to do," the elf said. "I do just what I've done each of the last three years—the sound of thunder and dragons roaring."

Grigg shot her a withering glare. "Yes," he said. "But don't forget that this year you *also* have to do the Great Earthquake."

Hasia nodded. For some reason she seemed a little more self-conscious all of a sudden.

"What am I supposed to do?" begged Sindri.

Finally Grigg turned to Sindri. "You have the most important job of all," he told the kender.

"I do?" Sindri said. He knew that Grigg could not be serious, but in his heart he hoped that his job was at least better than fetching water or cleaning up after the pageant was done.

"Yes," said Grigg. "Where is that grotesque little idol you brought back from the Cave of Abomination?"

Sindri fumbled through his pockets and then pulled out the item in question.

"Good," said Grigg. "Now keep it on your body at all times and be ready to do exactly what I tell you to."

Sindri frowned at him. "What are you going to tell me to do?" he asked. "I'm not throwing it at anyone."

Grigg laughed. "Why would I want you to do that? Then they'd just be able to get rid of it. In fact, put it back in your pocket. I don't want anyone to be able to see it at all."

"Wait a minute," said Sindri. "If you don't want anyone to see it, what good does it do?"

"It's cursed, you fool!" Grigg snapped. "It's an abomination before the sight of the gods."

"Yes," Sindri said. "I remember you saying that yesterday."

"Generally, the gods tend to withhold their blessings when they are offended," Grigg explained, waving his hand as if that one sentence clearly explained six other mysteries.

"So?"

Grigg shrieked with frustration.

"So," Hasia said calmly, "Grigg thinks that the acolytes will not actually be ordained unless Paladine grants them his blessing."

Sindri puffed out his chest. "That's terrible."

"Yes," said Hasia. "Accursed items can be pretty powerful deterrents for divine magic. While it's around I doubt that the acolytes or clerics will be able to heal a blister, let alone grant any major blessings or purifications. But as usual Grigg completely misunderstands the way things work. The ordination ceremony is completely non-magical. The acolytes already *have* Paladine's implicit blessing or they wouldn't be able to cast spells."

"So why are we bothering to bring the idol at all?" asked Sindri.

"Well, the acolytes are pretty haughty about their divinity," said Hasia. "And they do take the whole 'unholy idol' thing very seriously. So if they get too insulting to us, or if they refuse to let us start the Pageant of History, we can probably chase them away just by sticking it in their faces. They won't want to 'soil' themselves by being around such a horrible item."

"Oh," Sindri said. "I guess that's all right."

"Just wait," said Grigg. "You'll see."

"You're leaving?" Adyn's voice went up a notch. "Now?"

"Not right this minute," Cat said. She was still bent over her pack making sure that she had all her gear properly stowed. The backpack was fuller than it was when she arrived. Cat had taken advantage of the mercantile opportunities that Palanthas offered, replacing items and replenishing her basic supplies. She even bought a few small items that caught her fancy.

She stood and hoisted the pack onto her shoulders, testing to make sure she'd balanced the weight evenly.

"I swore to see you ordained," she said, "and I do not break promises lightly. After I have the honor of toasting you as Father Adyn, though, I will be on my way."

A shadow of indecision crossed Adyn's face. He seemed to be weighing whether or not to say something. Eventually he said, "Do you really have to go so quickly?"

"Yes," Cat answered. She knew how difficult goodbyes could be. "As entertaining and enlightening as spending time here at the temple has been, the clerical life is not for me."

Ansalon looked big on a map, but it was a surprisingly small place, especially for those who lived wandering lifestyles, and the gods had a way of making sure that good friends managed to cross paths every now and then. Catriona had the distinct feeling that Adyn had, in a relatively short period of time, become one of those people in her life.

"But what if another opportunity arose?" Adyn asked, still struggling with what to say. For a moment, Cat was worried that he might be preparing to propose marriage—there was no admonition against it among Paladinian priests.

"What sort of opportunity?" she asked cautiously.

Again Adyn hesitated, looking at the ceiling and moving his mouth without actually saying anything. "Oh, you know," he said. "An adventure or a quest or something heroic. You seem to be interested in such things again."

Cat breathed a silent sigh of relief. "I am always willing to bend my path to assist in a worthy cause," she said. "But with the Solamnic Order being so well represented in Palanthas, it is safe to say that the city will not suffer for my departure."

He smiled. "But you're open to possibilities," said Adyn.

"What do you have on your mind?" Cat asked. "What are you talking about?"

"Nothing," Adyn said quickly. "Nothing. Just making small talk. I am quite nervous about the ceremony."

Cat chuckled. "That is abundantly clear," she said. "But you will not have to worry much longer. In fact, I think it is about time to go to the Central Plaza."

Just then Tarrok and Fallstorm both tried to enter the room at the same instant. Predictably, they wedged themselves into the doorway so tightly that for a moment neither one could move. They exchanged glares, backed up, and each one made a sweeping gesture with his arm to motion the other through the door. Again they both began to step through at the same time. They likewise stopped, started, and stopped again with absolutely the same timing.

"It's time to go," they both said with the same breath.

Cat and Adyn burst into laughter.

"Yes," said Cat. "By all means, let us go before you two begin reciting all the Emperors of Ergoth in unison."

"Where is the medallion?" Tarrok asked.

Cat reached under her tunic and pulled the stone disk out. She wore it around her neck on a leather thong.

"I don't see why I have to wear it," she said. "You are the ones who are worried about the wizard apprentices causing trouble."

"Yes," said Tarrok. "But they're most likely to attack the ceremony itself. And each of us has various tasks and responsibilities that will take us away from the group during the ceremony."

"We'd like you to stand near at the front of the crowd," said Fallstorm. "That way the most number of participants will be protected."

"And Revered Son Elistan will not be able to blame any of you for going to such ridiculous lengths," Cat said with a wry tone.

The acolytes blushed but did not deny the charge.

Cat looked at them the way a parent looks at a child who has been seen reaching toward the cookie jar, but not caught reaching in yet.

"Very well," said Cat. Against my better judgment, and as an ordination present for you all, I will wear the medallion."

## 22    CHAOS ON CENTER STAGE

The great brick Central Plaza in Palanthas sat directly between the Lord's Palace and the Palanthas City Jail, and is bordered on one end by the Courthouse and on the other by the barracks for the City Guard.

On most days the plaza was a bustling place. It was the hub of the city's wheel-like map, so all the streets that served as major spokes began at Central Plaza. On Dragon Day, however, the crowd was so thick that it was virtually impossible to cross the plaza. People from all over the city as well as sailors from every ship in the harbor were gathered around the edges of the square talking with their neighbors, eating treats bought from the vendors whose carts lined the surrounding streets, and enjoying the glorious sunshine that Paladine had granted them for this celebration. The very center of the plaza stood empty except for a small stage where the ceremony would take place.

The apprentices from the Greeves Academy had to elbow their way through the crowd to get to the stage. Sindri simply stayed half a step behind Grigg and followed smoothly in the larger student's wake, accidentally stepping on his heels about once every twenty paces.

**199**

Finally Grigg stopped and Sindri walked full-speed into the back of his legs nearly knocking Grigg over.

"Sorry," the kender said.

Grigg muttered under his breath and then said through gritted teeth, "Just stay here and be sure nothing happens to that idol. I've got to go back and get some more incense to burn during the finale."

Sindri nodded his head vigorously, but he was already distracted by all the sights—the people, the towers of the Lord's Palace, but most of all the stage. It was a hastily built with support structures and extra lumber still visible underneath, but it was impressive if only because of the tremendous audience it would attract.

The kender imagined looking out from the stage and seeing a nearly endless sea of faces stretching away in every direction. He dearly wished that he had a more important part in the Pageant of History so that he could get to center stage, but only the instructors and most advanced apprentices got to do that. The rest of them would stand on the wings or stairs of the stage.

"I think the west side of the stage will be better," Sindri said.

"What?" said Hasia. She seemed distracted by the sheer volume of people filling the square.

"The west side," Sindri said again. "We're on the east side and that's okay for now. But by the time the day's done we'll want to be on the west side so that we can still see the stage and the crowd without having to stare into the setting sun."

"You want to see the crowd?" Hasia said incredulously.

"Oh sure," said Sindri. "There must be two thousand people out there already, and nothing has even happened yet. I bet there's twice that many by the time the Pageant begins!"

Hasia swallowed loudly enough that Sindri could hear it even over the crowd.

"You're doing the Great Earthquake, right?" he asked.

She nodded.

"That means you get to go to center stage, right?"

She swallowed again. "Get to?" Hasia said. "*Have* to is more like it."

"Oh, you'll do fine," Sindri assured her. "C'mon, I'll show you." He started to lead her up the stairs.

"What? Where are we going?"

"To center stage, of course," he said. "I want to see what it's like. Besides, it's the fastest way to get to the other side."

Hasia dug in her heels and tried to get her hand out from Sindri's grasp.

"We could go under the stage," she said. "That would be just as quick."

Sindri looked at her as though she had just told him she was really a minotaur.

"Where's the fun in that?" he asked. He let go of her hand and ran to the center of the stage.

Although she could not figure out exactly why, the crowd made Cat very nervous. There were plenty of possible explanations—the crowd was a good place for an ambush, the anxiety of the acolytes had finally rubbed off on her, there was a decent chance that she might run into someone she knew from her time as a squire, and, of course, the apprentices were around somewhere and, if the acolytes were correct, they would be looking for trouble.

Cat trusted the feeling more than the reason. Something bad was going to happen—soon.

"Isn't it exciting?" Adyn said. "Look at all the people."

"I hear this is twice as many people as usually come out for Dragon Day," said Tarrok. "I wonder what that says, eh?"

"Perhaps it says that people are in the mood to celebrate now that war is not raging across the continent," said Cat. She knew the acolytes wanted to believe that the large crowd was the result of people filled with love for the gods, but in her experience praise and worship were two things most folk preferred to do in the privacy of their homes. The crowd probably would be happy to share this important moment with the students from the new Temple of Paladine, but certainly they were here to enjoy the rewards of a world that was no longer at war.

Tarrok grumbled.

Then, just as the first of the acolytes neared the stage at the center of the plaza, a mighty cheer went up from the crowd.

"Aha!" said Tarrok. "You see? You see how they're cheering? Who do you think they're cheering for?"

Cat kept her face completely neutral. "Not for you," she said flatly.

"Can't you admit when you're wrong?" said Tarrok. "Can't you see that they're overjoyed that the namesake of their city has returned? Can't you see their love for Paladine? Can't you hear them cheering for—"

"The kender!" cried a young boy sitting on his father's shoulders. "Look at the kender!"

Tarrok's look of smug self-satisfaction dropped into one of shock and disbelief. He turned from Cat and looked up at that stage. There, jumping up and down on center stage, waving to the crowd and reveling in their adulation was not only *a* kender, but *the* kender—the very same one that been caught holding the stolen Crown of Paladine.

"The kender!" growled Tarrok. And before Cat could appeal to his better nature or attempt to physically restrain him, the dwarf began barreling through the crowd toward the stage.

"I can see the Tower of High Sorcery from here!" cried Sindri.

"You can see the Tower from anywhere in Palanthas," said Hasia as she tugged on the kender's arm trying to get him to move offstage.

"But it looks so much better from here," he said. "I wonder if it's the plaza, the stage, or the crowd."

"Can we talk about this somewhere else?" begged Hasia.

"Oh, certainly," Sindri said.

He was allowing his friend lead him off stage when a voice in the crowd shouted, "Look, a kender!"

"Where?" cried Sindri as he ran back to cente stage. He jumped straight in the air and shaded his eyes with his hands in order to get a better look. "Where?"

The people near the stage laughed.

It took three more jumps and three more corresponding laughs for Sindri to realize that he was the kender they were shouting about.

"Do a trick!" another voice from the crowd shouted.

"A trick?" said Sindri. "What sort of trick?" He fumbled at his belt for spell components.

"Make yourself disappear," shouted another voice. The crowd laughed approvingly.

"I haven't learned that spell yet," said Sindri. "But I can turn your hair green, and I can turn it back again. I finally learned that one."

The crowd laughed again.

"How about yellow," cried another voice. "Turn his hair yellow instead."

"Yellow it is!" Sindri said happily.

The crowd cheered mightily.

He'd already reached into his pouch and started to intone an arcane phrase when a hand grabbed him by the shoulder and spun him around. Instead of pulling out the proper powders, Sindri's hand emerged holding the cursed idol.

"Hey!" he cried, "You ruined my trick."

He looked up and noticed that it wasn't Hasia or even Grigg who had grabbed him. Instead it was a black-bearded dwarf wearing acolyte's robes.

"Sweet Paladine's grace!" Tarrok said, "What is that thing?"

"Oh, uh, nothing," said Sindri. He tried desperately to slip free from the dwarf's grip.

"What were you going to do with that?" demanded Tarrok. "Throw it at us during our ceremony?"

"No!" Sindri answered. "I'd never do that."

"Yes, just like you'd never steal our crown."

"I didn't!"

"Drop the idol, kender," Tarrok growled, "Drop it or as Paladine is my witness I'll give you a case of dragon-hide-rash where you can't possibly scratch."

"No, you let go," said Hasia, who had come back from where she'd been hiding in the wings. "You let go of my friend's arm right now or I'll make you the first victim of the Great Earthquake."

"Don't worry, Hasia," said Sindri. "He can't do anything to me because of the you-know-what." As he said those words, the kender's eyes went wide and he focused meaningfully on the idol.

Tarrok laughed long and hard.

"Do you really think your horrendous little idol can thwart the might of Paladine?" he asked, although he clearly did not want to hear Sindri's opinion because he continued talking without even taking a breath. "We'll just see about that. We'll see how you and your grotesquerie enjoy being caught in Paladine's righteous sight."

Tarrok raised his left hand to the sky and called out so that the crowd could hear. "Lord Paladine, in your name I call down the blessed light so that these defilers will feel the heat of their sins burning away at their very spirits!" He formed his hand into a fist and swung it back to his side as if calling all the light from heaven down at his command.

Nothing happened.

"What did you do?" demanded Tarrok. "Why didn't my spell go off?"

Sindri's mouth hung wide open and he stared blankly at the idol in his hand. "It actually worked," he said.

Tarrok grabbed the kender's arm. "Give me that thing!"

"I told you to leave Sindri alone," Hasia said as she in turn grabbed Tarrok's arm.

The three of them stood there, their arms entwined so that no one could do much of anything. The crowd thought it was hilarious and continued to egg them on with hoots and hollers.

It suddenly struck them exactly how ridiculous this looked and what a poor idea it was to have this argument on stage in front of thousands of onlookers. They loosened their grips on one another.

Hasia looked like she might be sick to her stomach now that she realized how many people were actually looking at her.

Tarrok folded his hands under his priestly robes and stood still.

Sindri turned to face the crowd, sank to one knee, threw his arms wide, the left one still holding the cursed idol, and sang out, "Ta-dah!"

When the people near the stage began to laugh and clap, Sindri stood up and said, "Now let's get out of here!"

Before they could take a step, though, twenty apprentices led by Grigg came storming onstage. "No one hits our kender but me!" he shouted. They all looked upset and several of them held staves or sticks of some sort, and some were shouting and pointing at Tarrok.

"It's all right," said Sindri. The kender held his hands up to show that Tarrok was no longer grasping him and that no harm was done.

"Cleric!" called out Grigg. "Is this the sort of behavior your god condones? Assaulting a simple kender who is entertaining the crowd? Do you really crave people's attention that badly?"

"Lying wizard!" Tarrok retorted. "You're behind this, I know it. You sent your kender out here with this abomination to sully our sacred rite!"

"I just wanted to see what it feels like to be on center stage," said Sindri. "Really, I'm ready to leave now. It isn't as nice as I'd hoped."

"Self-righteous theocrat!" Grigg yelled.

"Devious manipulator!" Tarrok shouted back.

"I'm leaving now," said Sindri, holding the idol over his head. "And I'm taking my grotesque thingy with me."

"Stop!" cried a voice from the far end of the stage.

Sindri did just that and turned to see Cat rushing toward them holding a stone medallion in her hand. As she got closer the kender noticed that the medallion began to glow—just slightly at first, but with each step that Cat took the glow got brighter and brighter. He also noticed that the idol began to grow warm in his grasp. And this feeling, too, got stronger as Cat approached.

"That's strange," Sindri said, but he never got the chance to tell anyone else about his discoveries.

Later on in the day Sindri would ask people from the crowd what happened at that exact moment, but every one told a different story. Some claimed that there was an earthquake, others said it was a sudden gust of wind, while others blamed the acolytes, the apprentices, or even the gods themselves. Whatever the cause, all the attendees agreed that some force or event suddenly and unexpectedly knocked every one of them off their feet. And when they managed to get back up there was a strange new figure standing on the stage.

The newcomer was nearly ten feet tall with skin as red as the setting sun, black horns on its head, and a thick tail growing from the base of its spine. Its mouth was filled with rows of short, yellow teeth, and its voice echoed like distant thunder.

"Now we're going to have some fun!" it said, then threw its head back and bellowed a raucous, bloodcurdling laugh.

# CHAPTER

## 23   WHEN THINGS FALL APART

W hile the Central Plaza rang with demonic laughter, the bowels of the Tower of High Sorcery echoed with cursing more vile and colorful than any you might hear from an Ergothian sailor.

Maddoc was in the same small room he'd been in for nearly a fortnight. He sat on a bench with the Aegis laid out on the table before him. Smoke rose from the silver sword, acrid black smoke that smelled of brimstone and decay. With only these clues, one might guess that the Aegis had somehow caught fire and the old man barely managed to save it from destruction. However, a closer inspection would reveal that in spite of the smoke and the smell not a single scorch or scratch marred the blade or any of the gems decorating it. It remained in pristine condition. Still, Maddoc sat there with his head buried in his hands, inventing new invectives with every breath.

"That should have worked," he grumbled. "There was no reason for it not to work."

"Mending a rupture is rarely as simple as putting all the pieces back in the right order," said a voice from the shadows.

"Don't you think I know that?" sniped Maddoc. He instantly 208 regretted his outburst.

Silence filled the room except for a faint crackle—the sound, the old man imagined, of small arcs of electricity leaping angrily between two golden, hourglass-shaped eyes.

"My apologies, Master," Maddoc said, his voice tinged with fear. "This problem vexes me. I've performed all the rites, gathered all the necessary materials, and crafted the spells with the utmost care, and still I cannot fully restore the Aegis."

The Master of the Tower stepped into the room, though from where exactly Maddoc could not say. As always, his comings and goings were as inexplicable as his words.

"It is notoriously difficult to restore a shattered item to its original state," said Raistlin. "It has no will to be whole again."

Maddoc looked at him incredulously. What did will have to do with it? They were talking about a thing, an inanimate object. It had no will.

"Unlike people, some things are perfect at the moment of their creation," said Raistlin. "The rest of their so-called lives are journeys to obsolescence. A chip here, a crack there, a scuff or a gouge—they spend their whole existences breaking little by little until they are done. Sometimes it is best to let them rest in pieces."

"But I can do it," Maddoc insisted. "I can fix the Aegis!"

"Yes," agreed Raistlin, his face entirely hidden within the shadows of his black robe. "Yes, you can. You can also crush a rock by smashing it against your skull if you keep at it for a sufficient period of time. That does not mean that doing so is a good idea."

Maddoc sneered. "Are you saying that having eliminated my only real opposition, I should abandon my efforts to salvage a plan that was years in the making?" he asked.

Raistlin sighed. "I am saying, that there is a balance to the world. And there are very often direct relationships between objects and events that, to the unlearned eye, seem completely disparate."

Maddoc sighed, obviously mimicking Raistlin. "I may not be Master of the Palanthas Tower," he said. "But I have been practicing sorcery since before you first gazed up at the moons. There is no need to speak to me as if I was an apprentice still wet behind the ears."

Raistlin pulled the hood of his robes off and fixed Maddoc with his hourglass eyes. "Apparently there is," he said. "Because you are either too senile or too incompetent to see the ripples caused by your own actions."

"Speak plainly, Master," Maddoc said with mock sincerity. "Your god-touched eyes see more than do these aged orbs and I would learn from your wisdom. What is it that I do not see?"

Raistlin did not answer. Instead he picked up the Aegis and examined it. "For every force in the world, there is a balancing factor."

"Yes, Master," Maddoc said, not bothering to hide his impatience.

"This Aegis was a mighty instrument," Raistlin continued.

"And if you will help me to finish my work, it will be again."

"Oh, you will succeed."

"I will?"

"Yes," said Raistin. "In fact, you already have, at least in part." He held the Aegis up and allowed lantern light to play along its edges. "What do you suppose was the balancing factor for such a marvelous item? In the great scheme of things, what was the force that countered this Aegis?"

Maddoc thought about it. "I'm sure I don't know," the old man said.

"No, you wouldn't," said Raistlin. "Well then, what do you suppose happened to the balancing factor when your Aegis was destroyed?"

"I would guess that it, too, was shattered," said Maddoc.

"A good guess," said Raistlin. "And now that you are repairing the trinket, what do you think will become of its opposing force?"

Again Maddoc thought before answering. "Logic suggests that it, too, would be repaired," he said. "But you have just finished telling me that broken items have no wish to be whole. If no one knows that I am reforging the Aegis, why would anyone go through the trouble to repair its counterpart?"

Raistlin pulled the hood of his cloak up again, hiding his face once more in shadow. "Not every set of balances come in matched pairs," said Raistlin. "A powerful item may be pitted against a heroic person or group. And while broken items do not repair themselves, sometimes broken people do."

Maddoc's eyes narrowed. "Are you saying that the reason the Aegis broke is because my idiotic son and his friends had a falling out?" the old man shouted.

Raistlin shrugged. "Or perhaps they parted ways because you allowed the Aegis to be broken. It is difficult to assess absolute cause and effect in these cases."

Maddoc laughed. It was a cold, mocking sound. "So then, by repairing the Aegis I am also bringing that company of fools back together?"

No," said Raistlin. "Because you are meddling with forces beyond your understanding, the very powers of nature are meddling with you and your plans."

"Are you talking about the gods?"

Now it was Raistlin's turn to laugh. "No," he said. "Nature, if nothing else, has a sense of humor. Your meddling and machinations will be set to balance through discord."

Maddoc narrowed his eyes and set his jaw at an angle. "You speak in riddles," he said.

"Sometimes, when it amuses me," said Raistlin. "But right now I speak plainly. At this very moment Iffrontic, a demon of discord, is loose on the Central Plaza creating pain and suffering, and sowing seeds that will correct the imbalance you have created."

Maddoc looked around as if suddenly, after two weeks of being featureless, the walls might suddenly grow windows so that he could see the events that Raistlin described. Of course, there were none. However, a door had appeared in the wall opposite Maddoc. It opened onto a stairwell lit by natural sunlight.

Maddoc stood and moved toward the door.

"Do not leave anything behind," Raistlin said, holding the Aegis and Maddoc's packed travel bag. "I do not think you will be returning. Indeed, I forbid it. Arcane might and reckless negligence are too dangerous a combination to be suffered in my tower. I would sooner trust a kender than a fool."

Raistlin stood silently as Maddoc retrieved his gear and mumbled insincere words of thanks for the use of the laboratory. Maddoc went through the door and up the stairs. And when the old man was gone, Raistin smiled for just a moment.

"A kender," he said, shaking his head ruefully. Then he stepped back into the shadows and left the room the same way he had entered.

# CHAPTER

# 24   THE SEEDS OF DISCORD

"Oh, wait!" said Sindri. "I've seen one of those before. It was in one of the textbooks."

The kender tried to get a better look at the creature, but he was too busy ducking a vicious punch thrown by Marta. Her face was contorted into a mask of hatred. She swung again, missing even more wildly. When Sindri tumbled more than a few steps away, she immediately turned her attention to the next closest person in wizard robes.

"It's a demon of some sort," Sindri said. He was now trying to avoid being crushed beneath the hooves of a centaur. Staying literally one step ahead of his opponent, he realized, was a very smart thing. Wherever the half-man/half-horse's hooves struck, they punched through the hastily erected stage.

"Stupid wizard!" the centaur shouted. Normal robes wouldn't fit over his body, so the centaur wore only the priestly shawl and cloak. "You're ruining our day!"

"I'm not the one stomping holes in the stage," cried Sindri, but the centaur was not listening. None of the acolytes were listening—they were too busy doing their level best to kill every apprentice they could get their hands on.

Of course, to be fair, the apprentices were trying to do the same thing to the acolytes in return. Everyone on the stage was gripped with a violent fury over which they seemed to have no control. Everyone, that is, except the ten-foot-tall demon standing in the middle of the chaos and laughing himself silly.

"A discord demon!" Sindri called out as he dodged between pairs and groups of acolytes and apprentices rolling around on the stage hitting one another with fists, sticks, and anything else they could get their hands on. "It's a discord demon!"

He skipped over a wild kick aimed at his knees. "Or maybe it was a 'dancing demon,'" said Sindri. Then, after looking around at the violence on the stage, he decided, "No, that's not right. It must be a discord demon."

Bolli seemed to be getting the better of his opponent, so Sindri moved to stand near his friend's ear.

"I saw it in one of your texts, Bolli," he said, staring straight down into the apprentice's angry face. "Some kind of 'planar bestiary' or something, but we haven't even started to study that sort of thing."

"C-can't you see I'm a l-little b-busy here?" Bolli grunted.

"But this is important," said Sindri. "Who would be able to tell me more about a discord demon?"

Bolli grunted as he tried to keep Trysdan from moving. "I d-don't know," Bolli said. "Ask Grigg."

Sindri looked around. "I would," he said. "But a dwarf and a barbarian are throttling him right now. Can you tell me anything?"

"W-well," Bolli said as he rolled on top of Trysdan, pinning the acolyte's arms. "They're d-demons. You s-summon them and t-try to convince them to do your b-bidding."

"But what if you didn't summon one?" asked Sindri. "What if it just showed up all on its own?"

STAN BROWN

"Then it c-could p-pretty well do what it w-wanted," Bolli answered. While his attention was turned, Trysdan managed to wriggle halfway free and now the apprentice was trying to reestablish his dominance. "Unl-less you kn-know its n-name. It can't d-do anything to you if you kn-know it's real n-name. Now d-do you mind g-giving me a few m-minutes? I really n-need to c-concentrate on th-this."

Sindri nodded. "Sure thing," he said. "Thanks for the help."

Common sense seemed to have fled the stage entirely. On both sides people were forgetting their own best interests and attacking anyone who wore the opposite type of robes.

Sindri realized that he might actually be safer if he took off his apprentice's robes, so he quickly pulled his robes up over his head.

"Real name," he said to himself. "How am I supposed to figure out this thing's real name?"

His head swaddled in cloth, Sindri's eyes were greeted by a soft, cool white light radiating from the stone idol he still held in his left hand.

"That's odd," he said. Then, in a fit of inspiration he added, "I wonder if the idol has anything to do with what's happening."

Throwing off the robes to reveal his traveling clothes underneath, Sindri held the idol aloft. In the daylight it was harder to tell, but it definitely was still glowing. He considered the blocky stone figure—triangular head, unnatural features, broad-shouldered body—it certainly could be a representation of the demon standing in the middle of the stage. The gouges in the head could be horns and fangs. The arms could be tapered to indicate long claws. Of course, the fact that it was such a primitive carving made it difficult to be certain.

"It would be different if it were painted red," Sindri said. Then he considered the writing etched into the idol's body. "If it is related, then these words must be important. But where can I find someone who can read this language?"

"Am I the only sane person left on this stage?" Cat asked as she defended herself from three skinny young men dressed in brown apprentice's robes.

The only answers they gave were more hopelessly inefficient strikes. One was trying to punch her, another was trying to grapple her, and a third was attempting to hit her with what looked like a broom handle. They hit one another more often, and more effectively, than they did Cat, but there was always the chance that one of them would land a lucky blow, so she took their threat seriously.

Cat presented her sword but left it in its scabbard. She didn't want to hurt the apprentices any more than was necessary, and there was absolutely no reason to draw blood. Thanks to the Medallion of Sanctuary, the apprentices couldn't use their magic, and that was just about the only way they could be truly threatening in a fight.

She spared a moment to glance down at the medallion, which still hung around her neck. It continued to glow steadily, as it had since . . . since . . . Cat tried hard to remember. In truth, her head had been a little fuzzy since she'd picked herself off the stage floor.

How had she come to be lying there?

She remembered climbing the stairs seeing the acolytes and apprentices squaring off against one another with Sindri stuck in the middle.

"Sindri!" Cat said to herself. While she did, she struck back at the apprentices around her, swinging her sword with abandon "That fool of a kender! I would be surprised to hear that he was not the cause of all this. I wish he were here right now so I could wring his scrawny little neck!"

Cat stopped. The three apprentices that had been menacing her, along with four others, lay on the ground either unconscious or holding bruises from where she had struck. The more she'd thought about Sindri, the harder she'd swung. But where had those violent thoughts come from? Certainly there were some unresolved issues between her and her kender friend, but nothing all that serious. And for all she knew, she was the one responsible for this mess. After all, it began right after the medallion began to glow.

And then she remembered.

She remembered how the Medallion of Sanctuary had started to glow when she approached the apprentices. That was not terribly surprising since its function was to counteract and negate arcane magic. And since the glow had brightened as she got closer, she guessed that the light was somehow related to how much magic the medallion was blocking. But what made it flash so brightly that it knocked her off her feet—not just her, but everyone on the stage.

Or was it just the medallion? Cat dimly recalled a second flash from among the apprentices near where Sindri had been standing.

"It must be his fault!" she growled.

This time she had to close her eyes and vigorously shake her head to clear away the anger. Something strange was going on here, something much worse than rivalry between wizards and clerics. But what?

"Can you help me with something?" an all too familiar voice said from directly behind her.

"Sindri!"

In a single, fluid motion Catriona unsheathed her blade, spun, and struck a killing blow at the spot the voice came from.

Sindri stepped forward so he was practically standing on his friend's feet.

Cat's sword passed harmlessly over his head.

"No, really," Sindri said, "I need help. Can you read this?" He thrust the idol up into Cat's face so she could get a better look.

She threw herself backwards as though he had waved a handful of stinkweed under her nose.

"Hey! Your medallion is glowing just like my idol!" he said.

"Are you crazy?" she said.

Sindri looked at her as though she had asked him if he were the Emperor of Ergoth. "No," he said. Then he paused and seemed to consider the question more carefully. "I mean, I don't think I'm crazy. But then how could I tell? I guess even if I was crazy, wouldn't I think I wasn't?"

"Sindri, how could I possibly read that . . . that . . . *thing*?"

He looked at his hand, studying the idol carefully. Sure it was ugly, but it wasn't *that* bad, and the letters were pretty clear—they just didn't make any sense.

"Well, the writing is strange. But tell me," he said shoving the thing in her direction again. "Do you think it's supposed to look like that demon over there?"

Cat started to answer, then shut her mouth and cocked her head.

"Demon?" she asked. "What demon?"

Sindri pointed toward the very center of the stage. "How many demons are there?" he said. "That one!"

Cat looked where he pointed, but rather than alarmed she only seemed confused. "Sindri, I don't see any demon."

Sindri blinked twice. "You don't?"

"No," she told him.

The demon laughed again and gave Sindri a vicious smile and terrible wink.

"You don't hear that horrible laughter?"

"No," Cat said.

"You don't see a red demon with black horns and sharp teeth standing in the middle of the stage?"

"Sindri," she said. "The only place I see anything even close to that description is that repulsive fetish you're holding. What is that thing made of, rotten meat?"

Sindri looked at the idol in his hand—it was clearly made of stone. What was Cat talking about? And how could she not see the demon towering over the chaos on the stage? What was wrong with her?

Or maybe, he realized, maybe he was the only one who could see the demon. That, at least, would explain why acolytes and apprentices were chasing one another around its spiky legs as though it was just a stage prop. And if he was the only one who could see the demon, perhaps he was also the only one who could see the idol for what it truly was. If that was the case, then he was the only one who could see the words carved on the idol—except he had no idea how to read them.

As these thoughts occurred to Sindri, the demon's laughter ceased. It's eyes narrowed and it growled at the kender. Then it focused its eyes on Cat.

"For Paladine's sake, Sindri, throw that disgusting thing away," she said. But rather than seeming frightened or distressed, Cat seemed angered. Her feet moved into a threatening position.

"No!" he cried. "The secret to solving this mess lies in the idol. Why can't you see that?"

The demon began to smile again. Its lips moved as though it was whispering an offensive joke.

"You stupid kender," shouted Cat. "You aren't a wizard and you aren't a scholar. Stop pretending you are. Hasn't there been enough heartache caused by your foolish games?"

The demon switched his gaze to Sindri.

Suddenly Sindri's shoulders tensed and his voice grew as dark and menacing as a kender's could.

"No, I don't think so," he said. "In fact, I think I've got quite a way to go before I've cause half as much heartache as you have, Catriona."

"Dozens of students at each other's throats, the Dragon Day celebrations ruined, two organizations that have been pillars of the Palanthan community for hundreds of years trying to tear each other apart," she yelled. "I don't see that there's even a comparison."

"Well, at least no one has died!" he shouted back.

The demon's grin fairly split its leering skull. It raised its blood-red hand and extended a single clawed finger, bouncing it up and down as if keeping tempo with an orchestra playing a jaunty tune.

Reaching into his belt, Sindri pulled out the dagger that he had been given by Cat. A snarl curled his upper lip and he growled like a wild animal.

She returned his call with a cry of her own and positioned her sword for a charge.

They stood there, each brandishing a weapon and measuring the other for weakness or hesitation, but finding none.

The demon's finger bounced again, and again, and again—and then it stopped.

With matching howls of pure, unfettered hate, the two friends leaped at one another swinging their blades with all their might.

# CHAPTER

# 25     Shackles and Bonds

T he sound of steel against stone rang out twice.

Cat's sword connected solidly with the idol in Sindri's left hand but Sindri seemed not to care. The length of Cat's blade let her strike while he was still three strides away, but he kept on coming, dagger cocked behind his ear ready to skewer his target. His iron blade chipped a corner off the medallion and severed the leather thong holding it around Cat's neck.

The two landed a few feet apart with their backs to one another.

Sindri slammed the Medallion of Sanctuary on the stage with all the strength in his body. The thin stone disk cracked but remained whole and continued to glow. The kender raised his dagger again and viciously slammed the blade through the medallion to the stage below.

He released the handle, shook his hand to ease the stinging, and surveyed his handiwork. Tiny fragments of stone were scattered in a roughly circular pattern around what seemed to be an iron rose growing out of the rough-cut planks of the stage.

When Cat looked at the piece of rotting flesh Sindri had been **221** holding, it had transformed into a simple stone idol with runes carved into its chest. They were similar enough to runes the Solamnic Order used that Cat could decipher their meaning.

"Iffrontic," she read aloud, "Fountain of Conflict and Dissonance."

A pained howl filled the air, and Cat looked up to see a demon standing in the middle of the stage. She could only presume that it had been there the whole time, but that seemed ridiculous. How could that massive creature remain unnoticed? And yet, the acolytes and apprentices continued to battle one another around and even underneath the giant, so that seemed to have been the case.

"Is that what it says?" asked Sindri, who now stood at Cat's side.

"Yes," she answered. "It appears our tormentor is named Iffrontic."

Again the demon howled. But it also reached out toward Sindri and Cat with its razor-sharp black claws.

"Iffrontic," Cat said one more time, and as the demon's name left her lips for the third time, the red giant became as insubstantial as smoke and faded into nothingness.

All across the stage and through the crowd, men and women shook their heads as though they were awakening from troubled sleep. They stopped hitting, kicking, grappling, and otherwise abusing one another and gazed around with confused expressions on their faces.

"Is that it?" asked Sindri.

"Not quite," said Cat.

She pointed down at the idol. It retained its stony shape, but the features carved into it seemed to writhe with unnatural life. It was now clear that this was an image of the red demon, its mouth and horns easier to identify now that they were moving across the face of the stone idol.

"Somehow, that is even more disturbing than when it looked like it was made of rancid meat," Cat said.

"Why would anyone make an idol from rancid meat?" asked Sindri.

"You don't want to know."

"Okay," he said. "So what's next?"

Cat lifted her sword in the air and stabbed it straight down at the idol. Rather than deflecting off the stone with a resounding clang, the blade slipped neatly through is as if it was made of butter.

The face on the idol mouthed a silent scream, and the arms seemed to wave about in small circles. Where the blade impaled the stone, black blood seeped from the wound and stained the stage below. Then the idol shivered and collapsed into a pile of gray ash.

"That is it," said Cat.

A circle of onlookers stood around Cat and Sindri at the center of the stage. Now that the spell had been broken, they all wanted to look at their tormentor. Only a few of them were able to see the destruction of Iftronic, but word of what had happened spread through the crowd quickly. They looked around the stage, broken, marred, and stained with sweat and blood from their conflicts, and hung their heads in shame.

"W-what do we do n-now?" asked Bolli.

"We'll have to cancel the ceremonies," said Marta.

"How will we explain this to our masters?" wondered Hasia.

"How will we explain it to the people?" said Tarrok who dropped his voice so no one in the crowd could hear.

"I don't know about the rest of you," said Modaar, "but I plan to blame the kender."

Hasia smacked him in the back of the head.

"That's it?" Sindri demanded. "That's the best solution you can come up with? Blame the kender?"

"It would seem that in spite of all that has happened here today, you haven't learned anything," said Cat.

"Well what would you have us take from this momentous occasion?" asked Tarrok. "A stirring faith in the fact that our forces are evenly matched when it comes to wrestling skills?"

"Or that without our spells we are ineffective?" said Grigg. "We already know that. It won't change anything. We know that we aren't great warriors and we never will be. We've just chosen different ways to compensate."

"And yet you have all chosen to view the world from the same warped perspective," Cat said. "It is amazing that, with all the things you acolytes and apprentices share in common, you choose to focus on your differences. That is what all this is about, isn't it? Demonic interference notwithstanding, your problem with one another is that rather than embracing your similarities—the fact that both groups, wizards and clerics, have ancient connections to the city, want to support and assist the people of Palanthas, and claim traditional association with the Dragon Day celebration—you resent one another because of your differences."

"Any kender can tell you that it's our differences that make life interesting," said Sindri.

"And any warrior can tell you that they are what make us strong," added Cat. "Even within your groups you divide yourselves up by smaller differences—colors of robes or levels of piety. Why are those differences are worth overlooking, but you feel it's necessary to fight over the difference of whether you worship Paladine or one of the moon gods?"

"Yeah," said Sindri. "I mean, the gods get along fine—well, except Takhisis, but she doesn't like anyone—so why can't we?"

"After all, who among you would have thought that a kender and a Solamnic warrior would ever be able to become traveling partners, let alone friends?" said Cat.

"And yet it was our friendship that saved the day!" said Sindri.

"Yes," said Cat. "Iffrontic may have been able to fan the flames of our disagreements, but he could not break the bond of friendship and trust that we share. He could make us argue, but he could not make us fight, let alone try to hurt one another. If even a glimmer of that sort of trust and friendship existed between the wizards and priests, this entire disturbance could have been avoided."

The apprentices and acolytes hung their heads.

"Well, they started—" began Tarrok.

"They wanted to take away our—" stammered Grigg.

"It doesn't matter," said Sindri. "We *all* make mistakes. We *all* get into trouble we don't want. And we *all* say things we wish we could take back."

"But that is not what defines us," said Cat. "The measure of a man or woman or priest or wizard is not what mistakes the person makes, but how he or she responds to those mistakes. In the end we are not judged by what enemies we have faced, how much wealth we have amassed, or which mountains we have climbed, we are judged by who stood by our side through our personal adventures."

"Who are your friends?" asked Sindri, looking up at Cat with a grin. "When the whole world has turned its back on you, who will you still be able to count on?"

"The friendships you forge today are the bedrock on which you will build the rest of your life," said Cat.

The acolytes and apprentices seemed be nodding their heads and weighing these words carefully. One by one they began to smile and offer their hands in friendship to the others, in particular to anyone they remembered having exchanged blows with earlier.

Sindri smoothed the wrinkles out of his clothes as best he could, pushed his wild hair back into a semblance of shape, and stood as tall as a kender could.

"Class dismissed," he said in his best imitation of Headmaster Greeves.

From all around them erupted a mighty round of applause, cheering, whistling, and even some laughter. Cat blushed. Many of the apprentices and acolytes moved quickly off the stage. But Sindri stepped front and center.

With a flourish of his arms he took a deep bow.

# Rewards and Responsibilities

The ordination ceremony was a joyous affair. Revered Son Elistan, looking much healthier than when Sindri had seen him last, presided. He began with a brief but moving speech about following your heart but allowing others the freedom to do the same. Either he was lucky enough to have written a speech that happened to reflect the day's events or Elistan was a good extemporaneous speaker. Sindri chose to believe the latter.

Then Elistan called the acolytes up to the stage one by one. Each bowed and promised to devote his or her life to Paladine's service, and Elistan placed the Crown of Paladine on the acolyte's head. When the crown was removed, a new cleric of Paladine stood on the stage, and the crowd cheered. But Sindri and Cat cheered loudest for Adyn.

Once the ordinations were complete, the staff and students of the Greeves Academy swept onto the stage and began preparing for their performance. Since Sindri's assignment was no longer required, he was free to spend time with Cat.

They walked through the crowd and wandered the streets surrounding the Central Plaza, passing vendors with stalls selling 227 everything from food to handmade crafts to items of interest from the four corners of Ansalon. Cat bought them both roasted cubes of meat served on sticks whittled to look like Huma's legendary dragonlance.

"You know," Sindri said as he finished his meat, "we never did solve the question of who stole the crown in the first place."

Cat stopped chewing and looked at him.

"Are you still saying it was not one of the apprentices?" she asked.

"No," he answered. "In fact, I'm pretty sure it was, but I never found evidence to prove anything."

Just then Grigg and Modaar pushed through the crowd and stalked up to Sindri.

"This is your fault!" shouted Grigg.

"Yeah, your fault," echoed the elf, but he added with a hiss, "kender!"

Sindri looked at Cat, who had no more clue what these two were mad about than he did.

"Is it?" said Sindri. For all he knew, they were correct and whatever was bothering them was his fault.

"What kind of wizard do you call yourself?" demanded Grigg. "You not only let the priests steal Dragon Day from us, you put on such a good 'show' that they cancelled the Pageant of History. Now all we get to do is put on a glorified fireworks display."

"We're no better than gnomes!" cried Modaar. Then he thought a bit and amended his statement. "You've made us seem no better than gnomes!"

"You are certainly better than gnomes," Cat said. "We can at least be reasonably sure that you will not blow yourselves or anyone else up during the show."

"We weren't talking to you, mercenary," said Grigg. "You may have everyone else fooled, but I know what you are and I'm not afraid of you."

"I can see that," she replied, her voice steeped in sarcasm. Despite his bravado, Grigg made sure that either Sindri or Modaar was always between Cat and himself.

Turning back to Sindri, Grigg said, "All by yourself you've managed to make wizards everywhere look like fools and weaklings. I'm going to see to it that they not only expel you from the Greeves Academy, but that the Conclave of High Sorcery brands you an outcast and forbids you from ever casting a spell for as long as you live."

Sindri opened his mouth, but before he could say anything a merchant with more chins than hair came waddling up to Grigg.

"There you are, sir," he said. "I'm glad I found you. I saved three of the daggers as you requested, but it wasn't easy. Since the little kender's performance they have been my most popular item—I've been able to get four times the usual rate. However, since you are a regular customer, I will only double the previous price."

"Not now," said Grigg. A fine line of sweat suddenly covering his forehead. "And as for you, Sindri, I'll deal with you later!"

"Kender?" Sindri asked, tugging on the merchant's tunic to get his attention. "What kender?"

The merchant slapped Sindri's fingers. It was an automatic reaction—exactly what every merchant does whenever a kender's hand gets too close. But when he looked down and saw Sindri, his face became suddenly ashen.

"Forgive me, sir," he said.

"Um, okay, I guess," Sindri answered. He was uncertain what to do—this was the first time any merchant had ever talked to him using such polite language.

"Your actions today have made me a great deal of money. Allow me to give you a replacement for the dagger you lost." The dagger Sindri had used earlier was still stuck in the stage. "I'm sure your friend won't mind. I mean, I'm only replacing the gift he gave to you last time, eh?"

The dagger he handed Sindri was identical to the one Cat had given him onboard the *Miller's Dream* as well as the one that the acolytes had found in the Temple of Paladine the night the crown was stolen.

Grigg began to slink away into the crowd, but Cat snagged his sleeve and tugged him back.

"Wait," she said. "There's no need to rush off. Your merchant friend just made you a generous offer. You must at least thank him for it." She then turned to the merchant and said, "Tell us again about this dagger you have sold so many of, sir."

The merchant reached into his voluminous robe and pulled out two more identical daggers, their blades etched with thorny vines and the pommels carved to look like rosebuds.

"Just a few days ago I sold a dagger with this specific design to this young man for—what was it?—three steel pieces, I think."

"It was two," Grigg muttered under his breath.

"Of course, sir," said the merchant, then he continued. "He wanted to buy several, but I had only one on hand. So I brought two dozen with me today. However, since this brave kender used the dagger in your play, people have wanted to buy reproductions as souvenirs."

"Play?" Sindri whispered to Cat. "I thought no one could see the demon but me, and then you."

"No," said Cat. "He was plain enough unless you fell under his spell. As long as he was fomenting discord in our hearts, he was invisible to us."

"Unless you were holding the idol!" said Sindri.

"Correct," said Cat. Then she turned her attention back to the merchant. "So you have done a good deal of business today."

"Indeed," said the fat man. "And all because this apprentice bought a present for his classmate." He looked at Grigg again. "I have two left, sir, if you still want them."

"No," Grigg said almost under his breath. "I don't expect I will be needing those anymore."

"I'll buy them!" said Sindri happily.

"Oh no," said the merchant. "Consider it an additional present. I'll be selling copies of this dagger faster than I can reproduce them for the next month or more." He handed the blades to the kender and waddled back to his stall.

Sindri fixed Grigg with a hurt, insulted glare.

"It was you," he said. "You wanted people to blame me even though it would have reflected badly on the troupe."

Grigg laughed. "You can't prove anything," he said. "It is pure coincidence. I gave that dagger to . . . to Modaar . . . as a present. Besides, even if what you say is true, it would never have reflected badly on the rest of us. Everyone knows that kender are born thieves. No one would have blamed us for being unable to stop you from acting within your nature."

Cat stepped forward. She loomed over Grigg, her red hair falling around her face as she looked down into his eyes with a hateful stare.

"You have a great deal to answer for," she said. "You have dishonored yourself and your fellow students, and you very nearly got my friend killed in the process. Even then you didn't stop. *You* are among those most responsible for today's near disaster."

Grigg stood his ground, though it was clear he desperately wanted to run. "You still can't prove anything," he said.

Cat balled her hand into a fist and drew it back, but Sindri grabbed her arm before it could fly forward.

"No, Cat," he said. "He's right, you can't prove that he did anything to you. And how would you feel tomorrow if you allowed him to provoke you like this? Don't let him soil your honor. It's one of the many important things that are completely beyond his understanding."

Cat unballed her fist.

"When did you grow to be so wise, Sindri?"

The kender smiled at her. "Didn't you hear?" he said. "They let me into wizard school."

"You won't be there for long," Grigg sneered.

Without even a hint of warning Sindri turned, leaped straight up, and punched Grigg square on the chin. The apprentice's eyes rolled back and he fell on top of Modaar out cold.

"You're right," Sindri said. "I won't. But somehow I don't think you will either."

He laid one of the daggers the merchant had given him on Grigg's unconscious chest and handed the other one to Modaar. Then he said to the elf who was struggling to get out from underneath the unconscious boy, "Those are gifts for you two to remember me by."

With that, he turned and walked away. Cat followed close behind.

"You know what, Cat?" Sindri said when the crowd had closed behind them. "You're right. Sometimes doing things by hand is better than using magic."

"Congratulations, Adyn! I'm so proud of you!" Cat said scooping him up into her arms in a bear hug. She suddenly became aware that Tarrok, Fallstorm, Marta, and a half dozen of the newly ordained clerics were watching her, amused grins on their faces.

Embarrassed, she dropped her friend and smoothed out the

wrinkles she'd made in his crisp white robes. "What I mean is, I am very pleased that you have reached this plateau of achievement, Father Thinreed."

They all laughed, and Adyn laughed the hardest. He returned the hug with even more vigor.

"Thank you, Catriona," he said. "I—none of us—would have anything to celebrate today if not for you." He turned to Sindri. "And our thanks to you, Apprentice Suncatcher."

"Just 'Sindri' is fine," said the kender. "And pretty soon it's going to be more accurate, too."

Cat looked at him, her face turning somber. "You don't really think they're going to expel you from the school because of that fool Grigg, do you?"

Sindri shrugged. "I don't know," he said. "They might. But it doesn't matter. I'm thinking about leaving the academy anyway."

"But why?" asked Cat.

Sindri sighed. "Because in the end they really don't want me there," he said. "Oh, I've made a few true friends, but most of the students and staff think of me as nothing but an annoyance and a distraction. Headmaster Greeves only accepted me when he was basically forced to."

"What will you do now?" asked Adyn. All the newly ordained clerics gathered around, dozens of nearly identical concerned faces silently asking if there was anything they could do to help.

"Well, I'll stay in Palanthas for a little while," Sindri said. "I want to come to the temple and visit with Cat—we have to share stories about what we've done for the past fortnight."

Cat cleared her throat. "Actually," she said, "My time at the temple is through. I'm leaving Palanthas tonight."

"Oh," said Sindri. "Well, at least I can walk you to the city gate."

Adyn's face sank into a look of panic. "You haven't talked to the Revered Son yet, have you?" he asked.

"No," Cat said. "He seemed too busy placing crowns on heads this morning. And I wouldn't know where to find him in this crowd. Please, just convey my thanks for his hospitality."

"Oh no," said Adyn. His words flew out so quickly that Cat thought he might have kender or gully dwarf blood in his veins. "You can't leave without saying goodbye to him. I know he would be terribly offended and it could ruin Dragon Day for him."

The other priests all nodded and mumbled their agreement.

Cat, perplexed, looked down at Sindri. He shrugged his shoulders. Neither one could make sense of this strange behavior, but they knew it was not wise to insult someone as important as Father Elistan.

"Do you know where I could find—?" she began to ask.

Before the words were half out of her mouth, Adyn and all the priests spoke and pointed as one. "The temple," they said.

Cat and Sindri exchanged glances. Something unusual was going on, but the only way to figure out what was to play along.

"Very well," said Cat. "I will go there on my way to the South Gate. Thank you for your friendship and support."

"Oh, we'll go with you," said Adyn. "After all you've done for us, the least we can do is walk you to . . . errr . . . the South Gate." He smiled too broadly. So did all the other clerics, who also nodded their heads too vigorously.

Again Sindri and Cat exchanged glances. This was very strange. Now they wanted to get to the bottom of this so their new friends would stop behaving in such an odd fashion.

They made their way toward the Temple of Paladine the most direct way possible, but even that was slow because of all the people still celebrating Dragon Day. And every time they passed another of the newly ordained clerics the others would whisper something furtively or make strange hand signals and that person would join the group. By the time Cat could see the stairs of the temple, she and Sindri were at the head of a veritable parade of Paladinian clerics.

Revered Son Elistan stood at the top of the stairs leading to the Temple of Paladine, still wearing the ceremonial robes he had on that morning. He held a scroll in his hands and beside him stood a thin, balding man dressed in red wizard's robes.

"That's Headmaster Greeves!" cried Sindri. "I wonder what he's doing there."

The clerics seemed just as puzzled as the kender, so this was clearly not part of their plan, whatever that was.

When she reached the top of the stairs, Cat said, "Greetings, Revered Son," and made a deep, courtly bow.

"Greetings, Headmaster Greeves," Sindri said as he bowed and did his best imitation of Cat's arm flourish.

The two older men nodded and returned the bows.

"I have come to thank you for your generous hospitality," said Cat. "During my short visit here at the Temple my mind and body have had time to heal, and I have learned a great deal about myself. But the time has come for me to take my leave."

"So soon?" asked Elistan. "But it seems as if you have only just arrived. And your assistance, along with that of Apprentice Suncatcher, in instructing my junior clergy in the arts of patience and tolerance is hardly repaid by a few days' room and board. Will you not reconsider?"

"Thank you, but no," Cat said. "I have stayed in Palanthas too long already. In fact, I am on my way out of the city now. With your leave, of course."

"And I am going with her," said Sindri.

All eyes turned to the kender.

"Is this true?" said Headmaster Greeves. "Apprentice Suncatcher, this is no way for the student of the month to act."

"I'm sorry, Headmaster," Sindri said. "But you and I both know that things aren't really working out for me at the academy and—student of the what?"

"Student of the month," said Greeves. "It's a title we give to the student who has shown the most improvement as our way of encouragement. I see that in your case it has come too late."

"But . . . I . . . how?" Sindri stammered. "I've only been at the academy for barely a fortnight."

"Yes," said the headmaster. "And in that time you've shown more improvement than most beginning students do in their first six months. High Sorcery is not an easy thing to learn, Apprentice Suncatcher. Even 'the greatest kender wizard of all time' will only reach his full potential by applying himself to his studies over an extended period of time."

"So, I'm not expelled?"

"Good heavens, no," said Greeves. "What in the world gave you that idea? You may have made one or two mistakes, but that's what students do. Unlike most apprentices, though, you found a way to correct your errors as well as those made by a couple of your troupe mates. I would say that you are doing exemplary work—although I would encourage you to refrain from raiding the school's larder more than one night per week."

"I don't know what to say. Cat and I have to . . . that is . . . I have a friend who. . ."

"Sindri," Cat said, "this is your dream. Stay here. I'll go on alone. It's all right. I'm not even sure where I'll start looking for Davyn anyway."

"You're still planning to leave, eh?" asked Elistan. "Then it's a good thing this missive arrived when it did." He held aloft the scroll in his hands and read from it. "'It is the decision of the Whitestone Council, based on the information provided by Revered Son Elistan, that Catriona Goodlund has proven her courage and loyalty beyond any measure of doubt. We hereby extend clemency for all past transgressions and expunge any outstanding chastisements or sentences weighed against her. Furthermore, we entreat Lady Goodlund to forgive us for any injury our over-harsh judgments may have caused, and extend to her an invitation to rejoin the Order of the Rose as a squire in good standing.' It is signed and sealed by Lord Gunthar, the head of the Whitestone Council."

Cat stood unable to move or speak. In fact, for a few moments it seemed that she might even be unable to breathe. Then Sindri launched himself onto her and wrapped his arms around her.

"Cat, this is fantastic!" he yelled. "This is exactly what you've wanted—a second chance!"

She hugged him back, closing her eyes tightly as she did. Then Cat set him on the ground, turned to Revered Son Elistan and said, "Thank you for delivering that. Please send my apologies to Lord Gunthar, but I am unable at this time to accept his kind offer."

At first the surrounding group grew so quiet that they could hear the sounds of the Dragon Day celebration several blocks away. Then they all began talking at once, asking if she was joking, how could she possibly reject such an offer, did she hold a grudge for what happened before, shouldn't she take some time to reconsider.

She silenced them all by raising her hands.

"I deeply appreciate both the offer we have just heard, and Revered Son Elistan's efforts to acquire it," Cat said. "But as much as I want to be a squire again, as deeply as I long to rejoin the Solamnic Order, I cannot. At least not right now. I have made commitments to others—commitments that are measured in life and death—and I cannot shirk them. I must return to my friends, I must fulfill my obligations, and only then will my honor allow me to consider accepting this invitation."

"I am certain that Lord Gunthar will understand," said Elistan. "I will write to him and explain your situation. In the meanwhile, you take this," he rolled the scroll and handed it to Cat, "in case you need to be reminded in what high esteem you are held."

She took the scroll and bowed again.

Sindri hugged Cat again, and then turned to Headmaster Greeves.

"I made a promise to my friends, too," he said. "And even though I'm just an apprentice, they need me."

"Of course they do," said Greeves. "Members of the Solamnic Order are not the only ones who live their lives according to principles and honor. Your friends are counting on you, and you must go. But remember, there is no such thing as 'just an apprentice.' You are a member of the brotherhood of wizards. Let no one forget that."

"I am?" gasped Sindri.

"A very junior member," said Greeves. "But a member in good standing. You are welcome to resume your work at the Greeves Academy of Thaumaturgic Studies whenever your commitments allow it."

Now it was Sindri's turn to be speechless.

Cat took advantage of this rare moment to scoop her friend up in her arms and spin him around.

"It appears that you both have done quite well for yourselves during my absence," said a familiar gravelly voice. "Does this mean that it will be even harder to get you to listen to my advice in the future?"

"Maddoc!" Cat and Sindri said in unison.

She put the kender's feet on the ground and they both turned to look down the stairs. On the street below, not setting one foot on ground belonging to the Temple of Paladine stood the old man. He wore his usual black wizards robes and carried the same travel bag as always.

"How? Where? When?" Sindri seemed so full of questions that he could not actually complete any of them.

"After a few days of rest, I was able to extricate myself from Navarre," said Maddoc. "As I made my way back toward civilization, I encountered a merchant caravan bound for Palanthas and was able to secure transit in one of their wagons. We arrived not an hour ago and I was instantly treated to tales of a 'brave kender' and a 'fire-haired warrior' who either put on the best-staged battle scene ever or actually managed to save the city from a discord demon. I knew that these must be my two friends, and here you are." There was not a hint of surprise or astonishment in his manner. Despite the fact that they had left the old man trapped in the bowels of the earth, it was as though Maddoc had known exactly where he would find these two again.

"Yes," said Cat. "Here we are. But not for long."

"We're going to find Davyn," Sindri added. "And we're going to save Nearra."

Maddoc smiled.

"Of course we are," he said. "Wasn't that the plan all along?"

# Acknowledgments

As with any book, it took a lot of people to help get *Dragon Day* out of my brain and onto the page. My deepest thanks go out to: Mary Elizabeth Allen; The Alliterates (www.alliterates.com); Peter Archer; Wolf and Shelly Baur; Carrie Bebris; Jeff and Trish Brown; Neil and Mary Jo Brown; Cedar River Smokehouse (Renton, Washington); Jamie Chambers; Monte and Sue Cook; Jodi and Jonathan Goldberger; Dave Gross; Jeff Grubb; Miranda and Shaun Horner; Jess Lebow; Scott Magner; The Game Mechanics (www.thegamemechanics.com); Steve Miller; Christopher Perkins; John Rateliff and Janice Coulter; Rich Redman; Thomas, Teresa, Aidan, Galen, and Quinton Reid; Cindi Rice; Charles, Tammie, and Olivia Ryan; Marc Schmalz; George Strayton and Sam Shaber; Steve Sullivan; Margaret Weis; JD Wiker; and Steve Winter. Editors must like to go unthanked because they rarely seem to get the recognition they deserve, but in this case I insist on giving a very big and very public thank you to Nina Hess, whose editorial skill and literary insight are only outmatched by her incredible patience.

*Dragon Day* was written almost entirely on location at Starbucks #388 (Southcenter B&N) and the café in Borders Books (Tukwila). Thank you to Amy, Hibo, Malichi, Mary, Minh, Rick and the many fine baristas who helped to keep my teacup filled and my creative juices flowing.

The adventure continues in

# DRAGON KNIGHT

## by Dan Willis

Consumed by grief and haunted by nightmares, Davyn has given up on himself and his friends. But he cannot deny his destiny for long.

Shemnara rekindles Davyn's hope with a new vision. If Davyn can enlist the help of the dreaded Dragon Knight, Nearra may survive. Only Oddvar, the shifty Theiwar, has ever entered the Knight's home and lived to tell the tale. But even a Theiwar's secrets can be bought, for the right price. Soon, with old friends, new allies, and Oddvar by his side, Davyn enters the cursed keep. Nearra's fate rests in his hands. And all he has to do is make it out alive.

Available May 2005

# THE NEW ADVENTURES

## JOIN A GROUP OF FRIENDS AS THEY UNLOCK MYSTERIES OF THE **DRAGONLANCE**® WORLD!

### TEMPLE OF THE DRAGONSLAYER
Tim Waggoner

Nearra has lost all memory of who she is. With newfound friends, she ventures to an ancient temple where she may uncover her past. Visions of magic haunt her thoughts. And someone is watching.

### THE DYING KINGDOM
Stephen D. Sullivan

In a near-forgotten kingdom, an ancient evil lurks. As Nearra's dark visions grow stronger, her friends must fight for their lives.

### THE DRAGON WELL
Dan Willis

Battling a group of bandits, the heroes unleash the mystic power of a dragon well. And none of them will ever be the same.

### RETURN OF THE SORCERESS
Tim Waggoner

When Nearra and her friends confront the wizard who stole her memory, their faith in each other is put to the ultimate test.

For ages 10 and up

# KNIGHTS of the SILVER DRAGON™

## A young thief.
## A wizard's apprentice.
## A twelve-year-old boy.
## Meet the Knights of the Silver Dragon!

### SECRET OF THE SPIRITKEEPER
#### Matt Forbeck

Can Moyra, Kellach, and Driskoll unlock the secret of the spiritkeeper in time to rescue their beloved wizard friend?

### RIDDLE IN STONE
#### Ree Soesbee

Will the Knights unravel the statue's riddle before more people turn to stone?

### SIGN OF THE SHAPESHIFTER
#### Dale Donovan and Linda Johns

Can Kellach and Driskoll find the shapeshifter before he ruins their father?

### EYE OF FORTUNE
#### Denise R. Graham

Does the fortuneteller's prophecy spell doom for the Knights? Or unheard-of treasure?

## For ages 8 to 12

# Want to know how it all began?

# Want to know more about the **Dragonlance** world?

# Find out in this new boxed set of the first **Dragonlance** titles!

### A Rumor of Dragons
Volume 1

### Night of the Dragons
Volume 2

### The Nightmare Lands
Volume 3

### To the Gates of Palanthas
Volume 4

### Hope's Flame
Volume 5

### A Dawn of Dragons
Volume 6

Gift Set Available
By Margaret Weis & Tracy Hickman
For ages 10 and up

## Enter a World of Adventure

Do you want to learn more about the world of Krynn?
Look for these and other DRAGONLANCE® books in the fantasy section
of your local bookstore or library.

## Titles by Margaret Weis and Tracy Hickman

### Legends Trilogy

### Time of the Twins, War of the Twins,
### and Test of the Twins

A wizard weaves a plan to conquer darkness—
and bring it under his control.

### The Second Generation

The sword passes to a new generation of heroes—
the children of the Heroes of the Lance.

### Dragons of Summer Flame

A young mage seeks to enter the Abyss in search of his lost uncle,
the infamous Raistlin.

### The War of Souls Trilogy

### Dragons of a Fallen Star, Dragons of a Lost Star,
### Dragons of a Vanished Moon

A new war begins, one more terrible than any in Krynn have ever known.